TEN LITTLE FEN

A SPADE / PALADIN CONUNDRUM

KRISTINE KATHRYN RUSCH

THE SPADE/PALADIN CONUNDRUMS

TEN LITTLE FEN

In Memory of the World That Was

And dedicated to all the friends who now laugh and joke and expound at an amoeba table in that great sf convention in the sky

1

The snow started two days before. Light fluffy stuff at first, and then heavy flakes, filled with water.

At that point, the locals got worried. I don't worry until the locals worry. They know what's normal, after all.

I figure winter in the Sierra Nevada, you have to expect snow, and we've had snow every year since SierraCon started in the early 1980s. SierraCon does not take place anywhere near Donner Pass, although some attendees have been confused by that. The Sierra Nevada are 400 miles long, and most of that is *not* Donner Pass, although non-Californians don't seem to know that.

I haven't attended all of the SierraCons because I'm from the Pacific Northwest, but I've attended more than I wanted to, given that I don't like snow, I don't like mountains, and I'm really not as fond of California or Nevada as I pretend to be.

I was at this particular SierraCon because I had stepped in for Evelyn Zienert, a local SMoF who had received a cancer diagnosis in July. She was back working the convention—completely bald from the chemo—but supposedly in remission. She was weak, though, and unable to do most of the duties that the program director usually did.

I combined programming with finances on this con, since I had expected to be here anyway. I was supposed to have a meeting with Paladin about Casper.

I suppose in some weird way, Paladin and Casper have become my family, even though I only know one of their real names—and it's not Paladin's. Technically, Casper has family, but they abandoned her years ago. She was living on the streets when Paladin found her, and convinced me to sponsor Casper—who is smarter than anyone I know —into a school in San Francisco that specializes in prodigies in math and science.

Paladin and I act as her guardians, separately, with my name all over the paperwork. But if I ever screw up anything to do with Casper, I'd have to answer to Paladin—and I really don't want that.

I arrived at SierraCon almost two weeks early to clean up the mess that programming had become. I managed to get the right people on the right program items about a month before the convention, but I hadn't realized that no one had liaised with the hotel for the function space. Apparently, with SierraCon, the program director also acted as the hotel liaison in the last two months prior to the convention.

Of course, no one had told me that. But that wasn't entirely their fault. I didn't live in Reno or Tahoe or anywhere within driving distance. I missed all the in-person meetings, although I did Skype in when I could.

The problem was that I was also working on four other conventions that fall, and while I'm good at multi-tasking, I'm good at multi-tasking on finances and registration and things involving numbers, not things involving human interaction. I find that meetings take up more time than they're worth. I prefer emails and texts.

But sometimes emails and texts fall woefully short.

The hotel, named the Sierra Nev, was a grand old thing that had been around since the nineteenth century. The Sierra Nev had hosted the past twelve SierraCons, so the GM had set up the function space exactly the way they had set it up the year before, figuring that in lieu of new instructions, everything would remain the same.

He was mostly right, although I found myself dealing with tiny details—tiny *annoying* details—such as whether or not the hotel would provide water in the programming rooms.

I didn't pay attention to the things I normally paid attention to, since I was trying to decide how much coffee attendees would drink and whether or not we should pay extra for crudités in the con suite.

I certainly wasn't looking at the weather. Weather happened *outside* of the hotel. I was concerned only with the inside.

My mistake.

I had a suite on the upper floor of the hotel, but I kept my curtains closed. Because I was running (well, walking) all over the hotel, working with the staff, examining rooms, and making sure we had enough space for the big events like the art auction, I didn't notice the snow falling leisurely outside.

I do recall glancing out the window about a week before the convention, and thinking that we would end up with a nice dusting, the kind that kids wished for at Christmas.

That was as much thought as I gave to all of it. Instead, I handled crisis after crisis. No one had registered the permits for the Zombie/Reindeer Run that SierraCon had held for the past five years. No one had double-checked the course. No one had booked enough suites for the guests of honor. (Although I didn't know at the time that we would not need most of them.)

I was used to big city hotels, the kind that had an events manager and a sales person and a whole bunch of people invested in making certain our convention ran smoothly.

The Sierra Nev wasn't one of those hotels. Sure, it did weddings and big family events, although not usually at this time of year, which was why we got it so cheaply. At this time of year, travel to the Sierra Nev could turn chancy with a change in the forecast—something I knew as a con-goer, but hadn't registered with me, the con-planner. So the Sierra Nev gave its events staff rotating leave for the months of November and December. Three weeks before Thanksgiving, no one who had any clout remained in charge.

Once the GM realized that was a problem, he had assigned the Assistant GM, one Michael Shaye, to handle whatever came up. And

Michael Shaye couldn't find his way around his employees' filing systems. Nor could he figure out exactly what our contracts called for.

So it took me nearly two days to doublecheck *everything*. Most importantly, I had to coordinate with the managers of the Sierra Nev's three restaurants and two standalone bars. I had to make certain that *every* facility remained open during the long weekend, not just the twenty-four hour breakfast restaurant on the first floor. The fannish attendees of the convention would want to eat what they wanted to eat when they wanted to eat it. The fen (long-time fans) and gamers didn't pay attention to the time. When they were hungry, they would pay good money to eat.

That was especially important in a location like this one, miles from the nearest tourist town. Said town was decidedly uncomfortable, especially for people who looked like me.

I'm 6'6" and four hundred (plus) pounds, just like many fen. (Even though everyone calls me Spade, they probably should have named me Nero Wolfe, due to my size.) The rest of the tourists who came to the Sierra Nev during the fall and winter were usually athletes, either casual or professional. The nearby towns all catered to skiers who wanted to be on the slopes early (to enjoy the daylight) rather than the fen who wanted open restaurants late at night.

If the fen wanted to go to those towns and drink among the skinny in-shape folks giving them the stink-eye, there were plenty of good bars. Skiers liked to drink, even if they did roll up the sidewalks early.

But the old-time fen had learned early on that it was best to drink among their peers in the hotel. Less chance for a clash of cultures that might result in a good old-fashioned bar fight.

I figured once the con attendees got here, they would remain indoors. The last forecast I had heard had predicted a snowstorm, but every year I had come to SierraCon, there had been a snowstorm.

One thing about holding a con in a hotel that catered to skiers in the weeks before ski season officially began, we knew (and expected) the hotel to be geared up for any harsh weather that might come our way.

So, in addition to staying inside the hotel for the past week, I had stopped turning on the room's television. It was an old con-going habit for me. I never paid attention to the outside world when I was in my fannish bubble. Usually, staying out of the news cycle kept me sane and upbeat.

But this time, it meant that I missed the change in the forecast: it looked like one of the worst blizzards in decades would hit the Sierra Nevada just as the convention started.

Any sane person would have called off the convention. Had this been a regular convention, that is. Some kind of trade show, one of those daytime attendee things that people would come to from nine to five and then scramble home (or to nearby watering holes) for the evening.

But science fiction conventions weren't normal conventions. I was pretty typical of the fen. We came to the convention to *escape* our lives. The idea of being snowed in with each other was an ideal, not a nightmare. If we could live, breathe, and sleep fandom, we would.

And many of us do.

The proper beginning to the convention was Friday, but SierraCon scheduled events ahead of the regular con. One year, it had been a fannish wedding featuring the son of one of the biggest name female authors in the business. Another year, it had been a fannish funeral.

And a few years ago—for reasons that still escape me—it started to host the Zombie/Reindeer Run. I know how the tradition started.

Decades ago, half the convention showed up to ski Tahoe on Thursday. Then a large group of the skiers became snowboarders. Snowboarders fit in better. They were usually gamers.

But somewhere, that group of gamer-snowboarders morphed into all-around athletes, with a bit of a death wish.

And one of them, David Sligobah aka Zombie Killer, organized the Zombie/Reindeer Run. I think it came from some kind of running app or video game or something.

Initially, it had been called the Zombie Run until SierraCon got threatened with a cease-and-desist from some nationwide zombie marathon company that sponsored zombie runs all over the U.S. They had trademarked enough of the name that SierraCon thought of canceling the run until I—yeah, me, all 400 plus pounds of me—came up with the bright idea of adding "reindeer" to the name (since the run is squashed between Halloween and Christmas).

Someone suggested adding "turkey" as well, until someone made a joke about zombie reindeer and zombie turkeys, and the entire thing got dropped.

But not the run, which was more of a cross between a haunted house, a fake zombie attack, and a decathalon-ish event. Participants found things, "killed" things, and participated in things like running a something or other K (5? 10? I have no idea), snowball fights, snowboarding competitions, and somehow collecting important "things" across some vast expanse of snow I didn't even want to contemplate.

To the younger fen, this all sounded like fun. To me, it sounded like torture.

I still have trouble with the athletic side of fandom. "Athletic" is an alien concept to my fannish generation—and not "alien" as in "space alien." "Alien" as in if we had to do more than saunter from the con suite to the restaurant and back, we were doing too much.

Most of the fen of my generation look like me as well—maybe not as tall, but just as wide. The very idea of exercise still makes me nervous. (All that bullying in grade school did not help.)

The younger generation of fen, however, have taken that whole clean living thing to heart by taking their fannishness to whole new levels. There were running apps that simulated the zombie apocalypse, Pokémon style gaming events that occurred outdoors as well as in, and the aforementioned Zombie/Reindeer Run. The run brought in dozens (maybe a hundred) non-fen attendees, some of whom turned into actual con-going fans.

Over the years, I had heard about the event from the participants, who made it sound like they really had been wrestling zombies in the snow. They would describe the encounters as if each one had really happened. Of course, normal gamers (if gamers could ever be called normal) did the same thing: they would often talk about the time they took on an oversized orc in a dungeon using only a torch, a club, and their own cunning.

But I was used to that. I was used to the folks at sf cons using their imagination to great effect. I wasn't used to them using their bodies as well.

Because of the Zombie/Reindeer Run, half of the convention showed up on Tuesday night, including a couple of the guests of honor. The Editor Guest of Honor and the Toastmaster weren't due to arrive until late Thursday, but everyone else had shown up.

I got the notices, showing that the GoHs had arrived, and that they had checked into their hotel rooms without incident. I was running (walking) from incident to incident, doing triage, so I didn't pay a lot of attention.

The only reason I saw those first heavy snowflakes, in fact, was because I was up at the ridiculous hour of seven a.m. to make sure everything was in place for the Zombie/Reindeer Run. The thing made me nervous, because the liability issues were through the roof. Fen, running. That meant all kinds of injuries, from twisted ankles to broken legs. Fen, running, on a mountain side. That meant everything from them falling off a cliff (literally) to getting lost and freezing some-where. Fen, snowboarding. More falling, more frostbite. Fen...well, you get the picture.

I managed to commandeer a snowmobile with a side cart the day before, and had one of the Zombie/Reindeer Run organizers drive me across the course which, I have to say, looked impressive as hell.

The Run was on the hotel grounds, which were expansive, rather like the hotel grounds in the Jack Nicholson version of *The Shining*—sloped hills, perfectly shaped topiary (now covered in snow), and lots of winding paths.

My fear that fen would fall off cliffs had abated, but my fear that they might get lost remained until the organizer showed me the gigantic fence that encased the hotel's property. The fence had buzzers and beacons, things that would allow someone who was lost to notify the front desk that a) they had no idea how to return to the hotel and b) exactly what their location was.

If I had had my preference, there would have been no

Zombie/Reindeer Run, but I wasn't in charge of the convention. I was just helping out.

Still, I had gotten up the morning of the run so that I could do a count of the participants. I had developed a check-in/buddy system that I ordered the Zombie/Reindeer Run organizers to use. That way, if someone didn't return at the end of the run, we would send out a search party to find them. (Or rather, the hotel would.)

Everyone thought I was being overly cautious, but then, that's what I did. I had seen too many things go wrong at sf conventions to let much go to chance.

Or so I like to tell myself, since I'm the guy who missed the blizzard barreling down on SierraCon like a gigantic freight train zooming down the tracks, whistles blaring.

The flakes looked scenic to me at seven that morning, as I stood in the hotel lobby, showing Judita, one of the young organizers of the run, exactly how the check-in program worked. Judita was tiny and as thin as the runners, even though she wasn't one. She liked talking to the athletes, which I found weird, and she liked organizing them, which I found even weirder.

Even though she was the twenty-something and I was the (cough-cough)-something, she was the one who wanted to use a paper check-in (and out) system. I wanted paper *and* computer, so that there was a back-up if something went wrong.

As we argued, the participants threaded by, wearing their race bibs (at an sf convention!) and ridiculously thin thermal gear. They all had running boots and thick gloves and most of them wore ear muffs instead of hats.

The only exception was Horatio Dunnett, SierraCon's Writer Guest of Honor. He was wearing a gigantic fake (I hoped) fur coat that went all the way to the ground, big fur-lined boots, and a matching fur hat (which he once told me was called a "ushanka.") Despite the hat, he didn't look like a member of the Russian military or even some royalty heading for winter. He looked like an oversized furball.

Horatio wasn't as tall as I was, but he was as round as I was. He wore the weight with panache, especially after his writing made him filthy rich. I was richer, but only because I managed the money I had gotten as one of the Microsoft millionaires, employees in the company's early years who got paid in stock options as well as dollars.

Horatio wasn't managing his money. He was drowning in it. He had had his bestselling fantasy series picked up by a pay-cable network, and lucky enough to have the series turned into a classy—and popular—production that had caught the imagination of fantasy lovers and non-fantasy lovers alike.

It always amazed me that a fantasy series about a fake British legal system became a worldwide success. Of course, adding dragons to the Chancery Court helped.

Dragons helped with everything.

Horatio loved the attention, so he appeared on all kinds of television talk shows. But he was a longtime member of fandom, having been a fan before I was, and wouldn't give up his fannish ways.

The only thing he seemed to be giving up, in fact, was his writing. I had it on good authority that he hadn't written a word of fiction since the TV show premiered. Since the fantasy series still wasn't completed, this worried everyone involved in the production of the books—everyone except Horatio.

I'd seen him at dozens of conventions in the past two years, and he hadn't mentioned writing once. He seemed happier than I had ever seen him, and content to be Big Fan On Campus.

Like he was this morning.

In addition to his swanky fur suit, he carried an authentic-looking wooden hunting horn. If he'd had a pipe clenched between his teeth, he would have looked like a slightly drunk Santa on a hunting vacation.

He saw me from across the lobby and bellowed, "Spaaaaaade!"

Heads turned, fen and mundanes (non-sf people) alike stared at me as if I had suddenly become Somebody.

I'd known (and been friends with) much more famous Somebodies so I was used to this reaction. I could easily ignore it.

"Horatio," I said as he approached. Judita remained beside me, clutching her iPad and the paper sign-in sheets, staring goggle-eyed at Horatio as if she had never seen a man draped in fur before.

I'd seen that reaction before as well. People who ran across their idols usually had one of two reactions: they gushed and talked endlessly, or they vanished into themselves, staring as if Moses had brought God Himself down the mountain alongside the ten commandments.

Only a handful reacted like they were around the famous all the time, even if they weren't. And only that handful got a real reaction from the famous, because that reaction was the only one that was in no way threatening.

"Did you see the *sleigh* they got for me?" Horatio boomed. "It looks like something out of Currier and Ives."

I had seen the sleigh. I had also seen the bill for the sleigh. I hoped the damn sleigh was worth every penny of its price tag, because that one expense alone could have broken a convention that hadn't had me as the financial manager.

"It is lovely," I said without enthusiasm.

"And real antique Russian white fur blankets," Horatio said. "The kind the Romanovs would have used."

On the way to their deaths, most like, I thought but didn't say. I had learned long ago to pretend I knew nothing about history when I spoke to Horatio.

His love of history was well known. What was less well known was Horatio's credulousness. He preferred history books that told great stories, even if they were poorly sourced. He also preferred history books that didn't examine the darker side of the wars he so idolized. Genocide, torture, mass graves—if those were glossed over, Horatio enjoyed the book even more. He had gotten his start as a war gamer— the kind who played with miniatures and dice, not the kind who went outside in costume and re-enacted some famous battle. He cared about how the troops moved, not how many civilians they slaughtered or raped or rendered homeless along the way.

"I take it you won't be actually running in the race," I said in my driest voice. Horatio liked sarcastic banter, but not if he heard it as criticism.

"I had thought about it," he said with all seriousness, "but my schedule didn't allow time to train this year."

Well done, I thought so loudly that Horatio had to have heard me. He not only managed to take my statement seriously, but he also managed to remind me that he was Famous and Important and I was not.

Then he grinned at me, and the resemblance to drunk Santa increased a thousand times. I half expected his eyes to twinkle with real Hollywood glitter stars.

"You do know why I'm here, right?" he asked.

"You're the Writer Guest of Honor," I said, letting the annoyance into my voice. I had a lot to do without bantering with Horatio.

"I decided to accept SierraCon," he said, leaning toward me as if he were speaking confidentially. (He couldn't be, because his voice still boomed), "because of the Agatha Christie portion of the convention."

I didn't know there was an Agatha Christie portion of the convention and I had ended up doing the programming myself.

And because we had an audience, I couldn't quite gloss over what he had said. I hoped I hadn't missed a SierraCon tradition, and I was now terrified that I had. "The Agatha Christie portion?"

His grin widened. "You know," he said. "*Ten Little...*"

He stopped, because he knew that we both knew the original title of the Christie book whose modern title is *And Then There Were None*. The original title of the book, so offensive I'm not going to type it here, came from a British minstrel show of the 1920s—not a time known for its sensitivity to people of color.

Not that the second title of the book showed any sensitivity either, when it came out in the 1960s. Someone had changed the N word in the title to the word "Indians." No wonder some publisher eventually got a clue and got rid of the "Ten Little..." format altogether.

"We're not doing any kind of in-house murder mystery parlor game," I said, hoping that was the case.

"Huh," Horatio said. "Could've fooled me. SierraCon is known for its snowstorms."

It was, but not for *murders* during its snowstorms. Besides, I had it on good authority that the storms were never as bad as the attendees claimed afterward.

I must have been frowning, because Horatio's grin widened.

"Oh, all right," he said, as if I had pulled the truth from him (when I couldn't really care about "the truth"). "I said yes to the GOH spot because I haven't been to this con before and it's on my bucket list, particularly the run."

I really didn't need the vision of Horatio running in my head.

"But," he said, with a laugh in his voice, "as the convention approached, I figured with the forecast and your presence, we were in for one of those adventurous fake killing parties, as well as a zombie run. In fact, I expect it all to start this morning, after I sound the opening horn."

He lifted the hunting horn as if he was going to use it for a toast.

I had to use complete restraint to prevent my eyes from rolling. I also had to bite my tongue to prevent myself from saying, *If you're going to use that mighty imagination of yours, why not use it to write the long-overdue next book in your series instead of imagining a science fiction convention as a game of* Clue?

But Horatio had already moved on. Apparently he hadn't even noticed that my frown had gotten deeper.

Instead, he waved that horn at me. "Why don't you join us in the sleigh, Spade? They found me two of the most beautiful women in the Sierra to keep me warm under that blanket, but there would be room in the back of the sleigh for you and the lady of your choice."

I had no idea how, in the era of #MeToo, Horatio was still beloved. If anyone else in fandom had said anything like that in public, they would have immediately been shouted down, and maybe ostracized.

"I'm afraid I still have a lot of organizing to do," I said, glad I wasn't going to have to bundle up and venture into the snow. If there was anything I liked less than exercise, it was sitting in the snow wrapped up in warm clothing all except for my rather outsized nose, which I was deathly afraid of losing to frostbite.

"Your loss," Horatio said. "This is going to be one for the ages!"

And then he toddled toward the bar, as if he expected someone to serve him. To my surprise, a waiter greeted him with a steaming beer stein. Some kind of hot alcoholic drink was going to accompany him and the warming women into the sleigh.

I hoped that the hotel had approved the hot toddy or whatever it was. I didn't want anyone (meaning us) to get in trouble for serving alcohol during off hours.

No one else seemed interested in booze. The runners were stretching and bouncing on their toes and adjusting what minimal winter gear they were going to wear. They were setting their watches and comparing their singlets and laughing about the snow.

I wasn't laughing any more. The snow seemed thicker than it had fifteen minutes before, and Horatio's words about the forecast bothered me.

Horatio's comment about Agatha Christie hadn't helped. The book had haunted me from my childhood forward. I never really liked isolated places—and made it a point to avoid sf conventions that were held on islands, for example.

But Horatio had been implying that we could become isolated here. Because he certainly wasn't discussing the book in reference to the weather. The book had been set during a particularly hot summer, about as far from the Sierra Nevada in November as you could get.

I shook the thought from my mind and got back to work. We still had a lot of set-up to do.

The art show was half assembled. The artists who had shipped their work were already on display, but the artists who were driving had yet to arrive. All of the book dealers (or their minions) were driving and only a few of them had arrived. They were badgering the hotel staff, because that was what book dealers did, so I sent security to the large ballroom we were using as the Dealer's Room to settle everyone down.

I was setting up the registration tables when Ruth Harshaw, the convention chair, found me.

"The hotel talk to you?" she asked, looking more nervous than a convention chair should as the convention got under way.

"No," I said, opening the folding chairs. Usually someone else did this stuff, but during the Zombie/Reindeer Run this convention was always short-staffed. "Should they have?"

"We're having a ridiculous number of cancellations," she said. "The hotel doesn't want to count any of those cancellation charges toward our block."

I frowned. Cancellations at a convention with Horatio as the Writer Guest of Honor? I didn't know how that would be possible. These days, he brought in a good 500 or so mundanes, even to the smallest conventions, not to mention the handful of wannabe writers and screenwriters who somehow thought that touching his robe (literally) would make them as famous as he was.

"Why are people canceling?" I asked.

"The *storm*," Ruth said as if my IQ had dropped fifty points in the space of the conversation.

"I thought the storms on convention weekend were always overblown," I said, trying not to wince at my unintentional pun.

"Not this time," she said. "Where's your phone? I've been texting you about this all day."

I patted my pockets but didn't find a phone. Then I grimaced. The last time I remembered seeing said phone, it was plugged into an outlet in my room. Getting up early was always the bane of my existence. I tended to forget things, but usually the things I forgot weren't important...like a damn phone.

"Crap," I said, then stood up. My back twinged, like it always did when I was doing too much physical labor. "Bring me up to date."

Ruth planted herself near the table, arms crossed. She was a short woman with glasses so thick that her eyes were nearly invisible. Some people would think she was harmless because of her size and glasses, but those people wouldn't have been paying attention.

"Bree—" the editor guest of honor "—can't get a flight out of New York City until Monday."

"Monday?" I said. "That's ridiculous." Considering it was Thursday. "What happened to her original flight?"

"Jeez, Spade, haven't you looked at your phone at all?" Ruth snapped.

"Not since seven a.m. this morning," I said.

"Flights to the Tahoe airport have been canceled through at least Saturday," Ruth said. "As of five this afternoon, the airport will be closed."

"Closed?" I had never worked a convention in which the local airport closed down, and I had worked hundreds of conventions. "What about the Reno airport?"

"So far, they're still accepting flights. But they're re-evaluating hour by hour. And the major airlines are anticipating problems, so they're rerouting to San Francisco. Not that that will help people. Amtrak is shutting down through the mountains. People already on the trains are being bussed."

"Bussed?" I asked. "Here?"

"Hah, hah, very funny," she said. "Back to San Francisco. Every major system of transportation is avoiding the Sierra Nevada for the next few days."

"Crap," I said again.

"No kidding," she said. "Which makes me worried, since you know how fen are."

I did. They thought themselves invincible when it came to travel. Hell, *I* thought myself invincible when it came to travel.

"How many are driving?" I asked.

"Everyone who could," she said, "until the local car rental places ran out of four-wheel drive vehicles. They're not renting anything that's going to travel into the mountains unless the vehicle is big, heavy, has chains, and four-wheel drive."

Too bad they couldn't check to see if the fen could actually drive. So many of the East Coast fen thought they knew what mountains were (not likely unless they were from Upstate New York and Vermont), what mountain driving was like (see previous parenthetical phrase), and what a snowstorm was (it's really different in a city than it is in the mountains—especially these mountains).

"So," Ruth said, "I need you to talk to the hotel. We're going to lose tens of thousands of dollars if the hotel doesn't count cancellation fees."

That one I could handle. I had negotiated the hotel contract, and while I had left the Acts of God clause in it, I had specifically stated that snowstorms were not in that category. In fact, I had negotiated some snowstorm contingencies, especially concerning food.

I did know of SierraCon's reputation for bad weather, after all.

But the hotel staff was probably acting based on the standard contract without looking up ours. I would be able to settle this problem in less than fifteen minutes.

The other problems with the convention, well, those would take more time. And that didn't include the Zombie/Reindeer Run.

I had a bad feeling about that.

If I could have, I would have canceled it, and suffered the wrath of those young, in-shape fen. But it was too late.

The storm had started, and the fen were in the middle of it.

2

Before I went to my unscheduled fight with the hotel's GM, I stopped by the Zombie/Reindeer Run in the off chance that the starting gun hadn't gone off yet.

I found that part of the lobby empty, except for some volunteers and Judita, pacing because she was so nervous. The bar was silent. The windows, overlooking the great outdoors, seemed like a 1980s television that only operated with an antenna. Occasionally something would come into focus, but mostly the view was fuzzy white with the occasional brownish gray something that seemed like it had been added for color.

"They're out there now, aren't they?" I asked Judita.

She nodded at me, lips thin. "I talked to Zombie Killer, and he said it was too late to cancel. It didn't sound like he wanted to, either. He was..."

She looked away from me.

I had been handling a lot of #MeToo complaints at conventions of late, and so I was extra sensitive to looks like that coming from my volunteers.

"He was what?" I asked gently.

"Determined," she said with a frown. "And a little angry."

My heart jumped. The last thing I needed was some angry runner harassing my people. Not that I could imagine Zombie Killer to be that guy. He made toothpicks look fat, and he was one of those soft spoken witty types who never seemed to have a care in the world.

But in the past year, I'd kicked a lot of former fen out of conventions permanently for bad behavior and had a dozen actually arrested for everything from inappropriate touch to actual sexual assault—people I had known for years. I had thought them all prickly and abrasive, but never violent.

And I had been wrong.

"He didn't threaten you, did he?" I asked, trying to remember my training. We'd had a class a year ago in ways to question assault victims to get answers, without asking questions that would harm a future court case.

She looked at me in surprise. "Dave? Have you *met* Dave? He makes pine needles look huge."

"Even tiny guys can be dicks," I said, knowing as I said it that big fat guys could too. I tried not to be an asshole around women, but I also thought I failed at times. Mostly, I didn't talk much about anything except business. And while that had worked for me over the years on a corporate, and then a con, level, it hadn't really enabled me to have much in the way of interpersonal relationships.

"He wasn't a dick," she said. "But he was insulted."

I hadn't expected that. "Insulted?"

She squinched up her face in a spot-on impersonation of Dave's usual expression.

"'I'll have you know,'" she said, with an even better impersonation of Dave's usual speaking voice, "'that we have run this race through some of the worst weather the Sierra Nevada can throw at anyone. We might not help any serious runners qualify for Boston, but we have a good time, and no one gets hurt.'"

"You told him you thought someone would get hurt?" I asked.

"I told him it was a blizzard, one of the worst, if not *the* worst in the past twenty-five years, and he said he'd heard that before, and his people weren't scared of a bit of snow, and a bunch of other runners chimed in with really loud *yeahs!* and by then, Mr. Dunnett had taken his horn and shouted, 'Yippee Ki Yay, Motherfuckers! Let's go!' and they all did."

Yippee Ki Yay, Motherfuckers wasn't what I would have thought of, particularly when it came from the movie *Die Hard* and had nothing to do with running in the snow.

Although the movie was about people isolated in a building during the holiday season.

I shuddered. We were developing a theme, courtesy of Horatio, and I didn't like it.

"Well," I said, "let's hope our counting system works."

And that everyone would arrive back in the hotel safe and sound.

"Yeah," Judita said, her voice lowering a bit. "Why aren't these people more cautious?"

I looked out at the gray-white-gray blurry exterior. If I squinted, I could make out individual flakes, falling fast, like hard rain. The gray meant there was some ice in that snow.

"Cautious?" I said, thinking about everyone traveling here for a weekend of fun, everyone braving the snow whether they were in-shape and running in it, or built like me and driving through it. "They're fen, Judita. No matter what they look like. They're fen, after all."

3

My own words were running through my head as I headed to meet the GM. Fen weren't cautious, yet I was going to talk with the GM about a spate of cancellations.

It took a lot for fen to cancel anything. I would expect the mundanes who had come to see Horatio to cancel, but they would have canceled days out.

I did have a conversation with Ruth about a week before in which she had mentioned a bunch of cancellations, but we had laughed about them, saying they were probably a good thing. Mundanes always thought they'd love fannish conventions until they got here and saw adults running amok in costumes, having serious discussions about which superhero could take down the Hulk, and why Superman and Lois Lane never had sex. (The definitive essay on that, I have always thought, came from author Larry Niven, the title of which was "Man of Steel, Woman of Kleenex.")

I hadn't realized until I crossed the side lobby of the hotel, heading toward the hotel's business wing why those cancelations had happened. Yes, they were the mundanes, but they were also the canaries in the coal mine. And, I'd wager, they cancelled in greater numbers than Ruth and I had expected.

I was noodling all of that, and the looming financial disaster if I didn't come to an agreement with the GM when I arrived at his office.

You'd think that the general manager of a hotel the size of the Sierra Nev would have a palatial office. And maybe, back when the hotel was built, the GM had had an office of appropriate size.

But that office either hadn't existed or vanished in one of the hotel's many remodels. This office was tucked in the back of the hotel's ugly staff corridor, and could have once been a laundry room. The walls were concrete, the floor was covered with discarded and damaged rugs from the area around the main fireplace, and the only window was a single pane that let in the cold all the way to the door.

One of those modern oil space heaters sat beside the GM's ancient metal desk, and another space heater was unplugged near his feet.

The GM, a tall spindly man named Pachinski, was shoving papers and a laptop into a briefcase. He paused when he saw me, and said, "We'll discuss anything you need after the weekend."

I'd heard that ploy a million times before. After the weekend meant after we had incurred charges we couldn't get out of paying. No court in the land would let us renegotiate a contract after we had exercised the terms of that contract. Dozens of smaller cons had tried it—cons that hadn't had me involved—and had lost every time.

"We'll talk now," I said.

"No." He shoved the briefcase closed, and leaned on it with one hand while snapping its locks with the other. "I'm heading out, and nothing is going to stop me."

Then he looked aghast at the words that had just escaped his lips. He was fleeing, and leaving us up here.

I moved in front of the door. He had no other way out, and a tall spindly man was no match for a tall stately man. (Or a tall overstuffed man, if I was being a teensy bit more accurate.)

"We need to have a brief conversation before you go," I said, crossing my arms. "Your people are trying to charge us for cancellations on the room block, when those who canceled did so late yesterday and today, which means you got to charge those customers at least one night's stay."

One of the latches popped open. He leaned even harder on the briefcase, and closed the latch again.

"That's standard," he said. "You know that."

"And you should recall that I negotiated a different contract from the standard one," I said. "We spent most of a day at it."

He lifted his head then and squinted at me, as if trying to recall that conversation. He wasn't acting, but I felt surprised anyway. No one forgot me. I'm too large, too pushy, and too loud for that, particularly during contract negotiations.

Then his shoulders slumped. "That was *this* convention?" he asked.

I forgave him in that moment. I had been wearing a suit during that negotiation. My suits are silk and tailored and very expensive, because I testify in court a lot as a forensic accountant. (Hobby. One I love.) My con clothes are a little different.

At the moment, I was wearing baggy black jeans and a rumpled black sweatshirt that read *There are two types of people in this world: 1) Those who extrapolate from incomplete data*

He looked at the shirt, then at me, then back at the shirt, and I had the distinct sense that he did not understand it. Which made me happy I wasn't wearing my *Underestimate me. That'll be fun* sweatshirt. Because that would have just been insulting.

"Yes," I said, hoping he was remembering the same contract I was. Although hope was never really the best way to go at contract negotiations. So I added, "Our contract states that we get credit for the hotel block if the guest pays for at least one night's stay."

He leaned hard on the closed briefcase and closed his eyes. We both knew this hotel's policy. Late cancellations—any cancelation made for any reason 48 hours before check-in—would be required to pay for one night's stay.

That policy was emblazoned all over the hotel's website, and it was unusual enough that the reservations department mentioned it in any phone call as well. The reason for the policy was simple: The Sierra Nev was in an out-of-the-way location, so it didn't get many walk-ins. If a guest canceled, there was usually no one to take his place.

Over the years, the Sierra Nev had made a small fortune on that policy. They were going to lose a much smaller fortune this weekend because of it.

He waved his hand at me. "Fine. It's in the contract. We won't ding your room block for anyone who cancels within the 48-hour window."

"Thank you," I said.

"We good now?" he asked picking up the briefcase, and grabbing his coat.

He was leaving. And if he was leaving, then that meant a majority of the staff was leaving.

"I don't know," I said. "What's this hour's forecast?"

He stopped moving and looked out that single pane window. It was covered with ice, making it impossible to see anything.

He clearly didn't want to answer that question.

He took a deep breath, then turned to me, and said, "We have a full-fledged old-fashioned blizzard that's going to hit at any minute. I would like to get home to my family before it does."

I had no idea where his family was or why he thought he could make it home from here. I assumed he lived in one of the little towns ten to fifteen miles from here.

If a blizzard was about to hit, he wouldn't make it home any time soon.

"Does your staff know you're leaving?" I asked with a bit more edge than I intended. I'd run conventions with a short-staffed hotel, and it was never pleasant.

He leaned his head back, like a kid who had been caught stealing.

"I asked for volunteers yesterday," he said. "Most of our staff loves you people."

You people. I hated that phrase.

"Most of the regular staff volunteered to work the weekend. We're giving them hotel rooms to stay in so that they don't have to go home. We prepared with a lot of cold cuts and bread, just in case we have power issues."

"Power issues?" I asked. "The hotel could lose power?"

"Not on the main floors," he said. "And not in the wing housing the convention. We moved the generators to accommodate."

"I assume there's enough fuel for those generators."

"Yes," he said.

I was vibrating with anger. He should have been consulting with us on all of this.

"So why the cold cuts?" I asked, trying to keep my voice even.

"We've lost power in the walk-in a few times. When that happens, it locks down. It hasn't happened in a few years, but we haven't had a blizzard like this one in a long time."

His watery blue eyes met mine.

"You should have told us, so that we could have made some decisions for our people," I said.

"We've had big storms during your weekend before," he said. "You people have never canceled. Besides, our forty-eight-hour cancellation policy exists for another reason."

I waited, keeping that skeptical look on my face.

"Once people have started up this part of the mountain, they're committed," he said. "In the past, we have been considered liable when a convention cancels ahead of a major weather event and a customer who didn't get the memo showed up. The 48-hour policy covers us, not just financially, but legally."

It took me a moment to parse what he was saying. "You were sued," I said.

He didn't answer me—at least not verbally. He probably wasn't supposed to.

"Loss of life?" I asked. "Injury? Something. You were found liable because someone didn't...as you said...get the memo."

His gaze was flat. One of the boilerplate clauses of our contract nailed both the convention and the hotel for legal fees should something foreseeable harm a convention attendee.

A blizzard was foreseeable.

Maybe I wasn't the Great Wizard Negotiator I thought I was.

Or maybe I hadn't expected a blizzard, and he had.

"You need senior staff here," I said. "This could be a major event."

"I have senior staff assigned to your weekend," he said. "My Assistant GM is handling everything. Provided I can leave right now."

I didn't want him to leave. I was beginning to realize just what a disaster this was turning out to be.

"What about hotel security?" I asked.

"We have plenty. Not that you people need much. You're rowdy, but not destructive."

At least he saw us that way, which was a good thing.

"Cooking staff? Housekeeping? Wait staff?"

"All ready to go," he said. "Two shifts worth. Not the usual three, but everyone will get overtime."

Which was my concern only in that well-paid employees were motivated employees.

"Medical staff?" I asked, trying to think ahead. The hotel boasted a nursing staff and an on-call doctor to help with ski accidents and other bad things that happened at a swanky place this far away from a major hospital.

He rolled his eyes at me. "You people are made up of doctors and lawyers. I've seen the guest list."

He was right; there were a lot of professionals among the attendees —provided they all showed up.

"Is that all?" he asked.

"Not quite," I said. "Has anyone who is staying behind been in the hotel during an extreme weather event?"

"More than I have." He pointedly looked at his watch. "I really need to leave *now*."

It sounded like he had thought through everything. He had certainly thought through it more than I had, which I found deeply and personally embarrassing. It wasn't like me to make a mistake this big.

But, if I were being honest with myself, I wasn't the convention chair. Nor did I know much about the weather in the Sierra Nevada. I lived in the Pacific Northwest, and tried to go to November conventions in the Deep South or Southwest, where the only weather conditions I ran into were on the flight there and the flight back.

I had been reassured dozens of times (and at a half dozen Sierra-Cons) that the snowstorms in this part of the Sierra Nevada were never as bad as the weather forecasters said.

I shouldn't have listened. Or, rather, I shouldn't have relied on my starry-eyed friends. After all, the Donner Party had holed up for the entire winter of 1846-47, unable to move forward because of the snow.

No one would resort to cannibalism here. Even if the snow was piled high after the weekend, helicopters and snowmobiles would get through—options the good old Donners didn't have.

But still, the historical equivalency made me nervous.

This was one of those times when I wished I had a liking for cleaned-up history, like Horatio did, rather than a penchant for the gruesome.

Pachinski was looking at me, as if a glare could force me to move.

It sounded like he had done everything he could. I was the one —*we*, the concom, were the ones—who hadn't.

I stepped aside.

"You're coming with me," he said. "I'm locking this iceberg up."

He was right: the office was cold. I suspected the entire hotel would have cold pockets throughout the weekend. I was going to have to get used to that.

He pushed open the door, and held it, so that I could leave first.

I did. It was his office, after all.

I waited in the hallway, feeling even more disconcerted than I had when I had gone in. I had gone in expecting a fifteen minute disagreement over cancellations, and I had come out thirty minutes later, realizing that SierraCon was heading into one of the biggest convention disasters in fannish history.

I could only hope that it would turn into the stuff of legends, rather like MileHiCon 29, which got slammed with the Great Denver Blizzard of 1997, and became known thereafter as Donnercon. No one died there. The power hadn't even gone out. By all accounts, the fen barely noticed the blizzard at all—except for the lack of cleaning staff at the hotel, and the bizarre turn of events that forced congoers to cook their own meals.

I found it both ironic and reassuring that the name Donnercon was taken.

That meant that no matter what happened here, we wouldn't be confused with that fannish legend.

And things hadn't really gone awry there. It had only become the stuff of stories.

I hoped the same would be true of SierraCon.

That hope, unfortunately, turned out to be wrong.

4

By the time I made it back to the main lobby, the storm had stepped up its game. The whistling wind was actually audible through the hotel's stone walls. The double glass doors rattled. The bellmen stood on either side, holding the doors closed until an occasional hand came out of the whitish gray mess and pounded for entrance.

Those doors couldn't be locked, and I wasn't sure they would hold against the wind, even though they were recessed inside a great stone arch, and looked like they had been reinforced with some kind of powerful metal. If I had my druthers, the hotel would put wood or something around the doors to prevent them from blowing open.

But of course that would prevent the remaining fen from entering. I couldn't imagine the kind of drive they were having.

Because the wind had whipped its way around the doors, the lobby itself was colder than I had ever experienced it.

Michael Shaye, the Assistant GM, and a woman in one of the hotel's gray uniforms were crouched near the gigantic fireplace that dominated the half of the room behind the registration desk. They seemed to be consulting on how best to build a fire. One of the runners, shaking and bouncing from toe-to-toe was consulting with them. I would have thought the hotel would have kept everyone on staff who knew how to build a fire, but that would be a tad more sensible than they had already been.

A raggedy group of snow-covered fen stood in line at the registration desk, sniffling and rubbing their hands together. Maybe some of the chill in the room had come from them.

But they certainly proved my point from earlier. Fen did not give up easily. They rarely cancelled, no matter what they were faced with. Cons were too important; some of these folks had been looking forward to this convention all year.

More fen were tramping in, dragging snow-covered luggage, and looking goggle-eyed. More Zombie/Reindeer runners were clustered near the couch and some kind of gigantic fake plant, arguing with each other. Horatio's distinctive laugh echoed from the bar, and nearby someone was singing Monty Python's Spam Song at the top of their lungs for some unfathomable reason.

I had planned to stop at the front desk to talk with Betty, one of the long-time employees. Her husband worked at a grocery store about ten miles from here, and she had told Ruth that he would be coming up to join her for the weekend, and was willing to bring extra groceries in case we needed things.

But as I got to the desk and saw the extended line of fen, I didn't have the heart to ask her for yet another favor. She and a woman I didn't recognize were working quickly and efficiently, but they were dealing with cold, wet sf fans, who really wanted nothing more than a change of clothing and something hot to eat.

I decided I would come back later, and was about to leave when a movement caught my eye.

Paladin staggered across the lobby, looking like an angry Elfquest heroine who had been left in the snow to die. Her face was ruddy with cold. The tips of her naturally pointed ears were bright red, and her nose was dripping.

She wiped at it with the sleeve of a jacket that looked like it had seen better days. It also looked like it had been made for a slightly cool rainy evening, not for a snowstorm that was blowing into a blizzard.

She scanned the lobby, saw me, and beckoned.

I knew that movement and decided that obeying it was the better part of valor. I managed to maneuver my way around the front desk, wind past the growing circle of Zombie/Reindeer runners (who seemed somehow dissatisfied with the course), and to Paladin's side within thirty seconds.

"You better have a room for us," Paladin said, shaking her inadequate coat. The snow fell in big chunks and hit the floor with an audible thud. So, not just snow. Snow and ice.

Not good, especially with that blowing wind.

"Us?" I asked.

"I have Casper," she said. "And we need help getting her stuff out of the truck."

Truck, stuff, Paladin, Casper. My mind was functioning on too little sleep, too much caffeine, and weird storm prep.

"Don't tell me," I said, "she got kicked out of school."

"Ah, *no-oo-o*," said an offended voice behind me. I turned around. Casper stood near the end of the line, holding two suitcases. She looked more like the Winter Queen's kid sister, wrapped in fake fur, her cheeks red with the cold, her eyes like little chips of ice.

She and Paladin looked enough alike to be sisters, even though Paladin swore they weren't related to each other.

I blinked, trying to put it all together. Paladin and I were supposed to *talk* about Casper and her future, not visit with her—or so I thought.

"I don't recall getting a notice from the school about vacation days." I sounded churlish. I didn't mean to, but I was tired, and I didn't need more to handle.

Not that Paladin or Casper were people I handled. They were people I cared about. I just didn't want the distraction.

And I didn't want to think about what they had been through to get here.

"In-service," Casper said. "You got that list at the beginning of the semester, remember? That's when we decided on SierraCon."

Actually, *I* had decided on SierraCon in the summer, so I was pretty sure Casper meant her and Paladin.

Paladin shook the moisture out of her hair like a wet dog, spraying all over the lobby. When she saw me watching, she raised her delicately drawn eyebrows.

"Hotel room?"

I had remembered to reserve a two-bedroom suite for Paladin. She had asked for that when she said we were meeting, and frankly, the request for a two-room suite should have been enough to make me think Casper was coming. Normally, Paladin didn't get a room at all. Sometimes, at cons, she slept in her truck.

"You have a room," I said. "It's in my name." Since this hotel, like so many others, didn't like the name Paladin. They wanted Paladin's full legal name, something she hadn't been willing to give me (or anyone).

I put up one stubby finger and walked over to the bellman nearest the door. He had a parka on the floor, and proper gloves. I waved a hundred at him.

"Would you be willing to get luggage from a truck?"

To my surprise, he stared out the door for a long moment. I was about to grab another hundred, when he said, "How close is it?"

"It's parked in the turnaround." That from Paladin. "I'll come with you."

"Not in that coat," I said, and winced. She had already been out in the snow. She had to know how bad it was. She didn't need me micromanaging her.

It was a sign of how exhausted she was that she didn't even give me a sideways look.

The bellman took the hundred, shoved it in his pocket, and put on the parka. He pulled open the door, and snow-covered wind whirled in, making eddies of white in the lobby. He grabbed the hood of his parka, and headed through the door.

Paladin followed in his wake, holding onto the edge of his coat.

It was really, really bad if she was willing to do that.

I went around the tired fen to the desk, and asked Betty for keycards to the suite. She made them while handling another check-in, and gave them to me without looking at me. I handed one card to Casper, and kept one for myself. I put the key for Paladin in my breast pocket, hoping she wouldn't mind that I had a key of my own.

Both Casper and I stood near the desk, watching the door. The remaining bellman held both doors closed with both hands, but he was getting buffeted by the wind.

He also looked really tense as he peered out into the snow, and his posture was making me tense.

I wondered if I should have let Paladin go, and then I realized I had not a single ounce of control over anything Paladin did.

"How long did it take you to get here?" I asked Casper quietly.

"Ten hours," she said.

"Ten?" It normally took a little over four hours to get here from San Francisco. "What time did you leave?"

"Too early to contemplate." Casper rolled her eyes.

"The storm was that bad?" I asked.

"Worse," she said.

"Not the last part? In the mountains?"

She didn't have a chance to answer me. The door opened, thanks to the remaining bellman, and the snow swirled inside, blocking my view across the lobby.

It took two of the runners and the bellman to get the door closed. When the snow stopped swirling, Paladin stood in the middle of the lobby as if she had been conjured out of thin air.

The bellman put the suitcases on a cart and wheeled it to us. He looked cold, but not severely so. Paladin looked even more wet and cold than she had a moment ago. Her lips were actually blue.

"Sooooooo," Casper said, finally sounding like the kid that she was. "As I was saying, it was bad. Stop-and-go traffic—"

"We were fine until we got to Placerville," Paladin said, clearly overhearing.

"We got there at eight this morning," Casper said.

I gave her a sideways look. On most days, Placerville was about an hour and a half from here. But after the first thirty minutes or so, it was all mountain roads.

"E-yeah," Casper said, seeing my surprise. "Stop-and-go traffic doesn't describe it, and it didn't help that the tiny superhero over there decided to help everyone and their grandmother put on chains."

I had never heard Casper sound quite so sarcastic about Paladin before. Usually Casper reserved the sarcasm for me and the rest of the planet.

"They don't have chains, we don't get up the mountain," Paladin said, rubbing her hands together. That's when I noticed how red and chapped they were.

Paladin lived in San Francisco. Her coat was inadequate, which probably meant her gloves were too. And she had been out in the weather, helping people put chains on their tires.

I wanted to take her hands and warm them in mine, but I didn't. Paladin and I had an understanding. The understanding was that we were friends who took care of Casper. If Paladin knew how much I wanted to touch her, she didn't let on. Which was just as well. Because if she knew how attracted I was to her, then she probably would have avoided me altogether.

That bellman's cart had more luggage on it than I expected. It looked like Casper was going to move into the hotel. I knew from experience that Paladin only carried one suitcase, and most of that was supplies for whatever case she was working at the time.

Paladin called herself a gun for hire. She took her name from the ancient Richard Boone TV show *Have Gun Will Travel*, but she wasn't quite as ruthless as that Paladin. And I'd never seen her use a gun.

But she was the most competent person I had ever met. The fact that this storm almost wiped her out worried me more than I can say.

I tipped the bellman, gave Paladin her key, and told them I would see them later. I had no idea how much later, so I wasn't going to give them a timetable.

I had just turned away when I heard Horatio's voice booming across the lobby:

"Paladin, my lovely! I had no idea you were coming here!"

He was still wearing his fur greatcoat. He reached Paladin's side in an instant and swooped her up in a hug so extreme that she seemed to disappear in the folds of fur.

Casper and I waited for a good twenty seconds. I had never seen anyone hug Paladin, not even in gratitude. I glanced at Casper, and saw some of my own emotions reflected on her face.

She was as surprised as I was, but I suspect the undercurrent of jealousy, which I was trying very hard to ignore, was not there. I was beginning to wonder if I needed to stage an intervention when the hug ended. Paladin stepped out of the fur, her short hair tousled, revealing the tips of her naturally pointed ears.

Horatio kept a possessive hand on her shoulder, or at least, to me, the hand seemed possessive.

"I didn't realize you knew Paladin, Spade," he said to me while looking at her. Was I mistaken? Did he seem a bit jealous as well?

"They more than know each other," Casper spoke, her voice filled with contempt. "They're my guardians."

Technically, it was more complicated than that, but I wasn't going to correct her. Particularly when Horatio's eyebrows went up just a little. He thought Paladin and I were a couple, just like Casper wanted him to.

Paladin opened her mouth to correct him, but stopped when Casper glared at her. I didn't have to do a thing.

"Well," Horatio said. "I've been out of the loop."

He kept his hand on Paladin's shoulder, though.

"I met Paladin at her very first con," he said. "She was so shy."

"Your definition of shy and mine differ," Paladin said, not seeming to mind that possessive hand. She looked at me, and for the first time since she arrived I saw the beginnings of a smile. "I kneed him in the balls."

"Apparently, I was a suspect," Horatio said.

"Actually," Paladin said with a pointed look at her shoulder, "you were handsy."

"Some things never change," Horatio said with a gleeful smile. He let his hand fall.

I had known him a long time, and yet I wasn't sure if that hand had been on her shoulder to tease her about their shared past or to irritate me. Or because there was more to this relationship than I initially thought.

34

"Oh, they change quite a bit," Paladin said. "Writer Guest of Honor. Back then, no one would have thought *that* was going to happen."

"I couldn't finish anything," Horatio said conspiratorially to Casper.

"Some things never change," she said, and I had to suppress a smile, since I had been thinking the same thing.

She clearly did not like him, which was unusual. Everyone liked Horatio. Even, apparently, Paladin.

Paladin shouldered a bag, and grabbed another. The bellman was standing nearby, looking confused.

I beckoned him over, took the bag off Paladin's shoulder, and set it on the bellman's cart. Then I gave him a big tip.

"Make sure they get to the room," I said.

He looked at Horatio, and I suddenly got it. The bellman recognized the famous guy.

"The women," I said. "Make sure the women get to the room."

"Yes, sir," the bellman said, pushing the cart forward.

"Take a nap, you two," I said to Casper and Paladin. "I'll join you when I can."

"Or," Horatio boomed, "if you don't feel like sleeping, join me in the bar, and tell me about all of these changes."

Paladin gave him a tired smile, but didn't make any promises. Casper was already trailing the bellman to the elevator.

Both Horatio and I watched them go.

"I never figured you for a ladies man," Horatio said to me.

I still wasn't going to disabuse him of the relationship. I usually wasn't this petty, but I couldn't help myself.

"I'm not," I said. "Sometimes relationships develop naturally."

Casper and Paladin got onto the elevator, and I turned away. Horatio was frowning at them still.

I patted him on his fur-lined arm. "I have a convention to run," I said, and walked away.

I wasn't sure if "run" was the right word any more. The world outside the windows had become a blanket of white. More and more fen were trailing in, looking exhausted, bedraggled, and half alive.

I didn't see the runners from the Zombie/Reindeer Run any longer. I was going to have to check in with Judita to see how it went.

After I made a few changes.

A lot of people had worked hard to get here, and we were going to be short-staffed. Not with the concom—everyone had arrived days before—but with guests.

Authors weren't as adventurous as fen, and it had become clear, from our editor guest of honor's problems with the airports, that some of the other guests weren't going to make it here either.

Time to revamp the programming.

And get some hot chocolate.

The hot chocolate wasn't for me. I wanted pots of it near the front door, with signs on them, offering something to keep everyone warm. The kitchen staff suggested coffee and hot chocolate, partly because they figured (and they were probably right) that we would run out of hot chocolate within the hour if they weren't a bit more judicious with it.

This hotel had hosted SierraCon forever, and apparently a lot of people on staff had learned the ways of my people. Which was good, because the concom was going to need all the help we could get.

Ruth and I hunkered down in Con Ops (short for convention operations) and made some serious snow-planning revisions. We added walkie-talkies for the entire staff, not just security. Walkie-talkies worked without cell towers, and since someone had mentioned power going out, I figured that meant that cell service might as well.

Then Ruth and I revamped some of the programming on the fly, using what we knew at the moment. We hadn't received all of the cancellations yet, but we'd received enough of them to know that programming would be extremely fluid this weekend.

Fortunately, Horatio was here, and he was game for every topic. We would probably use him more than we had planned.

We drew up some notices, letting people know that there was a good chance that programming could change. On this particular go-around, we dealt with the video schedule.

Mostly, we added movies and some snow-focused episodes of TV shows to the roster. Someone had both the James Arness and the John Carpenter versions of *The Thing From Another World* on their laptop, so even if we lost the hotel's Wi-Fi or cell service, we could still run the films. I also found a version of John W. Campbell's classic story "Who Goes There?" online, printed it up, and set up a panel of round robin reading of it, so everyone would know where the films came from. Half the concom suggested a few other snowed-in movies. I put my foot down at *Home Alone*, but did allow for *Planes, Trains, and Automobiles*, figuring everyone would see their own odyssey in that.

I revamped the program, marked it as Revamp 1, knowing that fen liked to collect convention oddities, and this convention's schedule would probably become an oddity.

I used the hotel business center to print out copies. Fortunately the printer there was a color printer, because in red and in bold I had added an important twice daily something to the program: I wanted a twice-daily check-in for everyone in attendance, just so we could keep track of our people.

Fen might be the brightest people in the room, but they aren't always the most practical. The last thing I wanted was for someone to get lost out in the snow.

The fact that Paladin had been willing to venture out for something as unimportant as luggage disturbed me. And then I remembered that she had parked her truck in the turnaround.

I shivered. She had gone out with the bellman and after he had gotten the luggage, she had parked the truck. No wonder she had looked cold.

I hoped she had found a nearby parking spot. I was glad I had let the valet park my van days ago. Because the late arrivals—if there were going to be any—would not be able to tell the difference between snow drifts and snow-covered vehicles.

I hoped the hotel had good liability insurance for its parking lot. They would need it.

I went back down to the lobby with the photocopied Revamp 1 programs in hand, and ran into Judita.

"There you are!" She was clutching her tablet and the paper clipboard, and she looked terrified. "We lost one."

That it took me a few minutes to realize what she meant by "one" was yet another sign of my exhaustion.

"A runner?" I asked, hoping it wasn't true.

"Yeah," she said, looking at the still-banging doors, now revealing nothing more than a coating of white. "They're out there alone, and I have no idea what to do."

5

I stared hard at that wall of windows. I knew what was beyond them—the stone walls, the cavernous walkway, the beautiful forest visible just past the parking turnaround. But I couldn't see any of it.

My heart clenched, and my hands closed around my walkie-talkie. For a moment, I, like Judita, also had no idea what to do.

Then wood snapped in the fireplace, sounding like nothing more than a tiny gunshot. I jumped, and my heart unclenched.

"Who's missing?" I asked, keeping my voice down. Horatio's distinctive laugh echoed from the nearby bar. Some of the runners were standing near that fireplace. I recognized them, not because they were still in their ridiculous Lycra clothing, but because they were thinner than the rest of us.

"David Sligobah," Judita said.

I whipped my head around and frowned at her. She misinterpreted the look.

"You know," she said. "Zombie Killer?"

"He can't be missing," I said. "He's the one who built the course."

Besides, Dave was one of those anal types, the kind who never missed a detail. He was a whippet thin guy who spent his non-con-going weekends running in charity races. He had three hobbies: science fiction conventions, gaming conventions, and marathoning.

I had come to rely on him at any convention he was at. Dave could match me, detail for detail, whenever he was involved in Con Ops.

"He hasn't checked back in," Judita said. "He's the only one."

I stared at that wall of white. The entry to the hotel was unrecognizable. What would an outdoor course be like? It would seem normal, but in weather like this, all of the landmarks would be gone.

The one thing I did know about this kind of weather came from the mountains of the Pacific Northwest. Climbers got trapped in blizzards up there a lot, and those that survived were usually prepared. They had some kind of weird tentlike structure and they hunkered down until the weather passed.

I would grimly read the accounts of survivors, who always mentioned the visibility or lack thereof, and I would silently congratulate myself on being smart enough not to participate in things like mountain climbing.

That should have included sponsoring runs in the mountains, but somehow, I found myself in charge of this one.

Which meant I was going to have to figure out how to rescue the guy who invented this run, and planned its course.

This was so far outside of my wheelhouse that I was momentarily stumped.

And then I leaned on what I did know. I knew that when you had no idea what to do, the best thing was to find an expert, and ask them.

"Okay," I said, straightening slightly. "What about the rangers or the state police?"

"They're all busy with the highways and lost tourists and some stuck train and a bunch of other things." She hugged the clipboard to herself, looking a little scared. "And no, I didn't call them myself without checking with you. They had a dispatch call the hotel to tell them to ask the guests to stay here until the weather system clears, so there wouldn't be more problems."

For them, anyway, I nearly said, but didn't. It irritated me that she listened to the dispatch call to the hotel and actually talked with the dispatch, but hadn't thought of contacting me. I had questions for the rangers and the state police.

"I suppose," I said, sounding a bit supercilious, and not sure how to stop myself, "that you spoke to the hotel about whether or not *they* could send someone."

She bit her upper lip and nodded. "They reminded me that the run was our idea, and then said that they weren't going to risk anyone's lives to rescue someone who should know better."

I closed my eyes. I could almost hear myself saying something like that to Dave, and maybe I had, back in the day. Not that it would have made a difference. A man who looked like me, talking to a man who looked like him, about what was safe and healthy—well, it took a blizzard to turn that on its ear.

I opened my eyes to find Judita staring at me. Were my eyes closed longer than I thought? Had I just caught a catnap, while standing here in the middle of a crisis?

I had legendary stamina. I wouldn't have done that. At least, not younger me. Older me...

"What are we going to do?" she asked.

"Have you called his room?" I asked.

She blinked at me, looking startled. "What?"

"His hotel room," I said, enunciating carefully. "Did you call it?"

"Oh, leave the girl alone!" Horatio swooped in, his fur coat swaying in the breeze created by his movements. He was swaying a little too. Too much beer already? It seemed early for that.

Then I glanced at my watch. The day was slipping away from me.

Horatio put his arm around me—which was impressive. Not many people had arms that could encircle me like that.

I didn't like it, but couldn't quite pull away.

He put his beery face in mine. "I have a sleigh," he said confidentially, as if the convention hadn't paid for it. As if I didn't know. "We could find him ourselves. Think on it, Spade! We would be heroes!"

I finally managed to pull away. I resisted the urge to wipe the stench of beer away from my face.

"We would be idiots, Horatio," I said. "That's an actual blizzard. We don't dare go out in it."

He swayed a bit more, then stared at the window as if he hadn't seen anything like it before.

"Ah, yes," he said. "The kind Pa Ingalls would have tied a rope around his waist to go from the house to the barn."

I had no idea where *The Little House on the Prairie* reference had come from, and I decided I didn't want to know.

I turned away from him and his enthusiastic confusion and said to Judita, "Well?"

She looked flustered, and it seemed to take her a minute to understand what I wanted. Then she put up a finger and headed to a house phone.

She set her clipboard down as she spoke to the operator. Then she wrapped the cord (a phone with a cord! How 1980s) around her hand as she waited. Then she spoke again, and as she did so, her shoulders relaxed visibly.

I didn't say anything. I needed those few minutes to bite back my *I told you so*. Young concom members in training didn't need arrogance from their colleagues.

She came back, looking relieved. "He's in his room," she said. "How did you know he'd be there?"

"He's been a fan for a long time," I said.

"So?" She looked confused.

"He set up the run," I said, speaking slowly, so she would understand this. "But not—"

"But not the check-in system!" Horatio shouted that last as if he had discovered it on his own. He wandered over to Judita and clapped her on the back. "Girlie, if you're going to run conventions, you have to understand that we're a strange and contrary bunch."

And then he wandered away.

Judita and I were quiet until he found his way back into the bar.

"Case in point?" she asked me.

"Yeah," I said. "Case in point."

6

By six p.m., the only people allowed in the dealer's room and the art show were dealers and artists, and we didn't have a lot of those. Some members of the concom were rearranging the layout, so that neither room looked sparse.

Some of the gamers had already taken over a room on the mezzanine, which did not make me happy. Gamers belonged in the basement of the hotel or on a floor not being used—somewhere far away from the rest of the convention.

By Sunday at a normal convention, the stench around the gaming area was legendary. I figured that by the end of this one, the stench could hit a level that would rival a fertilizer spill or maybe an overflowing city waste disposal system.

We would probably have the room to move them, but if I didn't do so soon, we would never again get the chance. Getting gamers to return to our reality was tough enough at the end of a convention; I'd only tried to interrupt them in the middle of a convention once, and it had not been pretty.

Technically, the convention hadn't really begun yet, but I wasn't sure that would matter to them.

The pre-programming had started elsewhere as well. Tommy Kaslowski, a long-time sf writer with a single bestseller five years back, taught using a schtick that reminded me of nothing more than Lawrence Block's old Write For Your Life seminars from the 1980s. Wannabe writers came out of this three-hour extravaganza bleary-eyed and inspired.

About fifty wannabes had signed up for the program, but only about twenty made it. The rest had canceled out or were still on the road. Kaslowski had asked me if he should start the class now, considering how many were still not here, but I had no idea how many were coming, so I said sure.

The attendees paid him directly. He rented the room from us. It wasn't part of the convention at all. Which probably explained the worried frown he had as he wandered toward his now too-big hotel conference room. Like so many one-hit bestsellers, he didn't have a lot of money; he'd spent the wave of cash that hit him as if he'd get paid like that for the rest of his life.

Unless a writer had an ongoing and unstoppable hit like Horatio, the money always dried up. And no first-time bestseller ever listened to me when I told them that, so I finally stopped trying.

I had managed a much-needed nap (so much for the legendary stamina), and I was heading to a dinner with Paladin and Casper. They had awakened me from that much-needed nap with a phone call, reminding me that I had promised to have a meal with them.

A meal the night before a convention was often necessary. At some conventions, though, meals in the first 24 hours were nearly impossible. I wasn't sure what kind of convention this one would be. I suspected it was the grab-food-now type, because I had no idea what was coming next.

I did know that programming started at noon tomorrow, and as of my naptime, only a handful of the local pros had arrived. Local pros were usually the ones who handled Friday afternoon programming, because the out-of-towners were arriving at various airports, and some on the concom were picking them up.

Only there was no arriving tomorrow because everything was shut down, and no one from the concom was going anywhere.

I was just going to wait until eleven or so before I planned the Friday afternoon programming, figuring whoever hadn't arrived by late Thursday night wasn't going to be here at all.

The main floor café was only a café by upscale hotel standards. Seating receded far into the building, with the prime seats the booths near a gated-off area near the main hallways. In most conventions, those were *not* the prime seats, as business deals got done in the dark in the back, but this wasn't most conventions.

The fen wanted to see and be seen and take any and all opportunities to greet the friends they hadn't visited with since the previous convention, whatever that was.

As I walked through the lobby, warmer than it had been thanks to the crackling fire in that gigantic hearth, the hotel had a Thursday-night-before-a-convention vibe. Several people sat in the uncomfortable chairs scattered around the front desk. The concierge desk was closed, as per agreement with the concom, who wanted its attendees to remain in the hotel, not off doing something sponsored by the hotel.

Two bellmen stood by the front door, while some other employees were still trying to hold those doors closed. Before the much-needed nap, I had spoken to Michael Shaye, the Assistant GM, and he told me that the hotel would bar its doors at midnight so the staff could sleep. I made him promise that security would post someone nearby in case a hand appeared out of the whiteness, grasping at the glass, as some intrepid fan made his way through sleet and snow and gloom of night, only to be barred from entry.

It took my entreaty combined with a threat of lawsuit if someone died of hypothermia in their car to make Shaye take me seriously. I was beginning to understand why Pachinski had left him here to handle everything.

A mess of untold proportions could be blamed on an inexperienced employee, and a lot of lawsuits could be dodged. Have the most experienced guy onsite in the crisis, and well, all lawsuits would easily go forward.

Paladin and Casper had managed to get one of the prime booths near the rounded corner of the little gate. They were studying the one-page menu as if it were written in Greek, and didn't see me in the lobby at all.

Which was good, because at that moment, the lobby doors blew open, and a stream of people staggered in. The man leading the charge —Forrest Dubek—saw me, and bellowed in his high-pitched nasal tenor, "Spaaaaade!"

Paladin and Casper looked up, as did everyone else in the lobby. It was hard to ignore Forrest, even when he wasn't shouting.

He looked the worse for wear. He was an East Coast creature, a native of Queens who had never learned how to drive. Yet he was one of the most well-traveled men in the entire science fiction field. How he ended up here was a mystery, until I watched the rest of the group stagger in with him.

There were nine others, all the Usual Set—a group of famous editors and writers who traveled the world together, going to conventions. The Usual Set often planned a long trip around a convention they'd heard of but hadn't attended before. I had seen their names on the guest list—had even programmed many of them—but had figured, given the preponderance of East Coast addresses among them—that they had been caught in the same airline hell that had trapped our editor guest of honor.

"Did you order this unfucking believable weather?" Forrest bellowed. "Horatio said—"

Forrest's wife, Carol Gaspard, put her hand on his arm, shutting him up. They were a round couple, loud and uncouth and extremely intelligent. They had been together forever, and seemed to read each other's minds.

She apparently realized that Forrest wasn't going to kid with me; he was going to excoriate me for the trip they had just had up the mountain.

Everyone else in their party looked like they'd been through the wringer, except for the one person who didn't fit, Wyatt Edwards. He was hiding, like he always did, beneath an expensive but battered cowboy hat. His longish dark hair was wet, which meant he had placed that hat back on his head the moment he had arrived inside.

I'd seen Edwards at countless West Coast sf conventions in the past year. He was maybe thirty-five, square-jawed, with movie-star good looks, not the kind of person who usually hung around at sf conventions at all. Because that bothered me, I looked into him and realized he was the W. Edwards who had started two Montana conventions, and was a well-known book collector, who had just turned his attention to writing.

He also knew his way around mountain roads.

His gaze from underneath the brim of that hat met mine, and I saw a flare of intelligence that Edwards usually took pains to conceal.

"Forrest, Carol, everyone," I said, nodding at all of them. "Let me assist you with check-in."

I was hoping we hadn't canceled their rooms yet, something Ruth had planned to do mid-afternoon before I convinced her to wait until evening. We had to cancel at a sweet-spot to avoid extra charges, but I wanted to make sure we still had part of the block in case, by some miracle, more fen arrived.

"You have no idea what we've been through!" Forrest said, leaning forward under the weight of the messenger bag he had slung around his neck. I knew from experience that the messenger bag had a laptop, that day's manuscripts piled inside, and any other project Forrest was working on.

He was the most award-winning short fiction editor in the field, and he somehow managed to maintain that despite a punishing travel schedule, and long nights as a convention raconteur.

I managed to get to the desk before he did, and asked for the list of hotel guests in our block.

I scanned it, saw all of the names from that group of ten on it, and sighed with relief.

"You're taken care of, Forrest," I said to him as I slid the paper back to the desk clerk. "The café's open 24/7, so you'll be able to get something to eat whenever you need it."

"Off the regular menu?" Forrest asked. He hated the con menus that we always approved so that the wait staff could get our people in and out of the café between panels.

"By eight," the desk clerk said primly, before I could answer. I would have insisted the café staff get Forrest whatever food he wanted when he wanted it, if possible. Not because he was intentionally difficult, but because he was difficult nonetheless, and one of the loudest humans it was my experience to encounter.

"Eight?" Forrest asked, loudly, of course. "What is this, a George Cukor movie?"

"I don't think Cukor ever set anything in the West," said Rochelle O'Reilly, a short ginger-haired woman who looked more like the librarian she had been than the editor she had become. She was witty enough to be in a Cukor film, which was one of the reasons she was part of Forrest's usual set.

"I'm sure no one does dinner at eight around here," said Wallace James Whitson, primarily to show off his knowledge of film.

"You'd be surprised," Edwards said softly, so softly that I was the only one who heard him.

The group lined up to check in, dripping just from their trip from the parking area to the front desk. They all had snow on their coats, and their shoes looked unsalvageable.

All except for Edwards who, except for the hat, was properly dressed for a blizzard in a ski parka and heavy boots. He held leather gloves in one hand, as he hung back, waiting for everyone else to finish with the desk before he moved forward.

"You drove them?" I asked as I moved closer to him.

"Yeah," he said. "Otherwise, it was going to Scott."

Scott Feldstein, a former comic book editor with DC who had given it all up to become a writer. He was the only one of the group who actually could drive, albeit not well. He lived in Philadelphia now, and told everyone who would listen how much he preferred public transportation.

"I don't see him," I said.

"He's in the second van."

I met Edwards' gaze. He wasn't as tall as I was, but he was close, something I hadn't realized before.

"There's another van?" I asked. "Who is driving?"

"Perry," Edwards said, and I took that one-word answer to mean Perry Stevens, another writer who had gotten his start in science fiction but who had moved onto thrillers set in the old west.

At least Perry could drive in this weather, just like Edwards.

"How far are they behind you?" I asked.

Edwards shrugged, then frowned as he glanced at the rattling doors. "We lost them at Placerville. We all got gas. I thought they were right behind us, but apparently someone in their group had gone inside the minimart to get snacks."

He sounded disapproving.

"Let me know who is in that van too," I said, "and I'll make sure they still have a room."

He gave me a flat look, which I couldn't decipher. Manly men like him (and Perry) made me a little nervous. Especially when they didn't fit into a typical sf box. It took me a while to realize that Edwards was as nerdy or maybe even more nerdy than the average fan. He just wasn't packaged like one.

I had yet to figure out Perry.

"Glad that you stepped in," I said.

"Glad that we saw them," Edwards said. "They'd had the bright idea to rent two gigantic vans that no one could really drive. I can't imagine what would have happened if they had actually tried to get up here on their own."

I could imagine it, and I suspected Edwards could too. I had a hunch half of the annual Hugo ballot had been spared an ignominious death, because of Edwards' and Perry's quick thinking.

Of course, I was counting those proverbial chickens. Perry's vehicle hadn't arrived yet.

"It's bad out there?" I asked, watching the Usual Set check in. They weren't chattering like they usually did, or even looking around much. They were leaning against their luggage, and looking like they had just gotten off the flight from hell.

"It's the worst I've ever seen," Edwards said, and somehow I believed him. One thing I knew about this guy was that he did not tend to exaggerate.

I nodded and squared my shoulders, trying not to think about that remaining van. I would have to let Shaye know about them, though, that we were expecting them tonight.

"You can call them, right?" I asked. "Maybe they stopped somewhere...?"

Edwards turned toward me, eyes glinting almost angrily. "Where is there to stop?"

I had no idea. I'd driven the road several times, but hadn't paid a lot of attention to other accommodations. "There's gotta be a hotel between here and Placerville."

"I thought you were from the West," he said.

"Seattle," I said.

"Oh," he said, as if I had suddenly lost all of my street cred...as if I'd ever had any street cred, at least of the tough, rugged, macho kind.

The two bellmen made their way to the Usual Set, bell carts in hand, and I turned away. I'd seen the Usual Set deal with bellmen before, and it was never pretty. Not that they were rich-people rude—they weren't—or that they thought themselves better than anyone else—they didn't—but because they were ditherers and they fiddled and they couldn't figure out what to do next and they changed their minds continually and took twice as long as necessary to make a decision (make that five times as long as necessary). They did over-tip, but that extra money rarely seemed worth all the hassle.

Once upon a convention, I'd stepped in, long ago in a land far away, and unless someone (read: in the hotel staff) broke down, I was never going to step in again.

I moved past Edwards, toward the café. Paladin was leaning back in her chair, one arm over its back, watching Casper intently. Casper was explaining something, not realizing that Paladin was also watching the scene around her unfold. The flimsy special paper menus had found their places between the condiments and the gate around the booth, so clearly Paladin and Casper had already ordered.

I started toward them, saying hi to the people I recognized, nodding at the ones I didn't. Everyone looked familiar in one way or another, including the hotel staff. As Pachinski had said, most of the hotel staff had worked this convention before, and some were in the spirit of the thing, wearing a small token like Starfleet badges next to their name tags or Tardis earrings.

A couple of the women wore headbands with little antennae waving as they moved, something I normally would have frowned at, but found enjoyable in this moment.

I had just reached Paladin and Casper on the hallway side of the gate, apologizing as I hurried toward the café's entrance, when the double doors blew open again.

The blast of cold air made it all the way to me. I resisted the urge to turn around, not quite sure why I believed that every time the door opened, it presaged a problem.

But I did turn, and winced as I saw what blew in.

It was the second part of the Usual Set, only they weren't leading their way in the door. Perry Stevens came in first, wearing a parka so big and thick that it looked like it weighed more than he did. The only reason I knew it was Stevens was because he'd pulled his hood down.

He was half helping, half steering people inside. Mick Renny, who was usually all bluster and smiles at the beginning of a convention, looked wrung out. His round face was red from the cold, and he wore an incongruous blue stocking cap that said *Rams* in white, with a gold sheep logo thingie behind it. I didn't know football well—just enough to make sure I didn't step into it with fen whose interests extended to sport—but I knew that Renny was a longtime Bengals fan. His straights had to be dire if he would deign to wear anything with another NFL team's logo on it.

His wife Jean followed him inside, looking lost. She was wrapped in a blanket that was covered in chunks of snow, as if she had fallen asleep in a drift.

She was abnormally silent. On a normal night, she would have been telling everyone where to stand and what to do, even if she had no idea what was going on.

The rest of the group included a couple of new writers Mick was sponsoring (he was always helping out the new talent), a few Big Name Midwestern fans who were lifelong friends of Mick's (and who also wore Rams paraphernalia—which looked new and must have been worn under pain of death or at least frostbite), and Scott Feldstein, who had been deposed from his post as driver of the first van. He was white-faced, his eyes big round holes in his face. Apparently, he had seen the drive and understood what kind of bullet he had dodged. Or maybe the trip had scared him spitless.

Linus Gold, the editor of the field's most influential non-fiction magazine, tripped on the way in the door, and caught himself with the door frame. His lazy eye looked worse than usual, probably because what hair he had left was tousled all around his face.

Behind him, Richard Agberg, one of the local pros I'd been counting on, walked in as if the weather didn't bother him at all. Richard was a native New Yorker, so he'd been through blizzards before, and even though he lived in Oakland, he did understand mountain snow. His ankle-length winter coat somehow looked elegant. The wool glistened with moisture, but he wasn't covered with it, like everyone else. His silver hair wasn't even mussed by the wind, and the scarf he had around his neck looked like a fashion statement instead of something that would keep him warm.

As he came all the way inside, he stamped his stylish black leather boots, which had clearly been treated with some kind of sealant, because the snow slid off and didn't leave any damage.

His much-younger wife, Kalee Behar, didn't look quite as fresh, even though she wore the same kind of coat, boots and scarf. That didn't surprise me. She had never been the peacock in the relationship. That award had always gone to Richard.

It was Kalee who caught my eye.

"Spade," she said with a mixture of relief and concern. "I hope you're not expecting anyone else. The roads are a nightmare. We barely got through."

"We got stuck three times," Gold said, his voice flat with disapproval. "I seriously doubted we'd ever get out that last time."

"We almost didn't," Mick snarled. "If you had gotten out of the van to help push like the rest of us—"

"I had the wrong shoes," Gold said.

"So did the rest of us," said Richard laconically, even though he didn't.

"Jean wasn't wearing the right shoes, and look where it got her," Gold said.

"She wouldn't have fallen if it weren't for the extra weight from your fat ass," Mick said, his right hand balling into a fist.

I moved closer, hoping to stave off the fight. Rather than confront both men, I stopped by Jean. She was gray and shivering. The blanket around her was wet.

"You need to get warm," I said, and led her to the big fireplace.

"Hey!" Mick said. "We need to check in."

"Come get her when you've finished," I said, figuring if he was strong enough to fight, he was strong enough to figure out the Sierra Nev's check-in procedure.

I moved Jean as close to the fire as I could. I draped the blanket away from the bricks in front of the fireplace, and debated whether or not to partially close the grate.

A movement caught the corner of my eye. Ruth had shown up out of nowhere, like any good Con chair, and said to me, "I got this."

She put her hand on Jean's arms, and eased her toward an overstuffed chair that hadn't been there a few minutes ago.

"Thanks," I said.

"Oh, don't thank me," Ruth said. "I'm not going to handle that group. It's on you."

The first half of the Usual Set had finally found their way to the elevators, confused bellmen in tow. The second half was standing in line, haphazardly, the anger and frustration surrounding them so strong that I was afraid a single spark would lead to what Mick would have once called fisticuffs.

I started toward them, but I wasn't the only one. Paladin had left the café and was heading toward the group, her mouth a determined line.

She hated Linus Gold for reasons she would never explain, and I was worried that she was going to do something rash.

I hurried toward the group, but Paladin reached them first. She spoke to Mick and Gold, who both stared at her as if they had never seen anything like her before. They both knew her, but they probably weren't used to small women stepping into the middle of their manly-men conflict.

As I got close, Paladin's voice became clear.

"...continue this, I will personally shut you both down. Do you understand?"

I hurried the rest of the way. Gold was glaring at her with his good eye. Mick grinned, deciding (as he usually did) that charm was the better part of valor.

"You're right, doll," he said.

I winced. I couldn't imagine anyone calling Paladin "doll" and living. Her eyes narrowed, but she didn't say anything. Apparently, she was used to Mick. Or maybe she had assessed that fighting him over the word "doll" was a bad idea at the moment.

Besides, he continued to talk, precluding any objection (except a loud one). "I guess I got a bit heated because Jean gave it her all out there in the snow, and this yahoo couldn't be bothered to help any of us—"

"My shoes—"

"Are not an excuse," Mick's voice went up. "My wife—"

"Is over there freezing," I said, mostly for Paladin, who looked like she was going to initiate the fisticuffs. "The faster you get through this line, the sooner Jean can have a nice warm shower and a change of clothes."

"Let me get ahead of you," Mick said to Gold.

"I'm cold too," Gold said.

At that moment, Paladin yanked Gold out of the line. He tripped toward her, and she stepped to the side, so that if he fell, she wouldn't catch him. He staggered a few more feet, then turned and glared at her.

"You can wait until everyone else has checked in," she said in a low tone. Then she looked pointedly at his feet. "And, by the way, those aren't shoes. They're called boots. They would have been fine in the snow."

Mick snarled. Apparently he hadn't noticed the boots. I moved him forward, away from Gold. Scott, who was ahead of them in line, smiled tiredly at Mick, and said, "Go ahead of me. Jean needs to get to her room."

The others murmured the same thing, and then, magically, Mick was standing at the check-in desk, fumbling for his wallet.

Gold was standing behind Paladin, his arms crossed. "You don't have to guard me," he said.

"Someone has to keep an eye on you," she said. "You clearly don't know how to behave in polite company."

I glanced at Casper, who was watching all of this avidly from the table in the café. I was torn between reminding Paladin that we were supposed to have dinner, and letting the scenario play out.

I wasn't that fond of Gold either.

As if she could read my thoughts, Paladin looked over at me.

"I got this," she said. "You need to order."

And with that, I was dismissed. I could hang around here, but I really didn't need to. None of the rooms had been cancelled, and soon everyone would head to the elevator. Paladin would make certain that Gold wasn't going to cause any more trouble.

I nodded at her, then went down the hallway to the café entrance. As I passed Casper, she ostentatiously grabbed the one-sheet menu and waved it at me, so that I would have it to look at when I got to the table.

I almost told her I didn't need to see the menu—I had approved the damn thing when the rest of the concom had been dithering about the name of the items on the menu—but I didn't. She almost looked happy to see me, and after the day I'd had, happy was an emotion I needed.

I smiled at her, and headed inside, my stomach rumbling at the scents of coffee and grilled hamburger.

I was hungry and I was already tired. I wished our table was in another part of the restaurant so that I couldn't see that snow-covered front door.

But every sf fan knew what happened to a man who made an idle wish. Things got worse instead of better.

So I checked my watch, saw that it was only 6:45, and grabbed the regular menu as I passed a rack of them. I needed something without a cute name. I needed a lot of food, because I had no idea when my next meal was coming—or if the electricity would stay on long enough for that meal to be hot.

7

I sank into the booth opposite Casper. She slid me the single-sheet menu, and I took it, even though I was clutching the other one. I was hungry, and tired, and a bit too worried about the line of the Usual Set still at check-in.

Paladin stood beside Gold, who was dead last. She wasn't letting him pull one of his usual tricks—going off to talk to someone at the front of the line, and then cutting in.

He looked even more unhappy than everyone else, which was quite a feat. They were all soggy and exhausted and probably chilled. At least Mick and Jean had left the lobby, heading to their palatial room on the far side of the hotel. Mick always bought in the block and then upgraded to something truly fancy, where he spent half the day writing and watching sports, so that he could spend the rest of the day downstairs in the most central place at the convention, telling stories and dominating any conversation he jumped into.

I half expected to see him down here already.

Casper was watching me watch them. I made myself focus on her, because we didn't get a lot of time together. I was also deeply aware of a well-hidden neediness in her. Her parents were early victims of what is now called the opioid epidemic, although I hesitate to call them victims. They could have put her first, got themselves into rehab, and figured out how to continue the nice middle-class life that they had had, but they hadn't.

They left her to fend for herself. I'd dealt with a lot of litigation getting me declared her guardian. Paladin was also part of that, although the agreement was between us because, again, she was unwilling to use her real name "unless it was absolutely necessary." There were ways to bend the law to avoid anything, and even though I was a forensic accountant, I knew more about bending the law than most people would think.

The waiter who took my order for chicken-fried steak off the main menu was one of the hotel staff who took the con seriously. He wore a propeller beanie that somehow looked good on him, and he actually smiled at me as he took the order.

Then he came back a few minutes later with the orders for Casper and Paladin. Casper had ordered a General Leia Organa salad—a large and fancy chef's salad that probably wasn't anything Carrie Fischer would ever have eaten. But Casper was going to school in San Francisco, and apparently good eating habits were part of the curriculum.

She eyed Paladin's Captain America burger—a two-inch thick hunk of prime ground sirloin, covered with mayonnaise, bacon, pickles, catsup and mustard, and sullied with American cheese. The fries half-covered the top part of the bun.

In the past, I would have wondered how Paladin was going to put away that much food, but nowadays, I no longer wondered. She had an amazing ability to fill her face and not gain any weight.

By the time Paladin finally came over to us, Casper and I were talking about a Rudy Rucker book she had discovered. I'd read *Mind Tools: The Five Levels of Mathematical Reality* years ago, when Rudy and William Gibson were co-guests of honor at a Vancouver B.C. convention, but I hadn't read the book since.

Casper had found the book in the school library and devoured it. Apparently, she'd been waiting for this trip to discuss the theories with me.

I could barely keep up. If this was an example of the kind of conversations I would have with Casper as she got older and more educated, I was going to have to brush up on my math and science. That would probably be good for me.

Paladin plunked down beside Casper and pulled the plate with the now-cooling burger closer to herself. She put the bun on top, ate the French fries that had been covering it, and cut the burger in half.

The waiter arrived at that moment with my chicken-fried steak, and his eyes grew wide at the food Paladin was about to consume.

Apparently, Casper saw the look he gave her.

"She's been pushing people out of snow drifts all day," Casper said.

The waiter nodded as if that made sense, and disappeared into the growing crowd in this portion of the café.

Paladin picked up half of the burger, and squished the sandwich between her fingers so that it would fit in her mouth. Her gaze met mine; I saw a challenge in it, that I didn't entirely understand.

"It was really that bad?" I asked again, and she looked at me with complete exasperation.

"Why do you keep asking me that?" she asked around the food. "I told you—*they've* all told you. It's worse than that bad."

"It's because Spade missed it," Casper said as she stabbed the ham in her salad. She sounded matter-of-fact, as if I always behaved like this when I missed something.

Did I? I wasn't sure.

But I nodded, needing to own up. "This is a big miss," I said quietly. I swept my hand around the café. "These people were all in serious jeopardy because of me. If I—"

"Oh, for God's sake," Paladin snapped. She started to put her burger down, then stopped herself, probably because it would be almost impossible to pick up properly again. "They're all adults, Spade. *We're* all adults—"

"I'm not," Casper said proudly, then grinned at me.

But she didn't derail Paladin. I wasn't even sure if that was Casper's intention.

"We all saw the weather forecast. We all chose to come up here anyway. A lot of people canceled, and they were probably a lot more sensible than we were, but here we are, and it's because *we* made the decision, not because you took care of us." She waved the half burger at me, as if to punctuate her point.

"It's my job to keep an eye on these things. It's my job to determine if the convention should continue or not. It's my job—"

"Actually, it's mine." Ruth stopped next to the table. She looked as weary as I felt. "I saw the forecast. The weather reports were wrong. They said the storm would arrive late Friday and blow out Sunday morning. The change in the forecast didn't happen until late last night, and I wasn't aware of it until this morning, not that that is an excuse. I just figured everyone would get here. They were planning to stay here for three days anyway, so what was the problem?"

"The problem," Casper started, but Paladin put a hand on her arm.

"I figured it would be like Donnercon," Ruth said. "An experience no one forgot, legendary in fannish circles. I didn't expect—"

"To be snowed in all winter?" Horatio had stopped next to the gate, putting his arms on it, looking forever like the Wizard leaning into Dorothy Gale's bedroom window at the end of *The Wizard of Oz*.

"That's not going to happen is it?" Casper asked with just a tinge of panic in her voice.

I rolled my eyes and shook my head. "Not even close."

"Oh, but it would be such an adventure," Horatio said. "We would have to check food stores and figure out who was in charge—"

"The concom is in charge," Ruth said.

Technically, I thought, the hotel was in charge. But I stayed quiet. Horatio was spinning a tale. He loved talking story more than he liked writing story. And he seemed to have overcome his beery morning. He looked energetic, excited even.

But he loved conventions. They were his element, and this one was now under way.

"I suppose it's in charge," Horatio said, "but if this disaster sprawls into next week, we might have to have a vote as to the actual structure of our little community."

"Let it go, Horatio," Paladin said flatly. She set down the remaining bites of the half burger. "You are never going to be in charge. None of us are that foolish."

"I have fans here," he said cheerfully.

"You can't finish a book," Paladin snapped. "All I have to do is remind them, and instantly, their joy in seeing you will turn to anger."

The smile left Horatio's face. "You're an unpleasant woman, you know that?"

She leaned back and crossed her arms. "Ah, the refuge of the ladies' man. Any woman who disagrees with him is 'unpleasant.'"

"It's not going to last into next week," Ruth said. "The roads will be clear by Monday."

"Monday?" Casper said. "But I have school—"

"And I'm sure they'll understand," I said. I paid them more than enough to understand, and if need be, I would remind them of that. But Casper didn't need to know the intricacies of expensive private school politics.

Suddenly, one of the tables in the middle of the room went over on its side. Rogers Carren, a Big Name Fan who ran a lot of West Coast conventions, was standing in the wreckage of his dinner, his chair on its side, his hand at his throat.

Paladin was out of her chair in a shot. I wasn't far behind, and neither were half of the other people in the restaurant. Paladin got to him first, somehow, and immediately grabbed him under his ribcage. She made a fist, grabbed it with her other arm, and yanked upward, once, twice, three times.

Something flew from his mouth across the dining room. People at a nearby table stood up, so that whatever it was didn't hit them.

Rogers was not a small man. He wasn't as big as me either, but he was much bigger than Paladin. I had no idea how she managed to do that so efficiently and so quickly.

Rogers stood up, his face red, sweat dripping off his chin.

"Thanks," he said, and then coughed. He coughed again, and struggled to catch his breath.

"Is there something else in your throat?" Paladin asked.

"No," he said, but his voice had become a raspy whisper. "I only had one bite."

I was up, my napkin still tucked under my chin. I had moved close enough that I could see his face, which was swelling. Faces didn't swell when someone choked on food.

"Anyone got an EpiPen?" I asked.

Half a dozen people waved EpiPens like flags over their heads. My people. I knew I could count on them. An older fan who went by the fannish moniker McCoy, because that was who inspired him to become a doctor, grabbed the nearest EpiPen, and as he hurried to Rogers's side, prepped the pen. When he reached Rogers, McCoy jammed the EpiPen into Rogers' thigh, and held the EpiPen in place as the epinephrine went into Rogers' system.

Then McCoy eased Rogers to a nearby booth. People crowded around, and McCoy told them to back off. A few fen were cleaning up the broken dishes on the floor.

There had been only one serving on the table. Rogers had been eating alone.

"Hey, Spade?" Paladin had moved to the other empty table. She was crouched near the item that Rogers had expelled. "Take a look at this."

I joined her and bent over, not really ready or able to crouch. The thing that had forcibly left Rogers' throat looked like a bit of white plastic, hidden inside of something brown and gushy and foodlike.

"What is that?" I asked.

Paladin grabbed a fork off the nearby table, and pushed at the white thing.

Then she looked up at me.

"I think," she said, "it's the number one."

8

I grabbed the seat of the nearest chair, and eased myself down. Me, crouching, wasn't the prettiest sight, but I didn't want to kneel. The carpet was soiled enough without whatever Rogers had expelled. I kept my hand on the chair and leaned forward, peering at the brown and white mass.

Paladin kept pushing at it with her fork, until the white part rose to the top. She was right: it was the number 1, about the size of the fingernail on my pinkie—maybe even smaller. The 1 was perfectly formed, like the kind of numbers you found in a children's educational game, only in miniature. If it were buried deep in his dinner, Rogers wouldn't have been able to see anything, almost like a tiny bone still embedded in an improperly cleaned fillet of fish.

"Is that food?" I asked, as Paladin kept pushing on it.

"No," she said. "I think it's plastic."

But she made no move to touch it. I didn't want to either. But I did need to document it. If Rogers decided to sue us and the hotel, I needed evidence that somebody screwed up. None of us would have been able to get close enough to put a number in Rogers' food. But someone in the kitchen might have screwed up.

I pulled out my phone and took pictures from several angles, which was about all my aching thighs and back could take. I didn't even want to think about my knees.

I put my entire forearm on the chair seat and levered myself up. Paladin put out her hands in that helpless way people did when they expected someone else to ask for help.

I'd be damned if I would ask for help standing up from one of the most in-shape people I knew. My cheeks warmed. I really didn't want Paladin to see me this way, but she had.

I managed to stand, then lumbered over to the still-overturned table. The nearby diners and at least one busser were picking up the shards of broken dishes. I photographed all of it, then looked at Rogers. I decided to photograph him, which I did discretely.

He was sweating and a weird shade of grayish pale, his eyes sunken in his face. McCoy was sitting next to him, talking to him softly. When McCoy saw me with the phone, he made a put-it-down motion. I did after shutting off the camera. As I pocketed the phone, McCoy beckoned me.

He got up as I approached, so that we weren't really talking in front of Rogers.

"This is one of those hotels that advertises onsite medical facilities, right?" McCoy asked. "Because we need something here. Otherwise we're going to have to fly him out."

I had signed a dozen waivers in the past month, and I remembered all of them. Sierra Nev did have onsite medical facilities for skiers and snowboarders mostly, so the place was filled with things that handled broken bones and frostbite.

The hotel was also clear about the fact that its on-site doctor lived in the nearby town, and could be here within fifteen minutes—on a good day. There was a helipad on the lawn for high-end guests and emergency medical flights, but I would wager any money (and I am not the gambling type) that the flights wouldn't be able to land in this storm.

Fortunately, we had, as GM Pachinski had said, a plethora of doctors among our attendees.

"Yeah, there's a medical area," I said. "I never really investigated it, but it's set up for skiing accidents. What's going on here?"

"I'm not going to say until I have a chance to investigate further," McCoy said. "But I'm concerned. Let's get him to that room."

I frowned. I had to let the front desk know, so that they would open the room.

"Can he walk?" I asked McCoy.

"Probably, with assistance," McCoy said. "I'll worry about that, but you need to get us in that room."

"I'll help," Paladin said from behind me.

"No," McCoy said, his voice soft. "I need you to collect food samples. Put them in separate bags or containers. Make sure they're well marked."

My gaze met his. Food samples. "Food poisoning?" I asked softly.

He grunted. I recognized the sound from my own doctor. It was a non-committal, *I'm not ready to tell you what I think sound.*

"Maybe a food allergy," he said, but his tone suggested it might be something more. "Just get the samples, okay?"

Paladin nodded. "Casper," she said, "go in the kitchen and ask them for to-go containers."

I turned. Casper had gotten too close to all of this. I didn't want her anywhere near this mess, and neither, apparently, did Paladin.

"How many?" Casper asked.

"As many as you can get," Paladin said.

Casper nodded and strode off, carefully avoiding the mess on the floor. Two other fen had joined McCoy and all of them managed to get him on his feet.

"You know where you're going?" I asked McCoy.

"Yeah," he said. "It's basement level, near that Starbucks wannabe."

The Starbucks wannabe was new. I had tried it once, and found "wannabe" to be the right description. McCoy wasn't far off. The medical area was right near the basement door.

"I'll be down with someone to unlock it as fast as I can," I said, and headed out of the café.

I probably should have gone to the Assistant GM, but I didn't want to take the time to find him. The front desk had all of the keys, and someone in security could let us in.

The whole thing bothered me, but only because I was tired. Having fen faint or get food poisoning or actually fall down because of some illness wasn't unusual. I'd learned long ago to leave the professional problems with the proper professional.

McCoy was a good doctor; Rogers was in good hands.

I went to the front desk, and caught Betty's eye. She had already been watching the proceedings with concern.

"We need the medical room," I said. "I know Harvey Richardson—" McCoy's real name "—isn't on your usage list, but—"

"It shouldn't be a problem," Betty said. "There's no way our staff doctor can make it here anyhow. If Mr. Richardson wants to access medications, though, we'll need some identification and the approval of our doctor and some staff."

"Then send someone who can engineer that as well as unlock the room," I said. "I have no idea what he'll need."

"I'll do it," Betty said. She grabbed a jumble of actual keys, plus a folder of key cards. "I'll be back."

I glanced over my shoulder at the café. Paladin was standing in the middle of the mess, holding a to-go container in one hand. Both of her hands were wrapped in plastic doggy bags. I had forgotten to ask about gloves, but Paladin seemed to have figured out a way to cope just fine.

I felt pulled in several directions. I should talk to Shaye, but he was so incompetent, I was afraid he'd get in the way. I needed to get to the kitchen, to make sure everything was all right there, and I needed to consult with Ruth. We didn't want this incident to dampen anyone's already strange but so-far adventurous convention.

I also needed to make sure that McCoy ignored all those patient confidentiality rules. I needed to know what had happened here.

That decided me. Paladin could handle the kitchen. I would talk to Shaye when I knew what was going on. Ruth could take care of herself.

But McCoy might think that following privacy rules was important here, and I needed to tell him otherwise. Rather than give him an order or ask him to break his oath, it would be better if I just "helped" out down in the medical room, and learned what I could in the process of treatment.

It sounded so logical inside my head. But like so many things I imagined without experiencing them first, it wasn't logical at all. It was a bit more difficult than I had ever expected it to be.

9

The medical room was in a corridor off a wide almost-lobby-sized hall, with the Starbucks wannabe on one side, a Subway wannabe on the other, and a to-go eating place with lots of prepackaged so-called healthy options that you could prepare in your room.

Most fen never saw the medical room; hell, most people who came to the hotel never saw it either. I had been shown where it was at as part of my initial tour of the hotel about a week ago, but I hadn't been allowed inside.

And I had forgotten about the fact that the basement was considered to be a daylight basement. The Sierra Nev was built into the mountain, with the bulk of the hotel on a flat plain (which, I assumed, had been flattened by bulldozers, not Mother Nature). There were two basement levels, the lower one staff-only. This one did have function space, but we hadn't rented it for this convention.

It also had locker rooms and changing areas for the skiers and snowboarders, another fireplace—this one not roaring—and several furniture groupings that were heavy on the sofas and the overstuffed chairs.

The entire basement smelled like old woodsmoke, though, and was weirdly lit. Or at least, I thought it was weirdly lit until I realized what I was seeing.

The wall of windows, complete with glass doors leading onto a stone patio that had a fire pit, and outdoor seating for the hardiest of ski bums, was covered in snow. Or buried in snow was probably more accurate, because I couldn't see the stone patio or the fire pit or the chairs.

All I saw was a wall of white, which, as I got close to it on my way to that corridor, looked like it was made of ice chunks and snow so porous that someone could have conducted an experiment to see if the old adage that no two snowflakes were alike was true.

It was extremely cold down here. I had always believed what I read about snow—that anything buried in snow stayed warm, but apparently that wasn't true at all. And then I shivered. Maybe it was true, and this was "warm."

Voices echoed from down the hall. I walked toward them, feeling a sense of urgency that I attributed to the chill. The hallway narrowed as I got deeper in it, which actually made the air slightly warmer.

The medical room's door was open, and light spilled out onto the industrial blue carpet. I knocked before going inside, even though I could see McCoy and Rogers inside. Rogers was propped up on the ultra-fancy bed, thick with mattress and linens which attempted to hide the fact that it was a high-end hospital bed in disguise. There was one more bed in the room—thankfully empty—and cabinets full of supplies. Another door, shut and locked with a keypad above the keycard slot, was just beyond the second bed.

Betty stood near the second bed, her back to the others in the room, talking softly on her cellphone.

She didn't even move at my knock, but McCoy raised his head and instead of beckoning me inside (where I would have loved to have gone, out of the chill), he raised one finger, commanding me to wait. Then he leaned over Rogers and said something softly. Rogers' bleary gaze met mine, then he looked back at McCoy. Rogers' lips moved in a distinct, but inaudible "yes."

McCoy smiled thinly and came into the hall, pulling the door partway closed.

"Rogers just gave me permission to talk to you," McCoy said. "I'll make sure he puts it in writing when I get back inside."

That sounded vaguely ominous to me, although I had no real idea why. The words were sensible, the permission necessary.

"We don't have all the tools we need," McCoy said. "Betty is working to get me on the hotel's medical department approved list, so I can access the storage closet."

He was being euphemistic, even though the two of us were the only ones in the hall. We both knew that the storage closet was really the drug closet, with all kinds of specialty drugs available by prescription only. There weren't any high-end opioids, though, because the previous doctor had overprescribed them to the hotel's skiing clientele. So the painkillers inside were decidedly old-school, pre-Oxy.

I remembered that detail from my tour, and I also remembered how relieved it made me. I was even more relieved now.

"This isn't acting like food poisoning or even some kind of allergic reaction," McCoy said. "I've taken blood, and I'm hoping there's a basic screening kit in that locked room. Otherwise, we're going to have to wait until we can get him out of here."

For a science fiction fan, I'm a reasonably healthy person. My weight causes some issues—I'm prediabetic and have under-control hypertension—but as long as I stay in touch with my doctor and follow her rules, I do all right.

As a result, I'm not all that up on medical stuff, nor was I all that interested—at least until that moment.

"Blood work?" I asked. "You think it's some kind of illness?"

McCoy shook his head. Apparently, he was used to some basic questions from the family and friends he talked to.

"No," he said. "He's not running a fever and he was feeling fine until he ate. The symptoms are familiar to me, but I don't like working without tests. I did Google them to make sure, though."

"Make sure of what?" I asked.

He let out a small breath. "I'm thinking," he said slowly, "that our friend here, Rogers, has been poisoned."

McCoy said the words portentously, as if he expected a theatrical Eb-C-F# combo—the old Dun-dun-Duuuuuuuun—to follow as terrifying musical punctuation.

I was beyond Dun-dun-Duuuuuun at the moment. The snowstorm had frozen me into a state of numbness. I just wanted to get through the next few hours.

"What kind of poison are we talking about?" I asked. "Rat poison? Arsenic?" (And, God help me, I had to force myself not to add, *Or old lace?*)

"It's too soon to tell," McCoy said. "I have a guess, but I'm not well-versed in modern poisons. I never saw any reason to study them."

He looked over his shoulder, as if checking on Rogers.

I followed McCoy's gaze. Rogers was a weird shade of gray, and his lips a strange blueish color. He seemed to be breathing all right, though.

"You don't have to worry too much," McCoy said. "He's lost the contents of his stomach twice since we brought him down here, which is also fortuitous, because now we have stomach contents too."

I suppressed a shudder, glad I didn't have to gather that stuff. There were many reasons I never considered medical school, but high on that list was the necessity of dealing with other people's bodily fluids.

"I suspect the vomiting is pretty much over," McCoy said. "I must tell you, though, that it startles me how very ill he is, because he only had one bite of food, and that got caught in his throat, so he expelled it. It never went all the way down."

I frowned. "Does that mean the poison was somewhere other than the food?"

"It might have been in the drink," McCoy said. "He had water, but not a lot of it. And he had ordered some wine with dinner, but he hadn't had any of the wine either."

I hoped Paladin picked up the glassware. The liquid would have absorbed into the carpet, but the glassware might still hold some residue.

"It's not a touch poison, is it?" I asked, remembering every damn cozy mystery series I'd ever read.

"I'm not sure," McCoy said. "I'm not up on modern poisons, as I said, but I suspect it was ingested, given the way that his body is responding. Touch poisons often show up in discoloration at the point of entry, and his fingertips look fine. I'll know more when—or if—we can test some of the fluids we do have."

I nodded.

"In the meantime," McCoy said, "I had Betty notify the kitchen that they needed to wear gloves at all times, and to scrub everything down."

I felt my heart sink at that. He had just asked them to destroy a lot of evidence.

"I'm trusting that Paladin photographed everything," McCoy said, "so we have that at least."

Either he could read my thoughts or my face was more expressive than I believed.

"I also asked them to bag any dishes used in Rogers' dinner and dinner prep, and I made sure that food prepared at the same time was thrown away."

I winced. We already had enough food issues during this storm. But McCoy was right to take that precaution. We didn't need any inadvertent poisons.

"Any open containers of ingredients have been set aside and bagged as well." McCoy took a deep breath. "I'm concerned about this, Spade. Either someone was excessively careless, or we have a much bigger problem on our hands."

I wasn't sure which I wanted it to be: carelessness was bad enough, but the "bigger problem" he alluded to was quite large indeed. If what happened to Rogers wasn't an accident, then someone had tried to kill him.

"Could this have happened before he got here?" I asked.

"A meal he had, say, on the trip?" McCoy asked.

I nodded.

McCoy shrugged. "As I've said..."

"'I'm not up on modern poisons,'" I said with him. "I know. I got it."

"Anything's possible, though," he said.

Betty peered around the door. "I finally got permission," she said to McCoy. "Everything's slow due to the storm. But your credentials came through. I'm going to give you the phone, and they'll give you the password to the storage closet."

McCoy glanced at me, then hurried inside. Betty sighed, ran a hand through her hair, and said, "I don't like any of this, Spade."

I nodded. I didn't either. Because as McCoy went inside that room, I'd had one more awful thought.

McCoy had been eating in that restaurant too. We were assuming that the source of the poison had come through the kitchen. But I'd seen enough bad TV cop shows to know that the bad guy could just as easily have tapped a few drops of something or other in Rogers' water when he wasn't looking.

McCoy had been sitting close enough for that. And ever since Agatha Christie, villains had been using their "Good Samaritan" routine to deflect suspicion off of them.

Then I shook myself. I couldn't believe I was suspecting McCoy of poisoning Rogers. If McCoy had been behind it, why tell me about the poison at all? Why not claim that Rogers had some virus or a bad heart or something else that was causing these symptoms?

Hell, McCoy had been alone with Rogers for a good fifteen minutes before I arrived, and who knew how long before Betty had come down. If McCoy actually wanted Rogers dead, that would have been the time to do so.

None of us would have suspected McCoy, and I could say that with authority, because I was one of the few who would probably suspect anyone of anything.

Based on that flimsy reed of logic, then, McCoy probably wasn't our prime suspect. I wasn't sure we had a prime suspect. I wished I knew something about modern poisons as well. Some took forever to get into the system. Many were a slow-build.

All it would take was a dab of poison on Rogers' daily pills, for example, and the poison would have built up over time.

If that was the case, the act of applying the poison wouldn't have happened here at all.

"Do you still need me down here?" Betty asked.

I shrugged. "It's not what I need. It's what McCoy needs."

"He said he wanted one more doctor down here. Do you know a Zula?"

I smiled in spite of myself. "You know," I said. "Phylicia Ransom."

"Oh!" Betty said. "Her. I was thinking the wrong way. I thought Zula was a man. You know, the Conan books?"

"I do know," I said. "They made him Grace Jones in the movies. I take it you've never seen them?"

Betty wrinkled her nose. "Not a big Schwarzenegger fan."

I nodded, keeping my own opinion to myself. I'd met the man a few times—we were in and out of the same circles on the philanthropy beat —and he was an interesting character. I seemed to collect interesting characters, so I wasn't as harsh a critic of them as some fen were.

"You do know who McCoy wants, then, right?" I asked.

"Hard to miss her." Betty eased around the door. "You want me to send her down?"

"If that's what McCoy wants," I said.

"It is." Betty waggled her fingers, and disappeared down the hallway —the opposite direction from the way I came. I mentally slapped myself on the forehead. Of course she did. She was heading toward the service elevators.

I hadn't seen Zula at this convention, although I did know her name was on the guest list. And Betty was right; Zula was hard to miss. Not just because she was one of the few long-term dark faces in the sea of whiteness that fandom had been for generations, but because she was literally built like the actress model Grace Jones.

Zula was six feet tall, muscular, and had the same kind of androgynous angular features that Jones had. Zula even kept her hair close-cropped to the sides of her head. On convention Saturdays, she usually wore some version of a Conan costume, strips of brown material over her bust and waist, with a bare midriff and often sandals or brown cloth boots.

That wouldn't be practical here, but fen often weren't practical.

Tonight, though, if she was at the convention, she was probably dressed like May Day from *A View To A Kill*. Zula made a mighty respectable Bond Girl as well.

I knew she was a doctor, because she'd helped out in emergencies at other conventions, but very few people in fandom knew what she did for a living. She preferred to keep her profession quiet; she liked to be able to relax at cons, and avoid discussing anything that even resembled work.

From what I'd heard, she was one of those doctors who put in seventeen-hour days, and a monthly convention served as her only time off.

Not this time, apparently.

I slipped inside the medical room. McCoy was clutching his cell phone in his left hand and writing down numbers with his right. If the day had gone slightly differently, I would have demanded that he memorize those numbers before chewing the paper and swallowing it, but on this day, I was afraid that McCoy would take me literally, instead of thinking of all those spy films that we both loved.

Rogers was watching me, his eyes sunk deeply in his face. I grabbed the wheeled stool that was apparently de rigueur in any doctor's office, fake or hotel or otherwise, and sat down heavily.

The stool bumped down a notch due to my weight, before settling, probably on its lowest setting.

"How are you doing?" I asked Rogers.

"I've had food poisoning at conventions before," he said, his voice raspy. "Usually my own damn fault."

Fen often brought their own food along, and kept it—unrefrigerated—in their rooms. If they brought perishables, then mild food poisoning often set in as early as Saturday.

"This does not feel like food poisoning," Rogers said.

I nodded. I did not know how to ask the detective question here, without sounding like a cliché. *How many people hate you, Rogers? Is there someone who wants you dead?*

"Did you eat something funky on the way here?" I asked.

"No," Rogers said, "and I live alone, just in case you were wondering. There's no way anyone could have tampered with my toothpaste or my meals or my medication."

But there was, Montressor, I almost said in my worst Poirot-Poe imitation. "You take medication?"

"A statin for my cholesterol. A blood pressure med." He gave me a weak smile, one heavy man to another. "You know. The usual."

I did know. "Vitamins? Daily aspirin? Tums, maybe?"

"No," Rogers said. "I have the stomach of an ox—or I did. And I eat pretty balanced when I'm not at a convention."

"Prescriptions filled at the same place?" I asked.

"No," he said. "I forgot my pills, so I had to call in an order to a Placerville pharmacy. They worked with my doc, and had my meds waiting for me as I drove through."

I frowned, trying to figure out how that worked, with the storm revving up.

"And I came through yesterday," he said. "Arrived last night. Went right to bed. Didn't eat anything here until this morning."

And those dishes would have been long gone, as would anything else. But he did have full prescription bottles in his room, so those pills could be tested too. Although I had no idea how some random pharmacist in Placerville, California, would have it out for a customer he'd never seen before.

Still, the pharmacist might've made an error.

"We'll need one of each of those pills," I said. "Properly marked. Just to see if they screwed up the prescription."

"Okay." Rogers sounded doubtful as to the wisdom of that idea. "I just keep thinking about it though. Did I hear Paladin right? Did I choke on a plastic number?"

I had no idea what to tell him. Was it better to give him all the information or none of it? Did he need to know how weird this was?

"Looks like it," I said. "But god knows what that really was. I'll look at it later."

He nodded, then sighed. If anything, he seemed pastier than before.

"Aren't you going to ask me?" he said, leaning his head back.

The question surprised me. "Ask you what?"

"Who hates me enough to kill me?" he said.

I guess he expected the clichéd detective question after all, and I wasn't delivering.

"All right, Rogers," I said. "I'll play. Who hates you enough to kill you?"

"Damn near half the planet," he said. "You do know what I do, right?"

"Lawyer," I said. "But I thought only Shakespeare wanted to kill all the lawyers."

"Not just any lawyer," Rogers said. "Divorce attorney. If I win, I piss off one half of the couple. If I lose, I piss off my client. The only people who like me are here, at a convention."

I frowned. He seemed too nice to be a divorce attorney. Which showed me just how deeply the cliché had gotten into my head too.

"Only they don't like me, do they, Spade?" Rogers said. "McCoy thinks they poisoned me. What do you think?"

I took a deep breath before telling him the truth.

"Right now, Rogers, I have no idea what to think," I said. "No idea at all."

10

By the time I made it back to the café, someone had thrown out my chicken fried steak. I was relieved about that, but I was incredibly hungry. I'd like to say that I wasn't the kind of man who could eat in a possibly tainted kitchen after all of that, but I'd be lying.

The café was bustling, as if nothing had gone wrong. Not that most of the fen eating in the café knew exactly what happened to Rogers. As far as they all were concerned, he'd choked on something and had an adverse reaction.

Normally, I would have disabused them of this notion, but I didn't. We only had limited places to eat, and I wasn't entirely sure that the problem was the kitchen here. I was kinda hoping that Rogers got poisoned over time, on his way to the hotel.

Casper still sat at our table, picking at a piece of apple pie. When she saw me, she waved at one of the waitstaff as if she'd been raised in privilege.

"Would you like your dinner now, sir?" the waiter asked as he approached.

"As long as it's newly cooked," I said. "I'll pay for both, since it was my issue but—"

"No, no," the waiter said. "The manager will comp your meal. He would like to talk with you when you're done."

My very hungry stomach clenched. Did the manager want to talk to me because he discovered that the problem was the kitchen? Or did he want to talk to me because he wanted an update?

I wanted an update too, but Paladin was nowhere to be seen. Neither was Rose. I could hear Horatio's laugh coming from the bar, and the low hum of conversation all around me.

"Where's Paladin?" I asked Casper.

"Taking the evidence upstairs," Casper said.

Evidence. That we would have to keep somewhere. I had no idea where some of it should be stored. I suppose I could ask McCoy or see if Betty would clean out an area of one of the walk-in refrigeration units. I hadn't done evidence storage, but I knew it couldn't be easy. Besides, by Monday, it would stink.

I put that on my to-do list as well, and wondered if I could farm it off on someone. This was outside of my expertise, though. I had no idea who to farm it to.

Paladin arrived just as I had that last thought, and slid into the booth next to Casper. Then Paladin picked up her fork and cut a slice of the apple pie.

Casper looked at her as if she was nuts, and I might have too.

"You can eat the food," Paladin said. "There was no apple pie on Rogers' table."

"I'm more concerned about the fresh cooked stuff," Casper said.

Paladin smiled at her, a natural smile, which was rare from Paladin. "I wouldn't worry about any of it," she said. "The kitchen's cleaner now than it's ever been, and it had an A+ rating from the health department before this."

I watched her face as she said that. She believed it.

"What do you think happened?" I asked her quietly.

"I have no idea," she said, "but I don't think he ate anything except that first bite, which I want to talk to you about when we've finished here."

At that moment, my food arrived and it looked better than anything I'd ever seen coming out of that kitchen. The gravy was thick and smooth, the potatoes perfectly mashed, the steak with its fried-chicken coating half the size of the dinner plate. The green beans were in their own little cup, so they wouldn't be sullied by the gravy, and someone had placed a sprig of parsley on the side, just like restaurants used to do in the old days.

My stomach growled, and while my brain protested that there might be a problem, my entirely olfactory system didn't care. The food smelled good and rich and oh, so fresh, and I dove in like a starving man on Donner Pass.

Okay, maybe not the best analogy in a historic snowstorm.

Casper watched me eat with something like incredulousness, but I couldn't tell if the reaction was from the kind of food I was eating (this was definitely not a salad) or if it was because that food came out of the kitchen.

"Casper says you put the evidence in your room," I said when I could finally take a breath.

"I *said* that she took the evidence *upstairs*," Casper said with grand disdain. "I *didn't* say she took it to our room."

That tone, which I had noticed earlier in reference to Paladin, was new. I had no idea if it was because Casper was hitting puberty or because she felt comfortable with us or because she truly felt the disdain.

Paladin's gaze met mine. She raised one of her pixieish eyebrows, Spocklike, in a silent comment on Casper's tone.

Then Paladin said, "I am using the mezzanine bar refrigerator. I asked, and the food and beverage manager agreed. He even let me reset the combination, so that only you and I will be able to get at the evidence."

She slid a piece of paper at me with numbers on it. I took the paper and put it in my wallet.

"We should probably call the authorities," she said.

"We will," I said. "As soon as McCoy finishes up a few things."

I didn't want to tell her in this public space about the possible poisoning, although it looked like she was coming to that on her own.

"Is Rogers better?" Paladin asked, her voice lower than it had been a moment ago.

"He seems to be," I said, scraping what gravy remained on my plate with one of the dinner rolls that had shown up with my food. "Time will tell."

"I don't like this," Paladin said. "Something feels really off to me."

"You mean besides the blizzard and what happened to Rogers?" I asked.

"Yeah, I do," Paladin said. "There's something I can't quite put my finger on."

"You ever been at a convention in crisis before, Paladin?" I asked.

She frowned at me. "Like what?"

"Let's see," I said, trying to remember some of the ones I'd experienced. "Earthquakes all weekend at the Nebula Award Ceremony in San Francisco—"

"I don't think the Nebula Awards count as an sf convention," Paladin said quietly.

"It was a convention," I said. "One of the first ones I worked. Just because it was geared to pros—"

"We don't caaaa-aaare," Casper said not as quietly as she thought.

I stopped, located my lost train of thought, and then said, "There was that record heat at the Phoenix Westercon. You might remember that."

Paladin frowned.

"The convention had been downtown," I said, trying to jog her memory as to which Phoenix Westercon. "Everything shut down during the Fourth of July weekend. We couldn't walk to food, and we didn't want to."

"Record heat doesn't sound like a blizzard," Casper said, leaning toward Paladin. Apparently that remark hadn't been addressed at me, so I didn't stop.

"Then there were the tornadoes touching down all around us and the severe thunderstorms all weekend, leading to flash flooding at the badly named and even more poorly run CrockettCon in San Antonio. That was the con where I realized that historic hotels, especially historic hotels near a controversial historic site, really shouldn't be con sites—"

"You know," the new, disdainful Casper said, "it's only old guys who reminisce about stuff no one else cares about."

"Um, Spade," Paladin said almost simultaneously. "You made your point."

"My point," I said, because they had annoyed me, "is that what's going on here is pretty similar to what happened at other weird-weather cons. The weather seems to take the energy out of the con itself. It's less fun and—"

"An earthquake isn't weather," Casper said.

I stopped and looked at her, resisting the urge to remind her that I had said *earthquakes*, not earthquake. And that Nebula ceremony had occurred six months after the Loma Prieta quake which had caused a highway to collapse. Everyone had been on edge.

It had been as strange as the other cons, maybe even stranger, because Gardner Dozois, the editor of *Asimov's SF Magazine* at the time, had sprinted from the balcony of a con suite to a doorway, which was just about as startling as watching me sprint...well, anywhere.

People talked about that for years. Years. But, apparently, not in the presence of Paladin. And Casper was too young.

I bit my lower lip, realizing that, in the moment, I had become one of the old-time fen, telling a story that no one remembered but me, and everyone else pretended interest. Or didn't pretend interest, as the case may be.

"So," Paladin said with a sideways look at Casper, "your point is that the feeling I have is being caused by the circumstances of this convention, not by some kind of valid hunch of my own."

I froze. Had I just mansplained something? I hadn't meant to.

"It's just that weather—" and then I looked at Casper, and corrected myself. "*Disaster*-challenged conventions feel different than other conventions. That's all."

Paladin raised both eyebrows, as if to dispute my thesis. But she didn't do so verbally, which actually told me how preoccupied she was.

"I'm still going to go with internal hunch," she said. "I just can't put my finger on what's causing it. I feel like I'm asking the wrong questions."

I sighed internally. What was causing it was the weather. We wouldn't have freaked out as badly about Rogers if this were a normal convention.

"What questions have you been asking?" I asked.

"I talked to the food and beverage manager when we were putting the evidence away." Her voice lowered even more, not that she needed to. The groups that had crowded every table in the café were gone now —except for an amoeba table across the café from us, with half of the Usual Set finally sitting down to dinner. (An amoeba table was one that continually absorbed other tables and diners, so it was a mish-mash of tables, chairs, and fen. Amoeba tables confused waitstaff, confounded restaurant managers, and were a staple of every sf convention since the 1939 Worldcon—and no, I wasn't there. I'm not that old.)

The Usual Set didn't appear to be listening to us. No one else was walking by in the corridor. Another amoeba table had formed near the gigantic fireplace, yards away from us, unable to hear. They appeared to be getting bar service.

No one, not even waitstaff, seemed close enough to overhear what Paladin, Casper, and I were talking about.

"I asked the F&B manager if they had new employees on this weekend in the café," Paladin was saying. "He said working this convention was hard enough every year, so he brought in regulars. This time, with the snow coming, he'd had to call a few past employees who had retired. They, in turn, reminded him of a few others who were still in the area and had moved on to other jobs. In other words, no one here is new, no one is a recent hire, and everyone has SierraCon experience."

"Well, technically," the new disdainful Casper said, "some of the returning staff would be considered recent hires."

Paladin and I looked at Casper. And finally, because I was paying for her education and because I wasn't the best at social interactions, I decided to say something—only to have Paladin beat me to it.

"What's your problem, Casper?" Paladin snapped. "That fancy school make you too good for us?"

Casper leaned back as if she had been slapped.

I wouldn't have added the second sentence, nor would I have asked the first quite so bluntly. But as Paladin often told me, she was a bulldozer. I was the one with finesse, for what good it did us.

Casper's eyes filled with tears. She looked at me balefully, and I had the sense she would have bolted from the table if Paladin wasn't blocking her way.

"I didn't mean...I'm...Can I leave now?" Casper asked, and she asked me, not Paladin.

I shook my head, feeling so far out of my depth that I couldn't find the surface if I wanted to.

"Did we do something to upset you?" I asked quietly.

Casper had made her eyes round. She hadn't blinked since they filled with tears, probably because she didn't want the tears to fall.

I resisted the urge to wipe the tears away with my thumb, because I'm an old fat guy and everyone on the planet would take that gesture wrong these days.

She shook her head ever so slightly. Tears sprayed across the table, and she looked appalled.

"I'm sorry," she whispered again. "Can I leave now?"

"No," Paladin said, apparently unmoved by tears. "You've been rude since we left this morning. What's going on?"

"Problems at school?" I asked, not sure what that could be. I was seeing Casper's grades in real time. Computers had made everything easier, and as her legal guardian, I was entitled to see test scores, attendance records, and everything else. I got notifications on my phone whenever something new was posted, and nothing was.

"They want to know who my parents are," Casper said, again, facing me, not Paladin. "They say I'm a charity case. And we all know that charity cases have no value."

I supposed that "we all know" was a refrain she'd heard, not something she expected us to agree with.

"We *do?*" Paladin asked, apparently not making the same leap I had.

Casper's face turned down into a misery that seemed deeper than any I'd seen from her.

"They won't talk to me, and they make me sit by myself, and they think I'm hiding something—and I *am*. I won't tell them about my parents, because you're right—" and here Casper looked at Paladin, "—my parents aren't worthy of the word. So I don't count them as parents anymore. But we all know that I'm your charity case, and you wouldn't do this if you didn't have to, and you *don't even trust me enough to tell me your name!*"

It was Paladin's turn to lean back as if she'd been slapped. The color left her face.

Casper had spoken so loudly that the conversation had ended at the amoeba table, and the Usual Set looked over at us with one single movement.

I waved a hand in an ironic *hello*, silently informing them all that there was *nothing to see here*, and they looked away. Or at least, most of them did. Rochelle O'Reilly frowned at me with something like concern.

I looked back at Casper. Tears flowed down her face now, and her breath hitched, which seemed to mortify her.

"No one knows Paladin's name," I said quietly. "I certainly don't."

Paladin's mouth thinned.

"And we—I—care about you," I said, wondering what the line was in this #MeToo world. Could I tell a girl child that I've known less than a year that I loved her? Hell, screw the permission. I wasn't even sure I was capable of telling her that I loved her. I had never uttered that sentence to anyone in my entire life.

Casper was staring at me, her eyes clearer than they had any right to be, given how she was still leaking tears.

"I took you on because I like you," I said. "Because I believe in you."

Was I getting mushy? I could feel my face heat. I had never felt this exposed with anyone. And Paladin was watching, as if she had never seen me before.

"Because you're one of the smartest people I've ever encountered," I said. "I'm honored to take a small part in your education and upbringing. I'm glad we met, and I—"

I almost said the *love* word. I wasn't sure how that would play, and as a result, it caught in my throat.

I cleared said throat, sounding weirdly like my father. I'd never realized he made that noise when he was getting emotional until right at this moment, and it made complete sense to me. Of course, I would channel him at the very wrong time.

"You're not a charity case, Casper," I said, sounding hoarse. "You and Paladin, you're my family."

The heat in my face grew. I probably shouldn't have included Paladin in that sentence, because she looked at me fiercely. She probably didn't even understand what I meant. But I couldn't take the words back.

I didn't want to take the words back. I meant them, each and every one of them.

"For real?" Casper whispered.

"For real," I said. "You want me to tell your friends that? I probably have more money than all their parents combined, and I have a lot of degrees, and I've put them all to use, but I don't present well, if, indeed, they even care what an adult looks like—"

"They're not my friends," she said in that same whisper.

"Well, that's pretty damn obvious," Paladin said, apparently recovering her poise. Or whatever she called it.

Casper winced.

Paladin frowned at her, and then Paladin's shoulders slumped. Apparently she was beginning to realize she was screwing up. Big time.

"I mean," Paladin said, "that friends wouldn't treat you like they're treating you. I didn't mean that there's something wrong with you."

Then she cursed, several heartfelt swear words combined with words I never thought were swear words, although she was making a convincing case for it.

Casper's tears had dried up, and her eyebrows were raised. She had clearly never heard Paladin do that, and I had only heard it once before, when Paladin thought she had screwed up.

Paladin took Casper's hand, squeezed it probably too hard, and then let go. "You're my family too, and I'll happily tell anyone that if they try to argue otherwise."

Casper folded her fingers into a fist, then stretched them out, like people often did when they were easing an ache. Paladin didn't seem to notice.

Instead, she was looking down, which was not something she normally did.

"As for my so-called real name," she said, "I doubt anyone knows it. I don't use it. It was given to me by people I have nothing to do with, and I reject it like I reject them."

Lesser people would have added, *Surely you understand*, or something like that, but Paladin wasn't that person. She didn't strive for sympathy. She was simply stating a fact.

Casper looked riveted. "You mean I can do that?" she asked in that same half-whisper.

"Not yet," I said, stopping myself before I added, *There are better ways to do so, legal ones.* I didn't want to insult Paladin.

"I suppose when I'm an adult, right?" Casper said. If she'd spoken that same sentence fifteen minutes ago, she would have said it with disdain. Now, she said it with a touch of wistfulness.

"We'll see," I said, and then my breath caught. Did I actually say the dreaded parental sentence? "I mean, you know, let's give it some time."

"Why?" she asked, her gaze meeting mine. "I don't like my parents. They did nothing for me. I can reject—"

"Yes, you can reject," I said. "But I'd rather have you do something positive. Choose a name because you like it, not because you need it."

I worked very hard at not looking at Paladin, but I saw her anyway. She was sitting up straighter than she had, and she looked very serious.

"Spade is right," she said. "You want a name that will reflect who you are for your whole life. That takes time to pick."

Then she looked at me. I nodded, understanding finally. Paladin was her name, not her moniker. She could live with that for the rest of her life.

I had a hunch young Paladin wouldn't have known how to live up to that name at all.

"Okay," Casper said with slightly less of a whisper. "But how do I get them to stop picking on me?"

I could get them to stop. I *would* get them to stop. I was going to talk with the school, because this was bullying.

"You don't," I said. "You don't get them to stop. They will continue as long as they know it hurts you. You keep doing what you do—"

"You just have them talk to me," Paladin said, with a little too much relish. "I can convince them—"

"No," I said. "We'll figure this out."

I made myself look at Casper, not Paladin. Casper's tears had dried, but her skin was blotchy and her nose was red. I handed her my unused napkin so that she could wipe off her face.

"I have to fight my own battles, right?" Casper said.

I shook my head. "It's just that bullying is tough. There are no easy answers. If we can't solve this, we'll move you to a different school. You—"

"No," Casper said, this time with strength. "I like the school."

Paladin frowned. She didn't seem to understand that. "You do?"

Casper nodded. "The classes. They're hard. I've never had hard classes before. I'm good at hard. They're not."

The *they're* probably referred to the other students. They were probably jealous.

"Grades matter at this school right?" I asked.

Paladin frowned at me. She didn't understand where I was going with this.

But Casper was nodding.

"And you all know each other's grades?" I asked.

"It's on a curve," she said.

"You blow out the curve," Paladin breathed, then smiled at me.

"Yeah?" Casper said. "So?"

"So they're trying to get you off your game," Paladin said. "Make you uncomfortable. Make you pay more attention to them than to your schoolwork."

It wasn't that simple. It was never that simple. But Paladin's words seemed to buck Casper up.

"Really?" Casper asked.

"Probably," I said, not wanting that to be the definitive answer. I gave Paladin my fiercest *don't contradict me* look.

Casper bit her lower lip, then nodded slowly. She looked forever like Paladin, and I wondered how much of that was imitation (the sincerest form of flattery).

"I can work with that," Casper said, more to herself than to us.

I put out my hand, not quite touching hers. "You let us know what's happening, though," I said.

"I'll come down there," Paladin said. "I'll talk to them—"

"Just let us know," I said, not wanting the bulldozer involved at all. "We have a lot of options. You aren't going through this alone."

Casper breathed out again, just enough to reveal the relief. She had been thinking she was alone, that we didn't care for her, that she meant nothing to anyone.

How did we let that happen? Or had it been there all along, and I missed it?

I'd have to talk with Paladin later. Or maybe with one of the experts around here. There were doctors, yes, and psychologists too, and damn near everyone in fandom had been bullied at one point or another. We all had our tricks for dealing with it.

And our aches from living with it.

"We got you, kid," I said, and I meant it.

She smiled, and that might've been her first real smile of the entire convention.

"Thanks, you guys," she said, and then she looked at the paper menu. "Anyone else want ice cream?"

"In a snowstorm?" Paladin asked.

"Sure," I said, and ordered some. With hot fudge for Paladin. Just because.

11

Well, that had been an unexpected detour at dinner. Late dinner, since the other two had eaten before I arrived. We had ice cream, and somehow we laughed, and the tension left the table, and the discomfort I'd been feeling all day disappeared...

For an hour or so.

It all came flooding back when I saw McCoy go by, pushing Rogers in one of the two wheelchairs that had been in the medical room. McCoy and Rogers were heading to the elevators.

I signed the bill to my room, and excused myself, hurrying toward them. My entire demeanor must have registered concern because McCoy spoke before I could even ask what was going on.

"I'm taking Rogers to my room," McCoy said. "I upgraded to a suite, when it became clear no one was going to be here, so I can keep an eye on him. The medical room is locked up tight."

"Okay," I said. Then I looked at the wheelchair, and at Rogers. He expected me to say something.

Instead, McCoy added, "He can walk. He's just tired. And I figured since we have wheelchairs we may as well use one."

I nodded, registering the comment differently than perhaps McCoy intended. If McCoy thought he could remove a wheelchair from the medical room for an ambulatory patient, then McCoy thought this entire incident was a one-off.

That relieved me somehow.

"You doing okay?" I asked Rogers, then winced. He was still pale. His eyes were red-rimmed and his lips were a little blue, but less blue than they had been.

"I've been better," Rogers said, then he attempted a smile. "But I've been worse, just today."

"I'm, uh, glad you're better." I was too, even though I probably sounded insincere. Expressing well wishes, however well meant, was not my strong suit.

Rogers gave me a weak smile, and we stared awkwardly at each other for a moment. So I did what I always did when I had no idea what to say. I nodded and changed the subject.

"Did you ever find Zula?" I asked McCoy.

"Yeah," McCoy said. "She's going to spell me if I need it. We're okay right now."

And then the elevator dinged, and the door opened, disgorging eight fen, who probably took up the space of twelve people. I had no idea how they managed to fit into the elevator, but that only proved it was a convention. Overstuffed elevators were part of the experience.

One of them knocked a nearby standalone ashtray, something that reminded me we were technically in Nevada, not California, even though smoking wasn't legal in the corridors of either state. This ashtray had the look of some antique.

It was heavy as one, because I had to move it aside to make room for the wheelchair.

McCoy pushed Rogers inside, and the doors started to ease closed. But before they did, three more people pushed their way onto the elevator. I waved at everyone and watched the doors finally shut.

I turned away from the elevator, feeling disconcerted. The conversation with Casper and Paladin had put me off my game. I was used to handling convention problems, not real life problems. And I'd never dealt with any bullying but my own, back in the dark ages, when we were all told to suck it up and stop being babies about it.

A shudder ran through me. I knew that the research had come up with ways of dealing with bullying, but I didn't know what they were, and I needed to research it, although not at the moment.

At the moment, I had to find Ruth for an update. I figured she would know who had arrived and who had canceled, without me going through the entire hotel system to figure it out.

I still had a schedule to plan. Programming didn't officially start until noon the following day, but that was coming up a lot faster than any of us expected.

I started down the wide corridor by the café. The amoeba table had grown even more, although Ruth was not part of it. Now, the amoeba table included Tommy Kaslowski and a few of his brave students. I would have waved them away from that den of verbal vipers, but Kaslowski was oblivious. He figured it was good to introduce budding writers to the Usual Set, given the fact that the Usual Set had a lot of editors.

But the Usual Set, this late in a stressful evening, had a lot of witty, tired editors, whose tongues were sharp to begin with. They knew how to land a barb, but usually only did it with each other.

I frowned at them all, suddenly realizing how much their behavior resembled Casper's before Paladin confronted her. That overcompensating intellectualism, those barbed comments about other people's interests.

The Usual Set might've been the top of the heap here, but I would wager they hadn't been when they were in school either. And they learned to be sharp-tongued just to survive.

I decided in that moment I would take a lot less offense to whatever verbal shenanigans Casper pulled, and I would remember they came from a place of pain.

I'd remember for the weekend, anyway. I had no idea how long I could sustain that thought.

I passed the café and glanced at the amoeba table near the fireplace. It was hotter down here, but not a pleasant kind of hot. It was the uneven out-of-control hot that came from sitting too close to an open flame.

It also stank of woodsmoke, a scent most people loved, but one that reminded me of camping. And camping had never been my forte.

Ruth was not at that amoeba table either. I was about to leave when Zombie Killer stood up. He looked dead on his feet, making his nickname seem even more accurate.

"Hey, Spade," he said, his voice reedy with exhaustion. "Any idea when the hotel will open the exercise room?"

The entire amoeba table let out with cries of derision and laughter.

"...at a con, Dave? Really..."

"...there's better ways to get exercise..."

"...sit still for an entire weekend and see how it feels..."

I lifted a hand for quiet, but that didn't work. So I beckoned Zombie Killer to come closer.

"The hotel usually revamps the exercise room during a con weekend," I said.

"This isn't a normal con weekend," he said, "and I need to get in my five miles before I do anything else."

I had no words for that. None. Because whatever words I chose would be wrong.

Casper had me on edge. I was afraid anything I could say would be harmful.

"I'll ask them," I said, then pivoted. "You see Ruth anywhere?"

"She was heading Con Ops last I saw her," he said. "But that was an hour ago or more."

"Okay," I said. "Let's go to the desk and see what we can do about your five miles."

My mission at the hotel desk proved easier than expected. A couple of other people had already asked about the exercise room—thank you, Zombie/Reindeer Run—and the hotel had agreed to leave the exercise room open 24/7.

I got a sense from the attitude of the hotel staff that they'd do anything to keep us happy and occupied this weekend.

Still, I thanked them and said good-bye to a happy Zombie Killer. He was heading to bed—at eight, at a convention, so he could get up and run five miles on a treadmill. With all of the con activities available and one of the world's best breakfast buffets (should the power hold), I saw no reason to 1) get up early for any reason and 2) exercise.

The very thought made me shudder. Even though I knew there was a chance I would see him as he toddled to the exercise room. But if I did, I would see him because I hadn't gone to bed yet, not because I had gotten up early.

Still, he made me feel just a little guilty about that massive dinner I'd had, so I decided to forgo the elevator on my way to Con Ops. And okay, it was six of one, half dozen of another, because the elevators were far behind me, and Con Ops was just up the majestic staircase beyond the fireplace.

The stairs were pretty low and spaced far apart, so walking up them was almost like walking up a gentle ramp. The staircase curved around that side of the hotel, giving me a view of everything from the main desk to the fireplace to the lobby bar.

Horatio still held court there, but I noticed that his beer stein was empty, and his meaty fist was wrapped around a bottle of water. He was a long-time pro; he knew how to nurse a drink through the evening. That made me wonder if his beery afternoon had been a mistake, because he hadn't expected to start so early.

He didn't see me as I headed up the stairs, but a few of the Secret Masters of Fandom, seated at a second table in the bar, waggled their fingers at me. I was relieved to see them. Ruth and I were both SMoFs, so we knew how to run things, but in an emergency, it was always better to have some other hands on deck.

From above, the rest of the lobby looked like any hotel lobby on the night before a convention—amoeba tables, people greeting each other loudly, lots of hugging and laughter and promises to catch up.

It made me smile, even though I could see the storm battering the exterior of the hotel, keeping the windows and the big doorways an unnatural white.

One of the few mantras I'd been repeating to myself all day was that this hotel had been built to withstand heavy snows and bad weather. The power lines were underground, and there were more than enough emergency generators to keep us all warm.

I still didn't like the feeling of isolation, though, and I wasn't happy with another thread playing through my mind.

This hotel made me think of the hotel in the crappy (but artistic) Kubrick movie *The Shining*. That hotel was also massive and decorated in early hunting lodge browns and greens, just like this one. I half expected to see creepy little twin girls in the hallway outside my room every time I emerged.

When I reached the top of the stairs, I was relieved to see the mezzanine level was empty and expectant, with signs everywhere about the convention. Little bits of normality helped me remain calm. We would not only get through this, I kept repeating to myself, but we would probably have memorable fun along the way.

Rows of tables were set up near the walls, with folding chairs behind them, waiting for the registration volunteers to show up early— well, not Zombie-Killer early, but con early—and hand out packets.

Someone had already put flyers on the flyer table, and only one big sign was on the sign board, advertising a room party that would start at eleven p.m.

The sign boards got less usage these days. Private room parties often got established by text, which I found irritating, because I would have to plead ignorance if the hotel asked me to shut one down.

I headed behind the tables to the function space hallway. The sign boards were already out, ready for us to finalize the morning program so that the hotel could list which panels were in what rooms.

It felt odd to me that I hadn't even considered what panels would need to be changed. Usually I did a goodly part of that work in my head, negotiating the changes, figuring out who had arrived, who hadn't, who got along, and who didn't.

I turned the corner, saw the narrower hallway for the lesser function space, and cursed my overactive imagination. Of course, I had to think about those Stephen-King-Stanley-Kubrick evil twins as I had come up the stairs. I half-expected to see them here, now blocking my way.

That was all we needed on top of the stresses already at this convention—malevolent ghosts.

I shook off the feeling with the mental notation that Paladin had been right after all: something did decidedly feel off here. Maybe it was a combination of the storm, the emergency in the café, and the conversation with Casper, but I was oddly on edge in a way that was very unfamiliar to me.

The only door in this wing that was open was the door to Con Ops. The door to the Greenroom, which would be a few doors down, already had its "Private! Invitation Only!" paper pasted to the outside. Ruth had called that a hint to the hotel to have something more formal made up, the way that they usually did.

I stepped inside Con Ops, and braced myself for the smell. We were only one day into the unofficial part of the convention, so Con Ops shouldn't have been entirely overrun with stench—and it wasn't. Half the tables were empty, waiting for the hotel to lay out a cold food buffet starting in the morning.

Usually, at most cons I worked, the Thursday night dinner was too much pizza, but there was nowhere to call for pizza near this hotel, even pre-storm, and the hotel's pizza, while good, was not worth eating after a delicious meal.

My Tower of Terror was up, though, along with the Captain's Chair. I had set up my massive convention computer system the night before, and had promptly forgotten about it after I locked Con Ops for the night. I hadn't even checked on my baby since I got up this morning, which showed just how distracted I was.

Still, from a distance, it was clear no one had touched my system. When I met Paladin, she had been sleeping in my chair, but she was the only person, besides me, to ever use it for any length of time. I suspected Casper spent a bit too much time in it, but I'd never caught her at it.

Ruth sat on the floor, papers strewn around her. I'd seen her do this at dozens of conventions. She was old-fashioned enough to use paper to reorganize things, a process I didn't entirely understand.

Her walkie-talkie was propped up against her waist, looking forever like it was holding her upright. She was chewing on the ear piece of her glasses, and her face looked naked and vulnerable without them.

"Ruth?" I asked.

She jumped. She hadn't heard me come in.

"Spade," she said, her calm voice belying that startle reaction. "Did you know that all of the Usual Set would be here?"

"They were on the guest list," I said.

"But you hadn't put most of them on programming," she said.

"Yeah," I said. "No one would tell me when they were going to arrive."

It was my practice to leave off big names if I didn't have an arrival date. I would understaff the panels, and pencil in (metaphorically speaking) the big names until I knew their plans.

When I hadn't heard from anyone on the Usual Set, I figured they weren't sure they were going to arrive at all.

"I'm not sure how to fit them all in," she said.

"I'll take care of the last-minute programming," I said, not adding that it would be a lot quicker and easier to do it on the Tower of Terror than it would be by shuffling papers around. Besides, I really didn't want to sit on the floor.

"We've had so many personnel changes that I'm not sure what's going on." Ruth rubbed her eyes. "And then something happened to Rogers. You know about that, right?"

"I was there," I said.

She sighed, and said, "That's two."

I made a face. I understood fannish superstition, but that didn't mean I liked it. And by saying *that's two*, Ruth was referring to the superstition that bad luck ran in threes.

I assumed, from context, that the number one thing she was referring to was the blizzard itself.

"Oh, I don't know," I said before I could stop myself. "He coughed out the number one."

"What?" She looked up at me, startled.

"You didn't know? There was a tiny number one in the food that got lodged in his throat. McCoy thinks that might be what Rogers choked on." And probably saved his life, since the poison hadn't gotten into his

97

system...if, indeed, that mouthful of food had been what caused the poisoning.

"Well that's not any good," she said. "That means we have two more to wait for."

"Oh, I don't know," I said, wishing I hadn't said anything. "It depends on how you look at it. We lost our editor guest of honor to the storm, but gained the Usual Set. So is that a win or a loss? The hotel seems to be going out of its way to make us happy, and we still have power, so—"

"Stop!" she said. "Let's not count our blessings. Because Loki might hear, and then decide to mess everything up."

I shook my head at her. "Loki?"

She laughed. "Okay. I'm stressed, and not in a night-before-programming-starts way."

And that's three, I almost said, but didn't, because I didn't want to unnerve her more.

Instead, I said, "Let's go over our guest lists and figure out what we're doing tomorrow."

Her smile faded as she handed me copies of everything she had printed out. And, because she had worked with me half a million times, she also had notations about which papers were in the cloud and which ones weren't.

Not that it was hard for me to tell. The papers that were made up mostly of hand-scrawled scribbles weren't in the cloud, and the rest of them were.

"We are lucky," she said as I took the papers over to the Tower of Terror.

"How do you figure?" I asked.

"We only lost about fifty attendees and guests. Everyone else showed."

That surprised me. And it was lucky, because it meant that SierraCon was not only in the black, but it would probably make a profit—if the weekend went anything approximating normal, that is.

"I didn't think there was that big a crowd downstairs," I said.

"A lot of people arrived stressed and went to their rooms after that drive, figuring they would start fresh tomorrow," Ruth said.

I didn't blame them. If I had had to make that drive in the conditions that Paladin had described, I might've gone to bed too.

Ah, who the hell was I kidding? I would have mingled downstairs, had something to drink and much-too-big dinner, and spent time with old friends.

Con time always seemed long, but the weekends ended fast, and there was no guarantee that we'd see old friends again any time soon.

"You look serious," Ruth said.

I looked down at the papers just for show. "We're going to have to revamp everything."

And so we did.

12

I sent Ruth to bed around two a.m. She was a great help, but she had started to yawn, and whenever someone started to yawn in the middle of a programming revamp, the sleepies would hit everyone. Since there wasn't an everyone on this late night, just her and me, I didn't dare let the sleepies anywhere near me.

She thanked me and headed off to her room, after making me promise twice that I would upload the finished schedule to the cloud (as if I could forget. The Tower of Terror was state-of-the-art, and I had it set to upload everything while we were working on it).

After she left, I did plaster a few stickie notes around the room, reminding myself to send all of the information to the hotel's email account when I finished. They didn't have to set up the sign boards properly, but it was better if they actually had the chance.

Programming had proven harder than expected, not because we had so few choices, but because we ended up with so many. Anyone of the Usual Set was better than the new(ish) editor we were bringing in, the one who hadn't arrived. She was good, but had been invited only because she had a roster of up-and-coming stars, so the concom figured she had her finger on the pulse of the field, whatever that meant.

She didn't. She was just the hot young editor of the hot young things. (Well, writers are rarely young, even when they're new. But you know what I mean.)

I'd thrown in some late-night panels on convention horror stories, figuring there was nothing better than being snowed in—even if the power went out—and telling "real life" horror stories by gaslight. Or the light of cell phones or fake kerosine lamps or whatever we might end up with.

And, of course, if anyone could consider a convention "real life," besides me.

I finished up, sent the program to the Publications Committee, so they could try to print up the day's schedule, made sure I had emailed all of the panelists about any changes that might occur. I also emailed everything to the hotel, as promised. Then I mentally patted myself on the back.

I'd managed to keep the panels mostly the same. I had added to them, of course, but I hadn't changed all that much. Good planning paid off again.

I shut down the Tower of Terror. It wasn't my usual procedure, but with potential power issues, I didn't want a sudden surge to zap the Tower. And even though I had pooh-poohed it, I didn't want to admit that Ruth had added to my stress by mentioning that we were waiting on a third crisis.

For me, that third crisis would be a complete electronic evisceration of the Tower itself.

Before I shut down the Tower, I did something I hadn't done in a century or more (okay, maybe six months or so). I backed up all the new convention materials on a thumb drive. I was more concerned about the nearby cell towers remaining up, although Ruth had told me when she first booked this place years ago that one of the things she loved about it was that it was on the mountaintop along with half a dozen cell towers.

We were closer to the cell towers than all the major cities on either side of the Sierra Nevada. Which both reassured me and worried me. I did most of my work using a personal hotspot rather than the hotel's Wi-Fi, and the hotspot was dependent on cellular technology.

That made me nervous. Hell, everything was making me nervous, which I was starting to chalk up to all the Coke I'd been drinking. We'd run out of caffeine-free Diet early in the evening (well, earli*er* in the evening), and I hadn't minded since I found that stuff to be an abomination anyway.

I drank Coke, but when I normally would have switched to caffeine-free Diet, there wasn't any. So I was jittery.

I straightened my work area, because I always straightened my work area, tossed the cans in the growing black garbage bag of death, hoping the hotel janitorial staff was one of the few groups that had stayed at the hotel, and then let myself out of Con Ops. I locked the room, and double-checked it, because I was tired, and checked my watch as I trudged toward the elevators.

Three-thirty a.m. Not quite the time that Zombie Killer had said he would start his five-mile treadmill run, but damn close.

I went immediately to my room, saw that I had no real messages, and toppled on my bed, falling asleep facedown in my clothes.

My alarm woke me four hours later, which was a heck of a lot of sleep for a person on the concom at a major convention in the middle of a blizzard. My face was smashed against one of the hotel pillows, my cheek was covered in drool and somehow my entire body had gotten entombed in the hotel bedspread. Well, if that wouldn't give me the con crud next week, nothing would. I should have peeled the bedspread off earlier in the night when I'd actually thought about it.

I got up, wiped my hand over my mouth, and decided against checking my phone right away. I needed a shower.

The rules for any sf convention were 6/3/2—at least six hours of sleep (well, failed that), at least three meals per day (usually not a problem), and at least two showers for the entire weekend.

I usually missed on sleep and overcompensated with both food and showers. I was large and noticeable as it was; I didn't need to wear my clothes for three days and not shower to make me even more difficult to be around.

The shower was deliciously hot, making me realize the room had just an edge of cold. I hadn't looked outside the window before taking the shower, and I didn't now. I didn't want to know, even though I was sure I would find out soon enough.

The shower had awakened me just enough that I would be able to make it to the World's Best Breakfast Buffet and be relatively witty. I had a reputation to maintain, after all.

I pulled on black jeans and my Official Day One T-shirt for this (and damn near any other) convention. The T-shirt was black with bright orange lettering and read, *I'm not trying to be difficult. It just comes naturally.*

I figured the T-shirt would cover me should I be inadvertently rude to the wrong person. Although most of the people here knew me and knew to stay out of my way on Official Day One.

Technically, it was day God Knows How Many because we'd been in intense prep now for more than a week. But all of the attendees were here, which was a weird feature of this particular convention, because of the snow.

Usually we had day-people, who generally showed up for Saturday. Since Horatio was the guest of honor, we had hoped for a large group of day-trippers to arrive for Saturday, and had scheduled his big signing accordingly.

In fact, Saturday was Horatio's big programming day. In addition to the signing, he would give a reading and a GOH speech, and he would judge the Masquerade that night.

He was busy enough on this day, though, primarily because Horatio loved science fiction conventions, and loved being the center of attention at them. He had signed up for more than his fair share of programming, and we (or I) had obligingly put him on as many programming items as we could, and still have room for other panelists.

I expected Horatio to still be asleep when I went down for breakfast, but he was there, in line at the café, a heaping plate of food in one hand. He was standing in front of the omelet bar, picking ingredients. I overheard ham and sausage and tomatoes and three kinds of cheese, although he did opt to forgo the onions "in consideration of others."

I doubted that consideration would last the weekend. It rarely did.

The café was nearly empty at this time of the morning, except for those of us who had concom duties and the unnaturally awake, like Zombie Killer.

He was sitting by himself at a booth, with a meager ration of food in front of him, considering the exercise he had already done. One omelet in front of him, some fruit on a plate, and a single jelly donut sitting forlornly in the middle of the table.

Maybe there was more than one reason that Zombie Killer was so thin. Then I smiled to myself. Maybe that reason was because he didn't run conventions.

I grabbed two jelly donuts and a chocolate éclair, as well as an actual slab of ham, au gratin potatoes, some sauteed asparagus that I had no intention of eating, and watermelon. I set all of that on the table the host had chosen for me after I requested something behind one of the plants.

Before I even ate any of it, I went back, ordered two of the special plate-sized pancakes, and one two-egg omelet with cheddar and even more ham.

No one even questioned how much food I got. Not everyone in fandom ate like I did, but most of the concom did, at least at breakfast, because we never knew when we might get another meal.

So I grabbed my pancakes and three different kinds of syrup, and more butter than I probably should have, and went back for the omelet. As I did, Horatio got his, which looked more like a stack of food covered in egg than an omelet.

"Figured you'd still be asleep," I said.

"My God, Spade, when did sleep become a word that people use indiscriminately at science fiction conventions?" he boomed, then laughed.

I smiled. There was a time that I would have been like the gamers, and gone three days without more than an hour per night, and that hour would have been inadvertent. But those days were long gone, and besides, I go to too many conventions now for them to feel special enough to forgo sleep over.

My omelet and I joined my feast at the table, and I started in with the hot food, instructing the waiter to leave a pot of coffee on the table so he didn't have to worry about refills.

The early morning crowd was mostly loners, except for Horatio's table, of course. That table was loud, and had a handful of the Usual Set—mostly the East Coast folks who apparently weren't on West Coast time yet. Although Mick and Jean Renner were always up at this time of the morning. Mick was like Horatio—he never slept much at conventions (maybe not ever) and he loved to hold court.

Right now, Mick and Horatio were holding a storytelling duel about some meal they had shared at ConDigeo years back. (That was the North American Science Fiction Convention in San Diego whose programming schedule went famously and hilariously unproofed.)

I had heard the duel before. Even though Mick and Horatio sounded spontaneous, they weren't. They had different recollections of that meal and they had made those different recollections into a schtick, which was funny the first three times I heard it. Now, I could repeat the lines, like an HBO comedy special I'd seen one too many times.

"Hey, Spade?" Zombie Killer stopped next to my table, a frown on his face. He wore a delightfully tasteless bright red T-shirt that read: *Red Shirt Running Team: I Probably Won't Make It...*, and clutched his food bill in his left hand.

I had to chase some blueberry-syrup covered pancake out of my mouth with lukewarm coffee before I could acknowledge him with more than a nod.

"Get your run in?" I asked after I swallowed.

"Yeah." He sounded dismissive, as if the run wasn't important. Then he pulled one of the chairs back and squeezed into the tiny space between the gigantic potted plant and the wall. "You know Jessica-6, right?"

I did. She was a well-known West Coast fan who named herself after Jenny Agutter's character in the abysmal 1976 movie *Logan's Run*. I could never figure out if she called herself that because there are very few sf movies about running, and she, as a runner, wanted some kind of sf nickname, or if she called herself that because she looked a lot like

Jenny Agutter in that movie—or did, back when she took on the nickname.

"Yeah," I said. "Why?"

Zombie Killer leaned in. "She went to Devon this morning, against my advice, and hasn't come back. I was wondering if you could tell the hotel...?"

I blinked at him. Was *went to Devon* some kind of code I didn't understand? Was my mind working that slowly from the strange night's sleep and the stress of the day before? Or was Devon a person I should know of and probably didn't?

"Devon?" I repeated stupidly.

"Oh, sorry," Zombie Killer said, actually whapping his forehead with his fingertips. "Devon is her truck."

"Oh." So Jessica-6 was one of those fen who named her vehicles. I had no idea why anyone would name a truck Devon, but I'd let that go for the moment.

I blinked, trying to comprehend the urgency, and then it all hit me. I looked over at the outside doors—which were still white and still closed. No one stood near them now, because the snow had clearly piled up so very high that the wind couldn't get through.

"How did she...?" I didn't even know how to finish the sentence.

"She was one of the few who got a space in the parking garage," Zombie Killer said.

The parking garage wasn't—a garage, that is. It was more like a parking alcove behind a big carport. The hotel actually charged for the handful of spaces tucked against the wall or bundled them into the luxury suites on the top floor of the building.

I had only been offered a space in the parking garage once, and fortunately, I had taken a look at it before driving my minivan into the back. The van would have fit, but I would have had a hell of a time getting in and out of it if anyone had parked next to me.

"When was this?" I asked.

"About thirty minutes ago," Zombie Killer said. "She finished breakfast first, and realized she'd left her hall costume in the front seat of her truck. I told her to forget it, but she'd worked on the damn thing for like three weeks, and she wasn't about to. She told me she'd be okay because the garage was underground."

It wasn't underground, but it was protected...somewhat. I had no idea if it really was.

"Did you call her?" I asked.

"Yeah," he said. "It keeps going to voicemail, which I'm hoping is because there's no reception in the garage."

"She was dressed to go outside, right?" There was an edge in my voice I didn't like. I wanted to sound calm, but I wasn't exactly calm.

SF fans were supposed to be smart, but often they were book-smart and common-sense stupid. Zombie Killer had been right. Jessica-6 should have left her costume in the truck, so she would wear the costume at some other convention.

I had a vague sense that if we sent someone to find her, and they didn't come back, then we sent someone else, and they didn't come back, that we'd be enacting a movie I only remembered dimly.

I swallowed hard. Suddenly the breakfast no longer looked as good as it had.

"I'll see what we can do," I said.

I signed my bill just in case I got too distracted to come back, stood up and put my cloth napkin on my chair like I did intend to return. The waiter was near the hostess station, and I said, as I strode out, "I'll be right back." This was an experienced crew. They would hold the table until they couldn't, and apologize to me later, if need be.

I went to the front desk, Zombie Killer trailing me like a partially deflated balloon.

Betty was there, looking like she'd slept as much as I had. Her gaze met mine, and I could read her thoughts without her actually speaking: *What fresh hell is this, Spade?*

"The parking garage," I said tentatively. "In weather like this, does it fill with snow?"

She looked at me sideways, as if trying to figure out where the question was going. "Not usually," she said. "But it depends on the wind. And you see what it's like out there."

Actually, I didn't *see* per se. I intuited. Because the snow had blocked every single first floor window.

"Why?" she asked, and in her tone, I heard her reluctance to even ask the question.

"Because one of our people went to her truck in the garage and hasn't come back."

"You've called her room?" Betty asked fiercely. She didn't want to deal with this any more than I did.

I turned toward Zombie Killer. He nodded. "You can try again, though," he said, and gave Jessica-6's real name to Betty.

Betty looked up the room number on her computer and punched the phone as if it had offended her somehow.

I hoped she would calm down as the day proceeded, because we had an entire weekend of this.

She held the phone receiver, playing with the cord. Seeing a phone with a cord heartened me. That meant if cell service went down, the phone service might still work here at the hotel.

"No answer," she said after a minute. "I can send someone to knock on the door."

I shook my head. "Do you have someone who can go to the garage and check on her?"

Betty frowned just a little, then gave me a glare. It was an *I'm only doing this for you, Spade*, glare, and I understood it. We were asking someone to go as close to outside as we could get right now.

"I'll see what I can do." She left the desk and headed into the office behind it, probably so I wouldn't overhear the conversation.

"I got gear," Zombie Killer said. "I could go."

"Let's see first," I said. I had the uncomfortable sense that I had just taken the first step into that movie scenario. Send one person, have them disappear; send another person, have *them* disappear; and on and on and on until everyone in the hotel except me was gone.

Only unlike the films I saw, there were more than 150 people here, not counting staff. It would take more than a weekend to get rid of all of us.

Zombie Killer bounced on the balls of his feet. I got the sense that he never stopped moving, even when he thought he was being still.

Betty came back, trailed by two hotel security people. Both were wearing brown parkas with the hoods down. One wore a ushanka that looked suspiciously like Horatio's and I wondered if Horatio had given it to him after yesterday's race ceremonies.

Both men were clutching big thick gloves, and one stopped near me. I recognized him. It was Marshall Kopeckne, who had worked hotel security every single time I had come to SierraCon. I loved his name, and told him that. It sounded appropriate for a man who lived and worked in the mountains—particularly a man who worked security.

He had a square jaw and the kind of blue eyes that faded to nothing in the right light. Which made him seem formidable, especially when he was angry.

He wasn't quite angry at the moment, but he was being formidable.

"You sure she's out there, Spade?" he asked, his voice rumbling in his muscular chest.

"I don't know where else she could be." This from Zombie Killer before I had a chance to say anything.

"Not entirely," I said, "but she was last seen going out there."

"Because," Marshall said, not looking at Zombie Killer at all, "I don't like risking my people's lives on a whim."

I bristled. This was not a whim. But then I made myself breathe. He had probably wanted me to bristle a little and re-evaluate the request. That was something I would have done.

Zombie Killer started, "It was the last place—" but my hand on his arm stopped him.

"I know it's dangerous," I said. "I'm only asking because your people would handle this better than mine."

"That's for damn sure," Marshall said. Then he glared at me with those ice-chip eyes. "But you tell your people that for this entire week-end, once they're in the hotel, they *stay* in the hotel. You got that?"

I nodded. "I do. I'll make sure we make extra announcements."

I couldn't quite believe that we'd failed to do so already. It showed just how far this storm had been from my personal radar. When we did a debrief on this entire convention, I would put some storm plans into place that kicked in immediately.

"All right," Marshall said, then he leaned over Betty's shoulder. "You got information on this girl's ride?"

Zombie Killer bristled. "She's not a gi—."

My hand on his arm tightened. "It's a truck," I said. "She left something important in the front seat."

"Nothing is so important that it's worth a life," Marshall growled, but he wasn't looking at me. I had the sense the growl was pro-forma.

"Here it is," Betty said. "Cherry red Ford F-150 with Colorado plates. Should be hard to miss. It's supposed to be in spot five."

"Okay." Marshall slipped on his gloves. "Make sure Carter is waiting for us with some blankets."

Blankets. I wasn't quite sure if those would be for Marshall and the other hotel security guy, or if those were for Jessica-6. Either way, I didn't like it.

Then Marshall tapped his gloved fingers on the top of the desk, presumably to get my attention.

"Since I won't be able to shed you until you know what's going on," Marshall said, speaking from clear experience, "Wait for me and Doug near the stairs to the garage. Under no circumstances are you to come into that garage, do you hear me?"

I had no desire to go into that garage. "Yes, sir."

But Zombie Killer didn't say anything.

"Am I clear?" Marshall said to Zombie Killer.

"Yeah," he said sullenly. I couldn't tell if he was being sullen because he was getting an order, or because he had planned to join them after all.

"All right, let's go," Marshall said. He beckoned the other security guy—Doug—who pulled up a muffler as they started down the corridor.

They walked at a fast clip that Zombie Killer had no trouble keeping pace with, but I sure did. I hadn't moved that quickly in a long, long time.

We marched behind the desk, around the bank of elevators, and toward the very back of the hotel. I hadn't been this way at this convention at all. There was no function space back here.

Three doors opened off the narrowing hallway. The center door had a sign that read *Employees Only*. The one to the right marked a stairwell. And the one to our left read *Parking Garage*.

"You stay here," Marshall said, giving Zombie Killer a particularly intense look.

Then Marshall put his parka hood over his head, adjusted his own muffler over his face, and glanced at Doug the Security Guy. Doug had pulled his own hood over his ushanka, making him seem even taller than he was.

Marshall tugged his gloves then used his entire body to push open the parking garage door.

Bitterly cold air blasted us. It smelled of ice and ancient musty gasoline and every cold winter that the Sierra had ever had.

Marshall bent slightly and headed into that chill, with Doug not far behind. Zombie Killer grabbed the door handle, and immediately let it go with a curse, shaking his hand.

"God, that's cold," he said.

Then he looked at me, as he realized what he had said. It was cold, and he thought Jessica-6 was out there. Had been out there.

My heart sank. I'd been hoping we wouldn't lose anyone to this storm.

But my hope was beginning to fade.

13

The chill wouldn't leave this part of the corridor. I resisted the urge to pull out my phone and check the weather news. I was afraid if I did pull out my phone, I would see dozens of text messages I had somehow missed.

This was the Official First Day, after all, and I had a million duties. But the most important was making sure we didn't lose anyone to this chaos.

Zombie Killer did pull out his phone, only to curse at it, and put it back in his pocket.

"Problem?" I asked.

"One bar," he said. "Barely."

One bar was better than I expected. Zombie Killer wrapped his arms around his torso and shifted from foot to foot. I remained as still as I could, trying not to let every disaster movie play in my head.

Was there swirling snow in that garage? Deadly cold winds? Drifts higher than a man's head?

I silently cursed my habit of watching deep, dark adventure films as entertainment. This wasn't entertaining. These men were risking their lives.

A third hotel security guy showed up, wearing an unzipped parka over his shoulders, with a stocking cap sticking out of one of the pockets. He had to be Carter. It wasn't my powers of deduction that made me intuit his name. It was the standard hotel blankets he had folded over his arms.

"No one back yet?" he asked, somewhat breathlessly.

I shook my head.

"Good," he said. "I was afraid I'd miss them."

He stood next to Zombie Killer and they both bounced on their toes, but not in unison. It was as if they couldn't see each other, so their rhythm was off, which was slowly starting to drive me crazy.

"How bad's the storm?" I asked, because what else could I do? Bounce with them?

"Worse today," Carter said. "This thing is going to blow for another 12 hours at least, followed by some record cold. It's one of the worst I've seen, and I've been through a lot."

Great, I thought, but didn't say. That was just what we needed.

At that moment, the door burst open. Doug, the ushanka guy, hurried in, his face mostly obscured by his muffler, ice crystals dotting the fur on his parka hood.

The air blowing in seemed even colder than before, but that might have been the power of suggestion.

"Stand back," Doug said.

Zombie Killer and I stepped as far back as we could go, but Carter held his ground.

Doug held the door open, and Marshall swept through it, staggering as he did so. It took me a moment to realize that he had a person in his arms, and the person was Jessica-6.

Thank God she was a small woman. Her brown hair extended down to the floor, her head flung back, her arms bouncing listlessly along the sides. She was wearing a bubble ski jacket and mittens, and her feet were encased in heavy fur boots.

She looked like she had dressed for the weather.

"What the hell is that?" Zombie Killer asked, pointing at her.

I blinked, stared in the direction he pointed. Her face was covered with something. It took a moment for that to resolve into a truly excellent Klingon mask, complete with brow ridges.

"I left it on," Marshall said. "Figured it would keep her warm. Need blankets here, Carter."

But he really didn't have to say that. Carter had already moved forward, and was enveloping Jessica-6 in layers of blanket.

"What happened?" Zombie Killer asked before I could.

"She was unconscious when we found her." Marshall had moved her forward to help with the blanket swaddling.

"Passed out from the cold?" I asked, almost hopefully.

Marshall raised his head, those ice-chip eyes taking me in. "I would probably have thought that, if she wasn't lying face down on the seat, with a bloody knot of hair on the back of her head. Someone kiboshed her, Spade, and then stuck the mask on her face."

"And *left* her there?" Zombie Killer asked. "She would have frozen to death."

I was certain that was the intention. My stomach had clenched. That was the second near-death experience of the convention, and I could almost hear Ruth. That meant there would be a third.

I wasn't superstitious, I reminded myself. I was not. But I didn't like this.

"Will she be okay?" Zombie Killer asked.

"I have no idea," Marshall snapped. "You have a doctor, yes?"

He directed that last at me.

"Yeah," I said. "Let's take her to the medical room."

I was beginning to have a hunch that place would get a lot of usage during this convention. I wasn't fond of that.

"On my way," Marshall said, taking the now-blanketed Jessica-6 toward the elevators.

"I'll be right there with you," I said.

Doug trailed along, but Carter headed back toward the desk, probably to update Betty.

I walked at a slightly slower pace, my phone in my hand, hoping for more bars. I finally got them as I rounded the corner near the elevators.

Fortunately, I had McCoy's number in my phone. I had no idea when I had gotten the number or how, but I was relieved to see it. I punched it with my thumb, and waited.

McCoy picked up on the second ring.

"Spade!" he sounded almost cheerful. "Listen, Rogers is doing better. He actually—"

"That's good," I said. "But we need you in the medical room. You or Zula."

"Another poisoning?"

"No," I said. "Exposure."

"Some asshole exposed themselves again? What in the hell—?"

"No," I said. "Expo*sure*. To the elements. The hotel knows how to deal with it better than I do, but they asked for medical help. Can you leave Rogers?"

"I'm sending Zula," McCoy said, which was an answer in and of itself. "You'll be there?"

"No," I said. "I'm not needed. Zombie Killer is down there with hotel staff—"

"Zombie Killer?" McCoy asked. "What'd he do, try to go running outside this morning?"

"Zombie Killer is fine. It's Jessica-6," I said, feeling like I had entered a kind of *Twilight Zone* from this conversation alone. "She went to her truck."

"In *this* weather?" McCoy clucked. "I'll send Zula right down."

And then he hung up. I clutched the phone tightly for a moment, staring down the corridor.

The café was almost full. Fen were lining up, getting food from the World's Best Breakfast Buffet and talking like nothing was happening besides the convention itself.

For them, that was true. We had one poisoning and one kibosh with intent to kill. Those made me nervous, and I wasn't sure what the connection was, besides the convention itself.

I needed to give my brain time to absorb all of this. Plus, we had a convention to start. I got into the elevator, and pressed the long bar for

Mezzanine. I'd get the convention started, and then, maybe, I would talk to Paladin, see what she thought of all of this.

The elevator took less than thirty seconds to reach the mezzanine. I got out, braced myself, and took a few steps into the wide empty expanse where registration was.

The lighting here was weird, kind of a grayish whitish darkish color, because of the snow still pressing against all the windows. The lights couldn't quite seem to cope with this strange kind of light. It almost felt like twilight instead of early morning.

But that didn't stop the fen. Lines had already formed. People were behind the tables, pulling out name badges and handouts, along with my revised programming schedule.

Judita was standing near the edge of one table, talking to two pros. She waved an arm in the direction of the greenroom, then turned to someone else and said something almost audible about signage.

I made my way around the line of fen and to the registration table. I already had my badge, but of course I had forgotten it in my room. I'd have to go back and get it.

I stopped and scanned all of the tables for Ruth, but didn't see her.

As if reading my mind, Judita appeared at my side. "You seen Ruth?" she asked.

"No," I said, that low-level feeling of alarm I'd had since we found Jessica-6 growing.

Ruth should have been here. She should have been supervising all of this. She was the chair, after all.

"I've tried her room, but she's not answering," Judita said. "And she missed the breakfast meeting in Con Ops."

"She did?" I said, not liking that at all. Ruth never missed meetings. "I'll go get her."

Because I couldn't do anything otherwise. I was too on edge.

I started back to the elevator, then stopped. "You need me for anything?"

Judita shook her head. She seemed to have it all well in hand, which was a relief, because Ruth and I had apparently dropped the ball.

"Just get Ruth, would you?" she said.

I nodded, got on the elevator, and paused, trying to remember what room Ruth was in. It didn't matter. I'd figure it out. I needed to go to my room anyway to get the key cards. We had a magic open-all-function-space-doors key card from the hotel, and then the concom had exchanged key cards for our own rooms when we got them.

We'd learned long ago that it was better to have backup, in case you left something important in your room, and couldn't go get it yourself.

I punched in my floor, and the elevator made its way up, functioning normally because this was still early morning convention time. It was weird to be in an elevator by myself at a convention, even in the early morning, but this entire convention would be underpopulated for the entire weekend.

My mind went to Jessica-6. Kiboshed, bleeding, left in the cold. Rogers, swallowing poison—either here or at some point on the way. Those couldn't be coincidences, but I didn't know either of them well, which meant I had no idea where (or if) anything in their lives besides SierraCon made them overlap.

And that went for Ruth. I'd worked with her on dozens of conventions, but we were con-friends, not real friends. We had a shared purpose, but we never really discussed our lives or anything outside of conventions.

I made myself breathe. For all I knew, she had slept through her alarm. But even as I thought that, my interior voice screamed at me. In all the years I'd known Ruth, she'd never slept through her alarm. Not ever.

The elevator opened on my floor and I hurried out. No one was in the corridor, not even housekeeping. I pulled out my phone, checked the bars, and used my thumb to scroll until I found Paladin's number.

She had answered just as I reached my room.

"Hey, Spade," she said by way of hello. "You meeting us for breakfast?"

"Already had breakfast," I said. "And I'm going to need you to meet me outside a hotel room."

The keycard locked in place, the little key card reader changed color, and the door clicked as the lock freed. I pushed the door open, scurried inside, and it banged behind me.

The room numbers were on an actual sheet of paper, on top of some convention handouts. Fortunately, my badge was nearby as well, propped against one of the lights in the seating area.

"What room?" Paladin asked, sounding annoyed.

I grabbed the paper, scanned it, and frowned. It took a moment to find Ruth's room, but I did, and gave Paladin the number.

"I'll be there in five," I said, and hung up. I almost shoved the paper in my pocket, then realized that losing it—with all this crap going on— was worse than having to come back for it.

I set the paper back on the table, grabbed my badge and put it over my head, my Concom and Programming ribbons catching on my collar. I untangled them with shaking fingers, then grabbed a power bar off the stash I had on the mirrored dresser. I stuck that power bar into one of my pockets, thinking the power bar might end up being lunch.

Then I headed out of the room, checking to make sure I had my key card and the key card with Ruth's room number on it before I locked myself out. (Because locking myself out would be all I needed.)

I would have sprinted for the elevator if I were the sprinting type, but I wasn't, so instead, I walked as fast as I could.

The elevator was still on this floor—more proof that we were in early morning at an underpopulated convention—so I got on and punched in Ruth's floor. This time, the elevator seemed to take years to get to its destination, even though I knew that the problem was simply my perception of time and not time itself.

The elevator bounced to a landing, which did not bode well for tonight when it would be packed with too many bodies like mine, and then the doors eased open.

Ruth's room was at the opposite end of the hall. I knew that because I could see Paladin, waiting, hands on her hips as she faced me. That's when I remembered she hadn't had breakfast yet.

Maybe that power bar wasn't lunch; maybe that power bar would tame the savage Paladin instead.

She was wearing a white shirt with a T-shirt over it, and a pair of tight black jeans tucked into a pair of leather boots. As I got closer, I could read the T-shirt. *A Wise Woman Once Said "Fuck This Shit," and She Lived Happily Ever After.*

I couldn't tell if that was Paladin's mood or just the shirt she had decided to wear today before things got entirely crazy.

"What's going on?" she asked as she got closer.

"A lot," I said. "This is Ruth's room. She's nowhere, and she's not answering the phone."

I didn't want to tell Paladin about Jessica-6, not yet anyway.

I shoved the key card in the locking device, and held my breath. For a half second, I thought it wasn't going to work, but Paladin slammed her palm on the front of the device, and it beeped in response. Then the door clicked open.

I knocked as I twisted the handle downward, half expecting the chain lock to be in place. It wasn't. I would have to chastise Ruth about that later...if indeed, she was inside.

"Ruth?" I asked. "Hey, Ruth, it's Spade. I think you overslept."

I pushed the door in farther, and a waft of hot air hit me. It smelled of peanut butter, unwashed socks, and something sickly sweet, like spilled soda.

The smell didn't surprise me: con hotel rooms often got their own somewhat fetid odor by day four or five, which was what it was for those of us on the convention committee.

The room was dark, with some of that weird grayish snow-light peeking in from the curtains. I could just barely make out a lump on the bed. My heart rose in my throat—and beat a million miles a minute, all at the same time. I could barely catch my breath.

"Ruth?" I asked. "Ruth?"

"Ruth!" Paladin projected her voice so loudly that I nearly jumped out of my skin. No one could sleep through that.

The overhead light came on, along with two lights in the living area. A laptop was open on the couch, and papers, like the ones in my room, were scattered all over the table.

Ruth was curled under the covers, on her side, her phone plugged into the lamp beside the bed. I turned the lamp on, and looked at Ruth.

She was gray, her lips almost blue.

With shaking fingers, I touched her skin, afraid I'd find it cold. It wasn't, but it was clammy and a tad damp.

Paladin had come up beside me. She had a Kleenex in her hand. She picked up the pill bottle with her Kleenex fingers, and shook the bottle. It didn't rattle.

"Sleeping pills," she said. "Prescription, but not in Ruth's name."

We looked at each other. Then I pulled the covers back. Ruth was wearing the outfit she had on the night before, all the way down to her sneakers.

"Take pictures," I said to Paladin as I struggled to get Ruth out of the bed. I had done this before, too many times, with old, old friends. Overdoses were difficult, and God knew how long Ruth had been here.

Paladin snapped photos as I levered Ruth upright, calling her name and slapping her face. She moaned, and I had never heard a better sound in the entire world.

Paladin kept taking pictures as I dragged Ruth to the bathroom. I pushed the bathroom door open with my foot, and noted with relief that the shower was a separate stall from the bath. I shifted Ruth's weight. Her head lolled, and her arms kept hitting me on the side.

I had no idea how I was going to get her into that small shower opening.

"I've got her," Paladin said. "You call McCoy."

She wasn't holding her phone any more. Instead, she slipped around me, and started the shower, then pulled Ruth out of my arms, and dragged her into the cold water.

Ruth sputtered, but wasn't entirely conscious.

"We need to get her to vomit," I said.

"Yeah," Paladin said dryly. "Not my first rodeo."

She propped Ruth up, and slapped her, not that gently.

"Call McCoy," Paladin repeated. She was struggling to remove Ruth's overshirt. "I got this."

I eased myself out of the bathroom. My back hurt. I hadn't lifted a person in a long time.

I wiped off my hands on a towel near the bar sink and microwave. A bag of microwave popcorn was inside, unpopped. A number was half typed into the microwave, blinking as if waiting for someone to finish.

An unopened can of Diet Coke sat next to the box of microwave popcorn. I studied the entire scene as I called McCoy for the second time that morning, dialing with my thumb.

"I'm beginning to get scared when I see your name, Spade," McCoy said, instead of hello.

"You should," I said. "Ruth overdosed. We need you. You got something in your medical bag of tricks that might induce vomiting."

"Ruth overdosed?" McCoy said. "Are we talking about the same Ruth? Ruth Harshaw? Con chair? Tough as nails? That Ruth?"

"That Ruth," I said. I didn't see her glasses anywhere. If she had gone to bed, even if she had decided to take too many pills, she would have put the glasses somewhere sensible.

"She's not suicidal," McCoy said.

"No, she's not," I said. "And we can debate her mental health all you want, but if you don't get your butt here, we might be using the past tense instead of the present."

"I'm already on my way," McCoy said. "If this continues, you might want to check the attendee list for more doctors. Because Zula has her hands full downstairs, and Rogers is better, but not great."

"Yeah," I said, sounding just like Paladin. I almost added, *Not my first rodeo,* but I understood that McCoy's comment was well-intentioned and born out of a panic I was already feeling. "Just get here."

Then I hung up. I turned on more lights, photographed the entire room, and searched for those glasses. They weren't anywhere logical, not the half-bath, not the table near the couch, not any of the bedside tables, where you'd think they'd be, given that she was blind without them.

I finally found them, kicked underneath the television across the room from the bed. I took more photos, because I knew we couldn't preserve this room for the cops' eventual arrival. But I also knew that they would need some kind of evidence.

Because Ruth hadn't done this to herself, any more than Jessica-6 had kiboshed herself on the head, or Rogers had poisoned himself.

We were in every horror movie cliché on the planet—a remote, isolated location, in the middle of a snowstorm, with no help possible... and a madman on the loose.

14

I pushed open the main bathroom door. The shower was on and the air was humid, but not steamy. Paladin had her arm around Ruth and was trying to guide her out of the shower.

The floor was covered in puddles. I grabbed the bathroom rug off the side of the bathtub and tossed it into the wet, hoping that would make them slide less instead of more.

"I got this," Paladin said through gritted teeth. She was soaked, her shirts plastered against her body, her jeans blacker than they'd been, and her boots most likely ruined. Her close-cropped hair was glued to her face, the points of her ears poking out of the wet strands.

Ruth was shivering and muttering, which was a step upward, and was probably why Paladin was going to move her around now.

"McCoy's on his way," I said.

"Not a moment too soon," Paladin said. "I can't get her to wake up all the way. This is bad, Spade."

"It's worse than you think," I said, and opened my arms. "Let me drag her around a bit."

"No," Paladin said. "I'm soaked. You're not. You're going to have to call the authorities."

"Yeah, I am," I said. "Because Ruth isn't the only one."

"Rogers, I know," Paladin said. She was hauling Ruth toward the door. I moved out of the way.

"And Jessica-6," I said. Then I told Paladin what happened, as she mostly dragged Ruth around the room. Ruth did occasionally put one foot in front of the other, but I couldn't quite tell if that was voluntary or if it was because of the way her feet were being pulled.

There was a knock on the door. I almost yelled, *Come In!* then realized this was no longer a friendly con. And we'd let the door close, so whoever it was (McCoy, I hoped) couldn't let themselves in.

I went to the door and actually used the peephole, feeling awkward. How many movies had I seen where someone got shot in the eye when they peered through the peephole? Or stabbed through the eye? Or...

It was McCoy, and he actually had a medical bag. I had no idea that was still A Thing, but I was grateful it was.

I pulled the door open, and he bustled in, noting the mess, and then his gaze alighted on Paladin, making a soggy circuit with Ruth in her arms.

"What did she take?" McCoy asked.

"She didn't," I said. "And I'm not sure the bottle we found is what was forced into her."

"Well, I don't have the equipment here or downstairs to pump her stomach," McCoy said. "So we go with the old-fashioned vomit response."

"I tried," Paladin said, "but I couldn't induce."

McCoy stopped the sog-parade and tilted Ruth's head back, peering at her eyes. They were dilated, and her mouth lolled open, but she did make a fluttery moan in protest.

"Okay," he said to Paladin, "let's get her back to the bathroom. If we're going to make a mess, we do it there."

He helped her get Ruth across the floor, but before they went inside, he turned toward me.

"You have to stop this," he said. "You've got to call the authorities."

"I will," I said, "but I can guarantee they won't be able to help us. They can't get here."

"Then tell the fen to lock themselves in their rooms or something," McCoy said, "because this isn't the way good conventions are run!"

Then he went in the door, leaving me gape-mouthed. Yes, I knew that this wasn't how conventions were run. Or even real life, really.

And he was right; I had to do something to stop this.

I leaned in the door as they wedged Ruth against the edge of the tub and McCoy brought some kind of bottle out of his bag.

"I'm going to see what I can do," I said lamely. "If you don't need me..."

"I need you to get this under control," McCoy snapped, "and if that means you can't help here, so be it."

He didn't even look at me. Paladin gave me an empathetic glance. She knew this wasn't my fault.

"I'll let you know what happens," she said. "Tell Casper I'm not joining her for breakfast."

And then she pushed her booted foot against the door, easing it closed.

I grabbed my phone and left, feeling even more urgency at the mention of Casper. I called her as I made my way down the hall.

"Where are you?" I asked after she said hello.

"In the café," she said. "I already got breakfast. You going to join me? I didn't get anything for Paladin."

"She's...helping me," I said. "And...I'll be right down."

I had almost told her to stay right there, but that would have been wrong. Casper didn't respond well to that tone, particularly the new Casper.

"What's going on, Spade?" she asked in a near whisper.

"I...um...I'll brief you when I get there," I said. "Order me a coffee."

And a million pastries. But I didn't say that.

I had to find someone to guard Casper as well as figure out what the hell was going on as well as run this convention.

If I had thought locking people in their rooms was the best, I would have done so, but all of the attacks—except maybe Rogers'—had come when people were alone. Telling fen to retreat was the worst thing I could do.

I actually needed time to investigate. I needed to figure out who was doing this, and why. And right now, I had no information at all, not even a clue as to who was going to be the next victim.

I needed to talk to Betty. I needed the hotel on board with this, because they already had been involved with some of the cleanup—or she had, anyway.

I reached the elevator, and went to the main level. As I did, I wracked my brain to see if I knew anyone in California or Nevada law enforcement, maybe someone to grease the wheels and get us some help up here. By snowmobile or helicopter, or something, as soon as this damn storm let up.

But I couldn't think of anyone, or at least, I couldn't think of anyone who was obvious. I might have known someone in law enforcement, but they hadn't identified themselves as such, so I couldn't work with it.

Most of the people I knew in California were fen (which often meant I didn't know their professions) or lawyers. I'd done a lot of testifying in court, but that had been for specific cases, and specific lawyers. Maybe one of them would know someone, and if I needed it, I would call.

Right now, though, I just needed to plant a flag, get in the queue, whatever the cliché was that would work best here.

I made it down to the first floor, which was bathed in that grayish white light. The entire first floor reeked of woodsmoke, because the fire was still burning in that giant hearth. It might have been burning all night—I couldn't exactly tell.

The café was full, and everyone was laughing and talking as if nothing had gone wrong. I scurried past it, hoping Casper didn't see me. I needed to talk to Betty first.

I reached the desk and thank God, Betty was at her post. She looked over at me, and her face fell.

"Something else happened, didn't it?"

"Let me back there," I said. "I'll tell you about it—after we call the authorities."

"They can't come up here, Spade. The storm is as bad as it's going to get."

"I know," I said, "but we need to be one of their first stops afterward."

Betty glanced over her shoulder, but none of the other employees were close. She opened the little door in the side of the desk and beckoned me in, then swept her hand toward the office.

"You call. I'll be right there."

I went inside the office, which barely deserved the name. It was a boxy little room with no windows, a gigantic computer and tall filing cabinets. There were mailbox cubbies that predated computers, and piles of paper on top of all of it, with a bulletin board for various OSHA notices and lots and lots and lots of notes from the California Board of Health.

I picked up the ancient phone, a little startled at the size of the receiver, and put it to my ear. The dial tone was reassuring. I hadn't expected it.

I dialed 911, expecting a wait, particularly out here. And as the phone rang, and rang, my stomach clenched. I hadn't figured out how to report what was happening here without sounding like a madman myself.

The dispatch picked up almost faster than I wanted them to.

"What is your emergency?" she asked.

I identified myself and my location, trying to keep my own tone somewhere between informative and slightly panicked. If I wasn't panicked, they wouldn't take me seriously.

"We're snowed in," I said, "which I expected, but it's caused one of the guests to snap. So far, he's hit another guest over the head and left her in the snow for dead, and attacked two other guests."

"Is everyone else safe?" The dispatch asked.

"Um, no. There's too many people for hotel security to watch everyone. The hotel will probably be contacting you, but I wanted this on the record so that when the roads open, you'll send the authorities up here as quickly as possible with at least one, maybe two ambulances. We have doctors among the guests, and they're doing what they can, but there aren't a lot of resources here."

"Have you subdued the suspect?" the dispatch asked.

"No," I said, deciding in that moment that I wouldn't tell her we didn't know who the suspect was. "This is a big hotel and there are lots of places to hide."

"I'm sorry to tell you, sir, but right now, we can't send anyone to your location. When the storm ends, we will be able to send someone."

I had no idea how she could sound so dispassionate, but I supposed it was part of the training for the job.

"I know," I said. "That's why I called. I want to be at the front of the line. We need someone at this hotel as soon as possible."

"I will do what I can, sir, but I can't guarantee anything."

"I understand," I said, my frustration growing. "But I'm sure you understand me. We need help here, as soon as you can provide it."

"I do understand, sir." I could hear the clacking of keys on the other side of the line. "I see that there is a helipad near the hotel. We might be able to send a helicopter when the winds die down, if someone can clear off the helipad."

The winds dying down seemed so far in the future that I had absolutely no idea what we would all be doing at that point. Clinging to each other and trying to survive? Reduced to feral games like the boys in *Lord of the Flies*? Sitting calmly together and watching yet another version of *The Thing*, happy we managed to control our crisis?

"I'll make sure the hotel makes that a priority," I said. "Let us know when the helicopter is coming, if it's coming."

"Can we contact you at this number?" she asked.

"Someone will answer this phone," I said. "And if the line isn't working for some reason—" (*because the bad guy severed it?*) "—here's my cell."

I rattled off the number, and repeated my name, and then added, "We have power right now, but I have no idea how long that will last."

"I understand, sir," she said. "We will do our best to contact you. If someone could update us on your progress in a few hours, that would be good."

I couldn't tell if that request came because she needed the update or because she wanted us to resolve this on our own or because she felt that silence from us would mean the situation was even worse than it had been.

I didn't ask either. I thanked her for her time—because I'm just that polite, I guess—and then I reiterated that we needed ambulances as soon as they could get something here.

"Any helicopter we send will have a medical team." She then doublechecked the phone numbers. Then she asked, "Do you need me to remain on the line?"

It was clear from the tone of the question that she didn't want to remain on the line, much as I wanted her to, much as I wanted her here *right now*.

But there was probably someone alone in a car under a snowdrift who was tying up another line of the 911 call center. We were a pressing emergency, but she couldn't talk us down or change anything by her continued presence on the phone.

"No, thanks," I said. "Just...make sure we stay a priority, okay?"

"I will do my best, sir," she said, and hung up.

I clung to the phone for a moment, feeling like I had just lost a major lifeline. I had never felt that way about the authorities—not that I hated them or even disliked them. They had their uses.

But I was beginning to feel all alone here, and I was slowly getting scared.

I was also probably the acting chair of the convention from hell, and that meant I actually had to do some things.

I put the phone in its cradle, and turned around. Betty wasn't there, but Marshall was. He looked smaller without his parka—except for the shoulders, which were probably the widest I'd ever seen on a normal human (not a Hollywood type).

"This is bad, isn't it?" he asked quietly.

I nodded. "I need to brief you and Betty and whoever else you deem necessary here at the hotel."

I didn't mention the Assistant GM. He could come if he wanted to, but I really didn't want him to gum up any works.

"I'll grab Betty," Marshall said. He started back out the door, and then stopped, and added, "We don't have a big security staff on normal days, and honestly, most of them are glorified bouncers. They aren't equipped to solve crime or anything."

There were two of us here with enough experience to find our madman. But I wasn't about to tell Marshall that.

From now on, I wasn't going to tell people outside my tight circle much of anything.

"I understand," I said, sounding like the dispatch. "We'll do what we can."

He studied me for a moment. "The woman we got out of the truck," he said. "Is she going to be all right?"

"I haven't had a chance to check," I said.

"You're going to tell the rest of the convention to stay inside, though, right?"

His words sent a slight alarm through me. I needed to take care of the con-goers as well as the problems I was encountering.

There was no one else to do it, at least at the start of the day.

I checked my watch. The first panels would start in forty-five minutes. They would be my best chance to warn the con-goers without alarming them.

I needed to think about how to do all of it.

"I'll tell them," I said. "I've been running from one crisis to another. Let's get Betty in here, so I can brief her, and then I'll take care of the next problem."

Marshall pointed his forefinger at me, his thumb up. The gesture looked too much like shooting a gun for my tastes, but he wasn't threatening me. Instead he said, "Got it," and disappeared out the door.

I stood there for a moment, letting myself feel overwhelmed for thirty seconds. It was an old technique that I had learned at an early convention, one I usually hauled out now before a court appearance, when the opposing side's attorney was known for a tight cross examination.

I shifted from foot to foot, going over my priorities in my head. A quick stop to get Casper, who wasn't going to leave my side until I could figure out who best to keep an eye on her, visiting registration and organizing the concom, and then notifying the gamers and the art show and anyone else I could think of.

By the time I'd made my mental list, Betty had arrived in the room, along with Marshall and Doug and a fussy looking man who had been the concierge as long as I had come to this hotel.

I took a deep breath, then briefed them on everything that had happened so far, and told them to stay in touch with the dispatch, emphasizing that we would need ambulances.

"How are we going to protect the guests, Spade?" Betty said, looking terrified.

How indeed? I wondered. "I'm open for suggestions," I said, but knew I wouldn't get the kind that I needed.

We just had to get through the weekend, one long hour at a time.

15

I finally joined Casper ten minutes later. She, bless her, had ordered a pastry plate to go, and was standing with one knee on the booth, watching the corridor as people went by. When she saw me, she grabbed the two white bags of pastries and coffee in a to-go cup, and headed out of the café.

She'd been coming to conventions long enough now to learn how to sign things to the room. At least, I hoped that was what she had done. We'd settle up later if we needed to.

"Where's Paladin?" she asked.

"Taking care of a friend," I said. "I'll explain later."

I didn't want to talk to Casper in the corridor, which was filling up with eager fen. Many were wearing hall costumes, some of which were alarming me.

SierraCon had never been a weapons-free convention, despite the fact that it was in California. The con predated the no-weapons policies that had come in during the 1990s, and the long-time con-goers had fought hard to maintain the weapons tradition.

Some of that was because the convention's dealers included a few locals who made beautiful swords and knives. Which normally didn't bother me at all—why stop someone from plying their trade—but suddenly sent yet another shiver through me—especially as I was being passed by Klingons with bat'leths, Dothrakis carrying arakh, and a few somewhat tame Vikings with their (probably historically incorrect) battle axes.

Even in normal times, weapons at a convention made me nervous, but today they were driving me absolutely crazy. I couldn't withdraw the weapons rule, though, not this late. All that would do was piss off the attendees, and right now, I needed them calm.

"We going to meet her?" Casper asked, and it took me a moment to realize she meant Paladin.

"No," I said. "There's some serious stuff going on right now. I need you beside me until I can figure out what's going to happen next."

"How about I just park myself in paneling until you resolve some of this?" Casper asked.

I looked at her as we headed to the staircase that would take us to the mezzanine. That was the best solution, and it was a sign of how preoccupied I was that I hadn't thought of it.

"As long as you don't go anywhere alone," I said, and realized as I said it, it sounded ominous.

"Even the ladies room?" she asked.

"You go whenever anyone else goes," I said. "Promise me."

She opened her hands, looking a little surprised. I'd never made her promise anything about personal stuff like peeing before.

"Okay," she said. "This is bad, huh?"

"Yeah," I said. "Tell me what panels you'll be at, so I can find you."

"I have my phone," she said.

"*Panels*," I growled.

"Jeez," she said, but ran down her list of panels anyway, and did so off the top of her head, which made me realize she really was interested in them.

"Call me at the end of the last one if you haven't heard from me or Paladin," I said. "In fact, call me before the last one if you haven't heard from us. The last thing I want you to do is stand in the hallway waiting for us."

"It's that bad?" she asked.

"Worse," I said.

We had reached the stairs. They were populated by con-goers, many coming down the stairs, badges around their necks and freebie bag in their hands Many were talking with each other, laughing and reconnecting. Some of the younger pros looked nervous, probably thinking about their panels.

The Usual Set was upstairs, talking in a group and comparing notes about their day, probably screwing up my programming plans with each sentence.

Normally, I would have stopped there and would have reminded them that their names were on the panels, so fans would expect them to be there. But I had more important things to do.

The registration line was even longer than it had been earlier, probably because the tables were short-staffed without Ruth. She usually manned at least one of the tables, making sure everything was going well.

As if I'd summoned her with that thought, Judita appeared at my side. I hadn't seen her coming.

"You find Ruth?" she asked.

"Yeah," I said. "She's not well. She won't be here. We're going to need to do some staff shuffling. I'd like to do it here."

Rather than have someone wait alone in Con Ops. Or (ahem) me wait alone in Con Ops until the rest of the committee showed up.

"Well," Judita said, "it's probably easier to do it here anyway, since most everyone has to go through here on the way to somewhere else."

"Gather them over near the plant," I said, nodding at a gigantic fiddle-leaf ficus near the railing, about as far from the elevators as we could get. I had wanted that plant removed, but the hotel wouldn't hear of it. Apparently the thing was ancient, and the staff was afraid to move it, not just because it weighed a ton, but they were worried that any change in scenery would kill the damn thing.

I had wanted to kill the damn thing just a day ago, but now I saw its leaves as a way to have a nice private little meeting, without someone being entirely alone.

"Can I come?" Casper asked.

I looked at her. She was smart, brilliant, and a teenager. She also would be mad if we kept her in the dark.

"As long as you remember that anything you hear is private," I said. "You can't tell anyone."

"Well, duh," she said.

But it really wasn't a well-duh as she would figure out.

She and I walked over to the plant, and she handed me a cruller, then turned the coffee so that I could grab and sip from it.

The coffee was typical hotel coffee heavily laced with cream and sugar, not the stuff from the Starbucks wannabe. Normally, I liked hotel coffee black, but I didn't say anything. The sugar would probably fortify me for an hour or more, and I liked to pretend that the cream had some nutrition.

It didn't take the concom long to gather around me, and I was happy to see that Andelusia Tran, who ran security, had made it as well.

Tran had run security for SierraCon for nearly a decade. She knew all the players. I had been afraid she was walking the halls, or dealing with some other kind of emergency.

She had two cell phones sticking out of the pocket of her plaid shirt, which also partly covered the two walkie talkies on her hips. She wore tight yoga pants and athletic shoes, and had a couple of probably not-legal weapons on her security belt. I knew that California police were no longer allowed to carry blackjacks, and I thought maybe mace wasn't allowed either. I also had no idea where she had gotten that stun gun. But I didn't mind them in her hands.

It was everyone else with weapons that had me worried.

"We have a situation," I said. "And none of this is for public consumption. Are we clear?"

Everyone nodded. That was one good thing about a concom. They knew how to keep things quiet.

"Okay," I said. "Here's what's going on. We've had three serious injuries so far at this convention, including Ruth—and no, I have no idea how she'll fare—and it seems to me and the hotel security that the con's being targeted. I've already talked to the authorities. They'll send help as soon as the snow lets up, but that's not for at least twelve hours, maybe more. We're on our own."

There was muttering all around me. Judita had put her hand over her mouth.

"We need to let the attendees know a couple of things. They need to employ the buddy system for the duration of the convention. No one should be alone."

"Jeez," someone whispered.

"And no one can leave the hotel. That's at the hotel's request. We nearly lost someone to the cold in the parking garage, so imagine how it would be in the actual blizzard."

"Spade, maybe we should shut down," said Cindy Ismay. She was one of the newer members of the concom, and I was pretty sure she'd never dealt with any kind of fannish emergency before. She kept flipping her badge over and over in her right hand, her green eyes big with fear.

"I'd rather keep the masses entertained than worried," I said. "We're not going to tell them about the attacks. But we are going to insist on the buddy system. I want notifications on all the boards, as well as texts sent. We need to have an announcement before each panel today at least, and I'll make a bigger announcement at opening ceremonies. This is going to be a balancing act. We need to make sure there's no panic, but we also have to make sure everyone is safe."

"I will make sure that we have paper notifications," said Joe Fitzcart. He was a short roundish man with a deep voice and a bushy graying beard, who looked every bit the lawyer that he was. He even wore a vest that cried out for the jacket to complete his three-piece suit. "I will work with the hotel to slide information under the doors of everyone attending."

"And put notices on the various boards," Judita said.

"That too, as well as next to the room announcements," Fitzcart said.

"We have to let people in the art show and dealer's room know," Cindy said somewhat breathlessly.

"I'll take care of it," Judita said. She was beginning to get my nomination for the person to replace Ruth as chair.

"I'll need someone to organize who is going to each panel to announce the buddy system and the stay indoors rule," I said. "Who will handle that?"

Cindy swallowed hard, then said, "I can do that."

"Good," I said. "That's all for now. We'll probably need to touch base in a few hours, and I'll let you know when and where. Let's just stay as positive and upbeat as we can, okay? And if someone questions your mood, remind them that there's a blizzard outside, and blame it for what's going on."

"I'm still wondering if we should let them know we have a crazy," Judita said, looking at me.

"Maybe at Opening Ceremonies," I said, only to put her off. I couldn't imagine announcing that some mad person was trying to kill us all in the middle of what was usually a jocular celebration of the convention.

But I'd seen strange things in Opening Ceremonies before, so such an announcement was within the realm of possibility. I just didn't want to do it. Not to mention the fact that most people didn't even come to Opening Ceremonies.

I made myself focus. We'd cross that bridge when we got to it. Right now, I needed the concom to handle the details I had thrown at them, and to (with luck) not panic.

It took all of my personal strength not to waggle my fingers at them and tell them to begone. Instead, I said, "That's all for now," as firmly as I could.

Judita and Fitzcart peeled off as if they were pursued by demons. Cindy shot me a terrified glance. The other concom members looked at each other, as if they wanted to say something more, but didn't feel like they dared.

I needed them to move before I could get away from that damn plant. Somehow they had backed me into a corner.

"You can leave now," Casper said, with an edge in her voice.

I looked down and sideways at her. She had not sounded that much like Paladin ever before.

Paladin. I felt the shiver that was beginning to take up permanent residence in my spine run through me again. I hoped the fact that I hadn't heard from her was a good thing.

The rest of the concom left, talking as they went.

Casper's gaze met mine. She didn't look scared so much as perplexed. "This is weird stuff," she said.

I nodded.

"I mean, why go through all this weird stuff, like poisoning someone or hitting them on the head and leaving them in the snow? If you're that angry at people, why not just bring a gun? That's what most people do."

I hated the matter-of-fact tone she used. "Most people?" I asked, my shock showing in my tone.

"You know," Casper said. "Those mass killers. They just bring a gun to, like, a bar or something, and that's that."

"You think this is a mass killer," I said flatly, trying the thought on for size.

"Well, not yet, but maybe by the end of the weekend," Casper said. "Unless they want to be caught or something."

Or something. She twinged something in my brain, but I wasn't sure what it was yet. Something familiar.

She wasn't wrong about the similarities. And it wouldn't have been hard for someone to bring a gun in here. No one searched the attendees, and because weapons were common at this convention, someone would have thought the gun (if they saw it) to be a fake.

"What?" Casper said. She clearly saw my expression.

"I have to think on this," I said.

"Well don't think much," Casper said. "Because no matter how you're downplaying this, this is serious."

Now, she sounded like me. Or at least the voice of my conscience.

My walkie-talkie crackled.

"Spade? Calling Spade."

The voice was tinny and far away, and uncertain, as if they'd never used a walkie before.

I grabbed mine off my belt and squeezed the side.

"Spade here," I said, feeling as ridiculous as I always felt when I said something like that.

"It's Judita." She sounded shaky. "I'm in the art show. We need you here right now."

Casper's expression—which had seemed so grown up a moment ago—fell, and suddenly I was looking at a scared little girl.

Before I even thought about it, I wrapped my free arm around her and pulled her close.

"I'll be right there," I said, and reattached the walkie to my belt.

Casper wrapped her arms around my waist—or as far around my waist as she could manage.

"I'm staying with you," she said against my chest.

"Yes, you are," I said. It was my turn to sound confident, even though I didn't feel confident. Judita, who was being a rock, was scared.

And if my rocks were getting scared, I had no idea what we'd do.

I slowly disentangled from Casper. "Let's go," I said, and started to move forward.

But she grabbed my hand as if it was a lifeline, which I guess it was. I'd been scrupulous in the past about touching her, but right now, holding her hand felt like the exact right thing to do.

She squeezed her hand around mine.

I looked down at her, and lied. "We'll be all right," I said. "I'm absolutely sure of it."

16

The art show wasn't too far from registration. Most fen would go down the main programming hallway and then turn right, but there was another, lesser used corridor near the stupid plant.

That was how Judita had gotten to the art show so quickly, and how Casper and I went right now. The nice thing about this corridor was that it trailed alongside the railing that overlooked the first floor, and was outside the usual path the convention goers took.

Casper was moving faster than I was, almost pulling me along. I let her. Because I wanted to get there quickly as well.

The mezzanine curved back in a half circle, and that particular corridor was mostly hidden, again with plants—two large scheffleras, almost as tall as I was. Their wide leaves made it hard to see the railing beyond.

Casper and I ducked behind them, and then I used one of my all-purpose key cards to get in the back of the art show.

From this angle, it looked sparse. Usually a SierraCon art show had to shove less worthy candidates far in the back because of a lack of space. This close to the major California cities meant some of the bigger name artists either sent their wares or attended themselves.

But, apparently, news of the storm had done its damage here as well. This back part of the art show was mostly empty. Someone had moved some of the fan art this far back, so that there were mediocre sculptures and some truly bad drawings of every single Doctor from the beginning of Dr. Who.

I worked my way around it all as I heard a familiar voice say, "I'm fine, really. Stop fussing."

Casper looked up at me, surprised. I wasn't sure if she recognized the voice since it wasn't booming or bombastic. But I knew Horatio's voice anywhere, and in particular, this version of it.

Back when Horatio was a poor writer, still hustling for every dollar, he used to sit in the back of con restaurants and actually research or write late at night. Sometimes I sat across from him and had quiet conversations about real issues, not about the made-up fantasy lands of what would become his bestselling novel series.

Casper and I rounded the horrible Doctors Who and stopped. Weapons were all over the floor, mixed in with some display panels and broken bits of metal. That didn't entirely compute—I had no idea how the metal broke—but I was willing to set that aside for the moment.

Three art show volunteers were hovering near the main entrance, looking terrified. Horatio was sitting on a nearby chair, clutching his lower leg, his right hand covered with blood.

"You're going to need stitches at least," Judita said. She was at his side.

"The great Horatio Dunnett, who writes about death and destruction, is terrified of needles," I said.

Horatio lifted his head. His shaggy hair, which looked appropriate under his various hats, was disheveled and graying. He actually looked his age, which was a lot older than most fen realized.

He saw Casper, and boomed, "I can just see the headline in the *New York Times*: 'Fantasy Writer Hoisted on His Own Petard.'"

"You're not hoisted," Casper said in an attempt at bravado, but her voice shook.

"Still." Horatio shrugged. His gaze met mine. "Hate to tell you this, old friend, but this was deliberate."

I looked at the mess around him, and tried to remember what had been there. And then I recalled it: a display of all the weapons in Horatio's Chancery Universe.

He wrote high fantasy which, back in the day, he used to claim he hated, and he was doing it all for money. Of course, it bit him on the ass now, because he had all the money in the world, and more angry fans than anyone else in the sf/f community because he couldn't bring himself to finish the work.

Angry fans meant moments like this.

"Let me see what's going on with your leg," I said, and made my way over to him.

"He won't let me see," Judita said.

"That's because, my dear," Horatio said, "I don't drop my drawers for just anyone, despite what the stories say."

"That's only because he's gotten older," I said as I crouched beside him. Blood was seeping through his fingers, not spurting, which was one good thing, but seeping wasn't great.

"You on blood-thinners?" I asked.

Horatio raised his chin at me, as if I'd offended him. But he was older and as heavy as the rest of us, and it wasn't an out-of-line question.

"Aspirin a day?" Casper asked.

He whipped his head toward her. "Well, yeah," he said.

"Then you're on blood thinners," she said, walking away from both of us. It took me a minute to understand where she was going. She was going to the check-in table where there should have been a medical kit.

We kept them in every big room, like the art show and the dealer's room. But this bad guy, whoever he was, might know that.

"She's got a mouth," Horatio said softly to me.

"Yeah, but she's right," I said. "Let me see what's going on."

His jeans were shredded, so all I had to do was peel them back. A long slice, the size of a battle axe blade, ran from the thick skin just below his knee to the bottom of his calf, missing—it looked like—all the major muscle groups.

"Did you walk over here?" I asked.

Something rebelled in Horatio's face. Apparently, he didn't like this kind of attention.

"No, I crawled," he said. "Of course I walked."

"Good," I said. "You put weight on it then."

Casper came back with the medical kit. I rummaged through it, found some butterfly bandages and superglue. I could work with that.

"I need wet towels and alcohol," I said to Casper.

She nodded, and started out of the room.

"Judita," I said, "you go with her. Casper, you promised. Nowhere alone."

She rolled her eyes, but waited for Judita to catch up to her. Then they left the art show.

"You want to tell me what happened?" I asked.

"I came in to inspect the display before the art show opened," Horatio said. "Half of this stuff comes from the studio, and I wanted to make sure it was secured."

The Hollywood studio that produced the Chancery series, one of the most popular shows on television.

I glanced at the mess. I couldn't tell if the weapons had been harmed or not. But there were a lot of strings and wires in the mix, and even more dangling from the ceiling.

"Did anyone know you were coming?" I asked.

"Pretty much the whole damn convention," Horatio said. "I'd been telling everyone that I'd make sure the display was perfect."

He twisted his leg so that he could see the injury. Even though more blood oozed out, he didn't seem to have trouble with the movement, confirming my first thought; he was damn lucky.

"This thing was booby trapped," he said more to his leg than to me. "If I'd been on a stage, I'd have seen someone was on the catwalk, with a release wire or something, so it all would collapse on me. And the thing is, Spade, the blades higher up were actually facing me. If I wasn't careful, I would've been chopped to bits."

Chopped. I frowned, feeling that same niggle I had felt earlier.

"Careful how?" I asked.

"I heard something," Horatio said, "and I jumped out of the way.

Yes, jumped. I can still do it. But that's why my leg took the brunt of it. I didn't get it out of the way in time, although my torso and the rest of me made it."

Damn lucky too, given what I could see.

"What did you hear?" I asked.

He shrugged, a frown on his broad face. "A sprooong and then a whoosh. I've been on TV and film sets where things have gone wrong. It's always preceded by a weird noise. And that noise was weird enough that my instincts made me jump."

He wasn't kidding about the sets. Back in the day, Starving Artist Horatio had decided to stop starving and—in his words—sold out. He'd gone Hollywood with the idea that he would make his fortune, and then return to the world of literature, which, in fact was what he did. Lots of banked money, but he didn't return to his literary roots. He kept writing what he thought the masses wanted and, it turned out he was right.

"Did you see anyone?" I asked.

"Besides them?" He waved his hand at the art show volunteers. "Not a soul."

"Did you touch the display?" I asked.

"What?" Horatio asked. "Why would I do that?"

"To make sure the weapons were secure," I said, thinking of the old booby-traps from haunted houses. Touching one of the display pieces in a place like that would have made the whole thing topple.

"I don't think so," Horatio said, frowning. Then he looked at his leg again. "This thing is starting to sting."

Maybe we would have to get him down to the medical room. Because what if one of the pieces was laced with something?

At that moment, Casper came back into the art show, carrying several dripping towels away from her body as if they'd contaminate her. Judita had a second medical kit and some dry towels.

They stopped next to us.

"Got scissors?" I asked.

One of the art show volunteers came over with a good pair of scissors, not one of those plastic things usually found in medical kits. I looked at all three of the volunteers and asked, "Any of you have any medical experience?"

They shook their heads in unison.

I sighed inwardly. I could handle things like cuts and burns because of conventions and working with notoriously doctor-shy computer geeks over the years, but this would tax my skills.

Still, I wanted to do what we could before we took Horatio out of the room.

"Cut his jeans at the knee," I said to Judita. She took the scissors, crouched on the other side of Horatio, and started cutting.

Casper held the wet towels as far from herself as she could. They dripped on the carpet. The mess was going to be something.

"Put those on that chair," I said to her, nodding at a chair beside Horatio. "And take as many pictures as you can of that ruined display. Maybe even the area around it. Be really careful. Don't get near any bit of it or the wires."

I handed her my phone as Judita finished cutting the last of the flayed jean leg. She tossed it aside.

I took the top towel. It was soaked and hot, which I didn't expect. I wrapped it quickly around Horatio's calf, and he hooted in surprise.

"Jey-sus," he said. "That hurts."

"Yeah," I said. "Everything I'm going to do is going to hurt."

I was beginning to rethink the super glue, hoping the butterfly bandages would be enough. But I didn't want to try to do stitches, even though there was thread and a needle inside the nearest medical kit.

"Maybe we should call someone for help," Judita said, her skin a little gray.

"McCoy and Paladin are trying to save Ruth," I said, "and I don't think Zula should leave Jessica-6 alone."

"What the hell?" Horatio asked. "What's going on here?"

I almost started to tell him, but then remembered my admonition to the concom. They were going to have enough trouble containing the news. If I was the first one to leak it, then I couldn't deal with them.

I looked at the art show volunteers. "I think we need to shut down the art show for the afternoon. We won't open it until tomorrow. Can you make signs to that effect? And let the concom know to put it in the bulletins we're sending out?"

"Us?" The volunteer who brought the scissors said.

"No one else is near you," I said, a little too pointedly. "Do any of you have key cards?"

They looked at each other, then shook their heads. That was good. That meant the concom was doing this part right, at least. Someone had unlocked the art show before the volunteers got here.

"Okay, then," I said. "Thanks."

One of them lingered. I made little wavy motions with my fingers, and the volunteers finally caught a clue. They left, talking quietly, but kept the door open.

I supposed that was all right.

"Judita, we're going to need a few garbage bags," I said, looking at the blood-soaked towel.

She was watching the door—anything except looking at Horatio's wound.

"Okay," Horatio said. "You got rid of the witnesses. *Now* tell me what's going on."

"We've had a rash of near-misses," I said. "First, Rogers Caron got poisoned. Then, Jessica-6 got hit over the head on the way to her truck and left to freeze. And finally, someone gave Ruth Harshaw an overdose of sleeping pills, we think. And now this."

"That's a lot of weird criminal activity," Horatio said. "Are you sure it was all meant to be lethal?"

Judita brought several garbage bags from the table, laid two on the floor and put the other on the side. I tossed the bloody towel on one of the floor bags, then grabbed another towel and used it to clean the area along the wound.

"You tell me," I said as I worked. "You're the one who just dodged a display filled with sharp objects."

Horatio stared at me, his mouth a thin line. His skin was paler than it had been a moment ago. "You're telling me someone just tried to kill me?"

"Yeah," I said. "Were those volunteers anywhere near you when it happened?"

"No," he said. "I was talking to them, pointing at some of the swords, telling stories—you know."

"I do," I said. I'd seen Horatio in action more times than I cared to contemplate.

"I could even see their hands. They weren't holding a cell phone. They weren't near any electronics at all. They were *listening*."

I blinked, thinking about what he had just said. He had thought that there was some kind of cellular or wireless trigger, just like there might have been for a bomb.

That would be worth investigating...when there was time to investigate.

"What's the point of doing something so elaborate?" Horatio said. "If you wanted to take someone out, there are a lot better ways to do it."

I tossed the second towel on top of the first. His leg looked pale and slightly puckered and vulnerable. The blood ooze had slowed to a seep.

Now, I couldn't put off the next step any longer. I grabbed the bottle of rubbing alcohol. I could dab or I could pour.

I elected to pour.

"Holy shit!" Horatio yelled and jerked back, nearly toppling out of his chair. "You could warn a guy."

"You can see what I'm doing," I said.

"You want me to look to see if there's any electronic stuff?" Casper asked, from near the ruined display. Apparently, she'd been listening in to our conversation.

"Not right now," I said. "You and Judita can get me more towels, though."

"I'm just going to call housekeeping," Judita said.

"No," I said. I didn't want them to see this mess. Or anyone else, for that matter. "Never mind. I'll make do with what I have."

Some of the skin was loose. The seeping blood made me feel better than the oozing blood, but it was still bad. No matter how much I wanted to avoid it, I was thinking superglue was our best option. That way Horatio could walk at least.

"Seriously, Spade," Horatio said. He was no longer looking at his leg, but at the mess near Casper. "Is this all because of the no-weapons policy? Someone could have snuck a gun in here. If they wanted to take me out, that would've been the way to do it."

I poured alcohol all over my hands. That stuff did sting in the little cuts around my nails. I couldn't quite imagine how it had felt around Horatio's leg.

I air-dried my hands, then grabbed the super glue. I looked at Judita, and was going to tell her to follow my fingers with butterfly bandages, but she was actually looking queasy.

Instead, Casper grabbed the medical kit. "This is a two-person job," she said. "I'll do the bandages."

"Do you know how?" I asked.

"My parents are drug addicts," she said. "What do you think?"

I nodded, realizing just how little I knew about her life. She tucked my phone back in the pocket of my shirt, then grabbed the first bandage. She raised her eyebrows and looked at me.

"I can probably do it myself, if you need me to," she said.

I saw the competent little girl who'd had to grow up too fast, the one that Paladin and I had sworn to protect.

Horatio was frowning at her. "Where did you find this kid?" he asked.

I didn't feel like answering him. But something he had said a moment ago caught my attention. This *was* elaborate. And there were easier ways to kill people. Casper had said the same thing.

What was the point?

Rogers hadn't died from that poison because he had choked first. And there was a number in the bit of food that he had eaten. A 1.

Was there anything in Jessica-6's truck? A 2, maybe? Only she wouldn't have been 2, would she? Her injury occurred in the morning.

Ruth's clearly had happened at night, after she left me. She had gone back to the room, opened her laptop to do a little more work or maybe watch a video, and she had put some popcorn in the microwave. If we looked—or maybe looked on the photos that Paladin took—we'd find a number 2.

I pulled the flap of skin near the top of Horatio's thigh closed, then dabbed some superglue on it.

He grimaced, but didn't say anything. As I worked my way down, Casper did as well, using butterfly bandages to hold the dabs of superglue in place.

I hoped to hell some EMT somewhere or some surgeon or someone would be able to undo what I was doing, without a lot of damage.

Rogers *choked*. Ruth had an overdose...of sleeping pills. That niggled at me.

Then I looked up at Horatio. He was resolutely looking at the mess of weapons.

"You said chopped," I said.

"Huh?" he asked.

"You would have been chopped up," I said.

He waved a hand. "Have you looked at that? I would have been in pieces."

I nodded, then continued working my way down. Jessica-6, though. A hit on the head seemed impromptu. I wasn't sure how she fit. Had she known the perpetrator?

Horatio's calves weren't as resilient as his thigh. I was working a little harder, letting my fingers do the dab-pinch while my brain worked. Something about her truck, something about—

"Oh, my God!" I said before I could stop myself. "She went to Devon."

"What?" Horatio asked, looking at me like I had gone insane.

"Her truck," I said. "It was named Devon."

"She named her truck?" Casper asked as she opened another bandage. "Why would you do that?"

I didn't answer that question, because my brain had finally solved the riddle. Why would someone go to such elaborate ends to kill people?

Because he wanted to be remembered, in a fannish kind of way. Mass shooters, generally speaking, were suicidal. They never planned to get out of that situation they shot up alive.

But someone in fandom would be smart enough to know that mass shooting situations had become all too common in the U.S. And anyone who wanted their name to be renowned in an icky villainous way would need to do so using a different method.

There was probably a good sf way to be remembered, but it probably required some kind of technology that our villain didn't have or which hadn't been invented yet.

But sf fandom and mystery fandom were linked. And they would know what he had done, later, when the news came out.

He was riffing off the horrid, horrid poem that had inspired the Agatha Christie novel that Horatio had mentioned yesterday. A poem that ended with the novel's current title, *And then there were none*.

None.

But there were only ten victims in that book. And there were potentially hundreds here.

It didn't compute. Unless he was actually not going for the mass killing, but was taking revenge before he took his own life.

Weirdly enough, that chill I'd been feeling left me. I felt better now. I had something to grab a hold of, something to work with—for the first time in two days.

17

I still had about three inches to close on Horatio's leg injury. Casper was running low on butterfly bandages, but we had at least closed up the wound, maybe enough to take care of it for a while. I'd get McCoy or Zula to look at it, and then prescribe some antibiotics. If we were lucky, there would be some here.

The art show seemed both empty and vast. Judita was bagging up the bloody towels. I grabbed one more. It was warm now, not hot, but still useful. I cleaned up as much of the wound as I could.

Then I took some antibacterial crème out of the medical kit, and just ran it along the wound. We needed something to wrap around this mess.

"Get me all the gauze," I said to Casper.

She nodded, almost as if she had already had that thought.

I had a moment to survey the art show. The armory display had been close to one of the walls, and it was visible from the main door. It would have been possible to rig up something and then trigger it from outside the room. All someone had to do was watch.

I needed to look at the hotel security cameras, and see what we had.

Casper handed me the gauze and some medical tape.

"You're in charge of the tape," I said, mostly because I was all thumbs when it came to that kind of stuff.

Horatio leaned over and stared at my handiwork. He looked a little dismayed, but managed, "At least it's not bleeding as much now."

"At least," I said.

Then I wrapped the gauze tightly around Horatio's upper thigh, and he hooted again, and swore, quite creatively.

"I didn't think writers were babies," Casper said, disapprovingly.

I glanced at her. I had forgotten that she hadn't liked Horatio when she met him.

"You do worse to your characters," she said, as she applied tape. "And they do just fine."

"Sometimes they die," he said.

She shrugged. "But they don't whine in pain. I'd think you'd be just like them."

"They're *fictional*," he said to her. "Fictional people have the luxury of continuing on after a grand injury. Mere mortals often cannot."

"So why make that stuff up, then?" Casper asked. "You give us all the wrong expectation."

He glared at her. She put some more tape on the gauze I was unraveling and, it looked to me, like she had used a bit too much force.

"You're a mean little thing, aren't you?" he asked.

"You're ungrateful," she said.

I had to stop this. "Horatio, when I saw you yesterday, you said you were here for the Agatha Christie portion of the convention."

He raised his head, finally distracted.

"And when I pressed you on it, you said you were just kidding because of the storm." I wrapped the last of the gauze along his ankle, then had Casper apply one more bit of tape, anchoring the gauze to his bare skin.

Horatio winced, but continued to look at me.

"I would have thought, though, if you were thinking about the storm, you would have said the Donner part of the convention."

"I was at Donnercon," Horatio said. "It was...well, not as exciting as this. I was trying for wit, Spade."

"I was just wondering if you knew something about the convention that I didn't." I put the gauze inside the medical kit. We'd made quite a mess.

Horatio leaned back a little in the chair, moving his leg gingerly. He didn't put any weight on it yet. Maybe I would go down to the medical area, and get him some crutches or that wheelchair.

"A bunch of us have always talked about doing something cozy-mystery-esque," Horatio said. "Maybe making a Chancery live-action mystery game, mixing something like *Clue* with my fantasy world. Or you know, or a version of *Ten Little...*"

He glanced at Casper. She looked confused.

"Um, you know, of *And Then There Were None*," he said. "I figured a remote con like this one would be best. But we had really stopped talking about it when we started doing cruise ships. I talked to my representation about it, and they believed that it would be better if we had a more *Chancery* specific game than some kind of murder mystery."

I stood up. My knees cracked and my back hurt. I was not built for the kind of work I had just done.

"Who were you discussing this with?" I asked Horatio.

He shrugged. "The Usual Set, mostly. They love cruises."

"And they're here. Again, is there something you're not telling me?"

"They're here because they wanted to do some kind of West Coast tour, and I told them to end it here, so we could all drink too much and have fun," he said. "Don't read anything more into that."

Casper was putting all the medical supplies back in the kit. She was rearranging them, now that we had used so much. Judita had bagged the dirty towels and put them near the garbage can.

There was a blood trail along the carpet. She put the remaining wet towels on it, so that it would soak up some of the blood. I almost protested, but there was no point.

By the time the authorities got here, everything would be different. We were on our own, quite literally, until this storm passed.

"Were there any fen in the discussion?" I asked Horatio.

"Millions of them," he said.

I gave him a look of disgust. "I'm serious, Horatio."

"I'm almost serious," he said. "A dozen, maybe two dozen, maybe more fen sat in on these conversations. Not counting the people who overheard. You know how it is."

I did. People sat close to their favorite celebrities—and Horatio counted as one now—and eavesdropped on every nugget they said. People also crashed conversations. I dragged a lot of well-meaning fans out of conversations that had nothing to do with them, but in which they drunkenly (or soberly) participated anyway.

Trying to find someone from a conversation Horatio had at conventions over the years—and yes, it would have been the same conversation, because con time is different from real time, conversations can stretch decades—would be impossible. Or nearly so.

"You've never been here before, though, right?" I asked.

"SierraCon?" Horatio said. "It's always been on my bucket list." He put a hand on his leg. "Maybe I need to rethink that list."

"Have you gone to conventions near here?"

"What are you, high, Spade?" he asked. "You've seen me at Baycon and Loscon and the San Francisco Worldcon. There was some Sacramento con whose name I can't remember, and a couple of Nasfics, not to mention Comic-Cons back before they became a Big Deal, and even afterward. When I was working on *Once Upon A Crime* and *Snackers*, I would go to any convention that was nearby, so I could stay in touch with my roots."

"And you were talking about your mystery-sf *Clue* idea then," I said.

"The Agatha Christie portion of the convention," he said with utmost seriousness.

"Have you made that joke a lot?" I asked.

"At damn near every convention I've gone to in the past decade," he said.

I felt a surge of disappointment. I had hoped I could figure out something, but it sounded like a dead end.

"So this is about you," Casper said, with an edge. "All these people are being hurt because of your joke."

"Enough," I said to her. Horatio was a victim here, not the perpetrator.

"No," she said. "He gave someone the idea."

"Casper," I said.

"Let me," Horatio said. He leaned toward Casper, and he had the most serious expression I'd ever seen him have.

Casper crossed her arms. Whatever he wanted to say, she didn't want to hear it.

"Look," Horatio said, "if I worried about some nutcase taking everything I wrote, every idea I had, and acting on it in some way, then I couldn't write. I'm not responsible for the insanity around me."

"Sounds like an excuse," Casper said.

"I work in mass entertainment," Horatio said. "Emphasis on 'mass.' That means there will be people who will take the wrong message out of what I do. What anyone does, really."

"Still sounds like an excuse," Casper said.

Horatio studied her for a moment. "Yeah, I understand how you can feel that way. Would you rather have entertainment that's all Smurfs and rainbow unicorns?"

Her mouth narrowed.

"Life is tough," Horatio said. "We have to acknowledge that in our art, and in our lives."

"People have gotten hurt," Casper said. "You haven't even asked how Ruth is doing, and she nearly died."

"You're right," Horatio said. "I haven't." He swept a hand down his leg. "I've been feeling a little self-involved."

"Have you heard from Paladin?" I asked Casper.

"Yeah," Casper said. "She says Ruth and Rogers are in the same room and McCoy is monitoring them, and the storm. He's called for a medevac as soon as the storm clears."

He should have told me about that before telling Casper. Then I realized he probably had.

"Did you get that from my phone?" I asked.

"Yeah," she said. "He texted you. I forgot to say."

I pulled the phone out of my pocket. I had texts from McCoy and from Paladin as well as a few members of the concom. I could ignore the concom. I didn't want to ignore Paladin and McCoy.

I tapped out an answer to the news, then tucked the phone back in my pocket.

"We're going to need to move you out of here," I said to Horatio. "And if you're going to be in your room, then we'll need someone to buddy with you."

"My *room?* You heathen, this is a *convention*," Horatio said. "I'm not going to my room."

"Well, let's get you down to the medical office and see if we can find some crutches." I also hoped Zula was still down there. She could look at my handiwork, and then she could maybe give him some antibiotics, if they had any.

"Judita," I said. "Leave the mess here, and lock up the room. Then you and Casper find Paladin. I don't want her alone either."

Judita nodded.

"I'd rather go with you," Casper said.

"Judita needs someone to accompany her while she's looking for Paladin," I said.

"Paladin is in our room, changing," Casper said. "It wouldn't take much—"

"No," I said, knowing where she was going with this. "No one is going anywhere alone, not even on a short journey. Is that clear?"

Casper made a face, but she nodded.

"It's hard, I know," I said. "But right now, we need the buddy system."

"The problem with your stupid buddy system," Casper said, "is that someone is going to end up buddying with the killer."

I'd already thought of that. But I knew it wasn't true. The villain—I couldn't call him a killer, because (fingers crossed) so far no one had died—would probably continue doing everything alone.

"Just partner up, kid," Horatio said tiredly. "Sometimes the smart thing is the only thing."

She looked at him. Then she looked back at me. "I'm going to call you after we get Paladin. Okay?"

"Okay," I said.

"What are we going to do?" Horatio asked.

"You and I are limping to the service elevator, and heading to the daylight basement," I said. "I'm your crutch, until we get down there."

Horatio sighed. He looked me up and down, and his expression found me wanting. I kinda felt like I was wanting. I wasn't sure I could handle his weight for all that distance, but I was going to give it the old college try.

The service elevator was off one of the side doors. I walked over to Horatio, and pointed. "We're going that way," I said.

Then I turned back to Casper and Judita.

"I was serious about not cleaning up. We have no idea if there are more booby-traps. Just go to Paladin right now."

Judita nodded. Casper's mouth maintained its thin disapproving line.

I smiled at her. "We'll see you shortly, kiddo," I said, using Paladin's nickname for her.

Casper's mouth grew even tighter, as if she had swallowed something bad.

I couldn't fight that, so I turned around, and slid a chair closer to Horatio. "We're going to get you upright first, and then you're going to lean on me—and hop."

"Hop," Horatio said. "I haven't hopped since I was...well, probably eighteen, and most likely high."

"Well," I said, "you can try putting weight on that leg, but I wouldn't recommend it."

He reached for the other chair, and levered himself upward, pinwheeling one arm so intently that I had to stay back to avoid getting hit.

He finally stopped, for just a moment, and I slid close to his injured side. "Put your hand on my shoulder," I said, noting for the first time that there was quite a disparity in our heights.

Horatio was such a vivid person that I thought he was taller than he actually was. But I had a good five inches on him or more. I thought it was less.

"I don't think the shoulder will work," Horatio said about the point I realized the same thing. So I wrapped an arm around his torso.

"Lean in," I said. "The first stage is getting to the elevator. You can lean once we're in there."

"Think of it like a military campaign," Casper said, with just an edge of asperity. "You know, one pincer movement at a time."

It was an odd thing to say, more so in that it made Horatio smile. "You read my books, kid."

"So?" she said.

"So, do they make you feel homicidal?"

"Yeah," she snapped. "I've been homicidal since you've taken your own sweet time writing the last book."

Oh. I finally understood. Casper was a fan of Horatio's. But she was a certain kind of fan, one who had loved the books until there were no more. And then, she felt betrayed—not by the books—but by their author, who was refusing (in her mind) to finish them.

"I'm working on it," Horatio said.

"By swanning around conventions," she said, and turned her back on him.

He swayed a little, leaning his body into me a bit too hard. It was going to be work to help him keep his balance.

"She's quite a kid," he said to me.

"She can hear you," Casper said.

"She is amazing," I said in a neutral tone. "We're going to have to turn now, and face that door I pointed at. Turning is probably going to be hard."

"Yeah, I'm gathering that," Horatio said, and he already sounded a bit breathless. "This is a lot harder than I expected. I'm thinking that if I had it to do again, I'd revise a scene or two, making injury harder on my characters."

"Why bother?" Casper said. "They're *fictional*."

I couldn't help it. I smiled. And I didn't say anything. Horatio was leaning on me harder than I expected and he didn't really seem to have a lot of balance. It was going to be work for the two of us to get downstairs, but I wasn't about to ask Judita or Casper for help.

They needed to shut this room down and get to Paladin. Right now, Paladin was alone and that worried me.

Everything was worrying me.

If I was right, we had someone who had a hell of an agenda, someone who probably had a list of potential victims, before he offed himself. And we needed to find him.

I needed to find him.

And soon.

18

We made it to the elevator in record time. Record *slow* time. Each step was agony. By the time we reached the little elevator alcove, I was seriously wondering if Horatio could make it all the way to the medical room.

He was sweating and breathing hard, and barely able to keep his balance. He seemed to recover a little after I hit the elevator button, and we waited for its arrival.

To be fair, I was sweating too. I was overheated and working too hard, and if I were honest with myself, I was probably suffering from too much stress.

The elevator arrived with a ding, and the door eased open. It was empty. I helped Horatio into the carriage, which was large enough to handle at least two housekeeper's carts, so it could definitely handle two very large men.

I eased Horatio toward the wall, and pressed the B button for that daylight basement.

"I was thinking," Horatio said, "about what you asked."

I blinked. I had asked a number of things.

"About the Agatha Christie Portion," he said. "You think someone is acting out that awful poem?"

I wasn't going to lie to him. "Possible," I said.

"But you said Rogers was poisoned." Horatio leaned his head against the elevator's wall. He sounded tired.

"He choked first," I said. "That's how we know."

"How does it go?" Horatio asked. "'Ten little...'"

He looked at me as he searched for a way to avoid the N-word which had initially been in the poem.

"They've changed it a lot. I have no idea what it is now," I said.

The elevator was lurching downward, which was making me uncomfortable. I knew the service elevator was slow, but this was ridiculous.

"Soldiers, I think," Horatio said. "'Ten little...'"

And he stopped at the same place. Rather than listen to him start and stop like a recording stuck on loop, I prompted: "Fen."

He gave me a real Horatio smile. "Yeah. That'll work. 'Ten little fen went out to dine. One choked his little self and then there were nine.' So, that means he's going after ten people."

"No," I said. "If he's sticking to the poem, he's going after nine."

Horatio frowned at me. "Nine?"

"The last line," I said, "which really doesn't scan, except visually, even if you use a British accent."

"I don't remember it," Horatio said.

"'One little fan boy left all alone,'" I said. "'He went out and hanged himself and then there were none.'"

"Fan boy," Horatio said, almost to himself.

The elevator finally reached the ground floor, and shuddered to a stop. I moved into position next to Horatio. He balanced on his good foot as he pushed himself upright. He grabbed my shirt before slipping his arm around my waist.

We lurched forward, almost like the elevator had done. The door started to close before we could reach it, but I managed to lean sideways and hit the "door open" button.

The doors banged back. The hallway before us looked empty. It had that same grayish yellowish light that unnerved me yesterday. I was still unnerved, but not by the light. I was getting used to that.

"It doesn't really fit, though, does it?" Horatio asked, as we moved into that corridor. "The poem, I mean. You have Ruth, who was poisoned too, and out of order."

"No," I said. "Sleeping pills. And it wasn't out of order at all. It had to have happened second."

"'Nine little fen...'" he said, and stopped. "Ah, hell, I don't remember exactly."

"Something about being up late, and oversleeping oneself." I steered him toward the medical room. Using this elevator, the room was closer than it was with the main elevator, but right now "closer" was a technicality. I hadn't been dragging Horatio with me the last time I'd come down here.

It was pretty quiet down here. No con goers that I could see. The Starbucks wannabe was open, though, and the only employee behind the counter peered over it at us as if she had never seen anything that strange before.

"And then the one about going to Devon," Horatio said. "Followed by being chopped in half." He gestured toward his leg. "That could have happened, you know. I could have been chopped in half."

I wanted to tell him not to be so dramatic, but he was actually right. Any one of those weapons could have completely destroyed him. He had been lucky.

"I told the studio not to send anything. But they were flattered by the idea of the armory show, and honestly, I was kinda jealous of the way that HBO used to support George's show. That throne ended up everywhere."

He was referring to the iconic HBO version of the Throne in *Game of Thrones*. And he was right; damn near every single convention after the show became popular had a version of the throne either in the dealer's room or one of the fannish displays. And for years, every time you passed the damn thing, someone was sitting in it, getting their picture taken.

I had no idea how weapons compared; people didn't sit in weapons. They either loathed them (me) or admired them (Horatio—although I wondered if he would from now on).

"What I'm trying to do," I said, as I steered him away from the Star-bucks wannabe toward the medical room, "is remember what else is in that damn poem. There's a bumblebee, I think—"

"A bumblebee?" Horatio said.

"I think," I said. "And for sure, a gun. That's at the very end. I remember that because of some dumb movie I saw as a kid. The bad guy was holding a gun on the hero outside of a cave or something. I think that was made from the Christie book."

"Naw," Horatio said. "I'm pretty sure the movies made from it didn't have a cave. Where's IMDb when you need it?"

He laughed a little, but the laugh sounded strained.

"Remember when we used to debate all this crap without using IMDb?" he asked.

"Yeah," I said. Sometimes I was wistful about that. But right now, I needed to get Horatio to that room, and then look up the poem. It would help me figure out what was next. I hoped, anyway.

"How would someone get a bumblebee in here?" Horatio asked. "There's snow."

"The bee might be a metaphor," I said. "Devon wasn't quite what it was in the poem."

"I remember a bear," Horatio said. "But that can't be right. God, Spade. We need to see that poem."

"We will," I said.

We had finally reached the medical room's door—and it was closed. I had no idea if I still had my all-purpose key card, or if it was easily accessible, since I was essentially holding up Horatio.

Before I could search for it, though, Horatio leaned forward and knocked.

It took a few seconds, seconds in which I was trying to figure out what pocket I would have put the key card in.

Then the door swung open, and Zula was there. Zula loved Grace Jones, maybe because she looked like the 1980s Grace Jones. Her hair was cut in wedges around her head, which made her skull look almost square. Like Grace Jones, Zula was tall and angular and strong.

Usually Zula dressed like the character from the Conan movies, in some kind of metal bikini that showed off her abs and impressive muscles. Sometimes she added the wristbands and in the conventions that allowed weapons, she often wore those weird wristbands that had spikes sticking out the side.

So it was really strange to see her in a gray sweater that went to her mid-thighs and a pair of form-fitting blue jeans. Only the boots, which looked like they were made of leather, were some kind of reminder of the Conan character.

"Spade," Zula said, but her gaze was on Horatio. "What happened to him?"

"Accident," Horatio said as I said, "We had another attack."

"Clearly," Zula said, moving away from the door.

"He's cut up pretty bad," I said. "We bandaged him up and probably did some harm, but the bleeding has stopped for the time being. I'd like you to look at what I've done."

"Screw that," Horatio said. "I'm fine. I just need crutches and antibiotics."

Zula rolled her eyes, but stepped back, letting us in the room. Then she closed the door.

"You know about the buddy system right now, right?" I asked.

"I got the memo," Zula said, "although I don't think my buddy is going to help me."

She waved a hand toward one of those hospital beds. Jessica-6 lay on it, her head wrapped, and her eyes closed.

"Has she woken up yet?" I asked.

"No," Zula said. "I'm getting worried."

I was too. One more thing to think about, I guessed.

But I couldn't deal with that yet. I needed to get Horatio away from me. His weight was seriously torquing my back.

I eased him to the other bed, and he sat down heavily. The bed squeaked. Zula immediately crouched down next to the gauze bandages.

They were a little yellow near the wound, and there was some dried blood closer to his knee. Apparently I hadn't stopped the seepage entirely.

Zula looked at me. "No medical experience, right?"

"Some," I said. "But no training."

At least she didn't say, *Obviously,* but I suspected that was more out of deference to Horatio than to me.

"Antibiotics," Horatio said. "Crutches."

"Give me a chance to look this over," Zula said, waving her long fingers over his bandages.

"I'm going to leave him," I said, although as I spoke the words, I wasn't sure how I would do that, if I followed my own orders. I needed someone to accompany me.

"Oh, no, you're not," Horatio said. "How'm I supposed to get upstairs if there's a buddy system? Clearly Zula needs to stay here. And you're my buddy. You'll be breaking the rules too."

I sighed. The buddy system was a great idea, until it became inconvenient. And this was inconvenient. I didn't want to be tied to Horatio for the entire convention.

"Maybe you should stay here and rest," I said. "You don't have anything until opening ceremonies, if you're even up for that."

He glared at me. "People came to see me," he said. "I'm not going to disappoint. And—" he grabbed his badge and turned it over, peering at the schedule that we had glued to the back of each pro badge "—I have two panels this afternoon *before* opening ceremonies."

Two panels. I had a lot to check in on, and I needed to foist my duties onto someone else. If we had a—God, what do we call this guy (and why was I assuming it was a guy?)—A serial assaulter? A spree wannabe killer? A villain?—if we had one of those, and there were at least five potential victims out there, I needed to work on finding this guy.

"Spade?" Horatio said. "Earth to Spade."

Apparently, I hadn't been listening to him.

"Let's get out of here," Horatio said.

"Not until I check what Spade did to your leg," Zula said. "I want to know what happened here."

And I didn't want to look again. I grabbed my phone, and as I did, it actually emitted Casper's ringtone which was, unimaginatively, the theme song from *Casper The Friendly Ghost* TV show.

I held up a finger, and stepped into the hallway, wondering if—by my buddy-system rules—this counted as being alone or being with a buddy. To make my own conscience feel better, I propped the door open.

Zula looked up, about to correct me, and then rethought it.

I crossed the hall, so I could see inside, but have a measure of privacy.

"Everything okay?" I asked by way of hello.

"Where are you?" she asked.

"Medical office in the basement," I said.

"Me and Paladin are coming to you, after we drop Judita at registration."

So Paladin was all right. It had been a nagging worry that she hadn't been.

"You might want to bring Judita with you, so that Horatio has a buddy," I said.

"No!" Horatio shouted from the medical office, as Casper was saying, "She really doesn't want to be stuck with Horatio."

I peered around the door. Horatio was yelling at me, not Zula. He was on his back, but propped up on his elbows, and looking over his shoulder at me, rather than watching Zula painstakingly remove the bandages we had put around his leg.

He kept wincing, though, so I guessed it had to hurt.

"We can drop him at his panel or wherever," Casper was saying, as if she was repeating something someone else told her. She was speaking at the same time as Horatio.

"If I have to have a buddy," he said, "I get to pick who it is."

"None of us really get to pick," I said to Horatio.

"What?" Casper asked.

"I'm talking to Horatio," I said, hating these kinds of conversations. "When will you two get here?"

There was a pause and that rustly sound as Casper moved the phone away from her mouth.

"Spade—Yeowch!" That second word was involuntary. Horatio turned away from me, and said, "Really, Zula, there's no need—"

"You have superglue on your bandages," she said to him. "Spade, did anyone tell you superglue is very 1980s?"

"Tell the hotel that," I said. "It was in their medical kit."

"Fifteen minutes max," Casper said, and it took me a moment to remember what she was talking about. They would be here in fifteen minutes, which was fourteen minutes longer than I wanted.

But I had made the rules. I really didn't dare break them. They were sensible.

"Tell Paladin no side trips," I said. "I need you both down here fast."

"Okay," Casper said, and hung up.

Zula removed the last of the bandages and tossed them away. She put her hands on her hips and stood back, staring at the long wound.

"I'd prefer it if you didn't do anything else today," she said to Horatio. "This is some injury."

"I'm not going to be doing anything, really," he said. "I'll be sitting on panels pontificating. I can pontificate down here, to you, or up there, to fen. I prefer fen. No offense."

Zula looked at me. "There better not be a skit or anything at Opening Ceremonies. I don't want him on this leg at all."

A skit. We had planned one, and I had forgotten about it with everything else happening.

"No skit," I said.

"You're going to be one of those difficult patients, aren't you?" Zula said to Horatio.

"I prefer that to this." He waggled a finger at the unconscious Jessica-6.

Honestly, I preferred him conscious too, no matter how difficult he was. It worried me that Jessica-6 hadn't come to yet.

"Yeah." Zula's gaze met mine. "I'm not liking any of this, Spade."

"Me either," I said. I pocketed my phone and cross the empty hallway. As I did, I realized that the employees at the wannabe Starbucks and the sandwich shop were more or less alone too. Or did it count that they could see each other from across the narrow corridor?

I probably needed to warn them as well. And the hotel.

More things to do.

I let myself back into the medical room, but I left the door propped open. I sat on the opposite side of Horatio, so that I wouldn't be able to see what Zula was going to do to his leg. I had a hunch it wouldn't be pretty.

"You gotta look up that poem," Horatio said, shifting slightly so that he could see me.

"Stay still," Zula said. She had gathered some bottles, probably cleansers. "And what poem? What's so important about a poem?"

So we told her. Or rather, I did.

She stopped what she was doing and looked at me over Horatio's leg like I had lost my mind. "Someone is using that racist shit to try to kill us?"

"Yeah," Horatio said. "At a convention. Can you believe it?"

Her hands froze, and so did her expression. "Yeah," she said after a moment. "I can."

Horatio frowned at her. "SF conventions are the friendliest places in the world."

She grabbed one of the bottles and what appeared to be a clean rag. "For white people," she said.

"Granted, there aren't enough Black people in science fiction, but—"

"But what?" she asked. "Black people read. They read a lot of sf. I thought sf would be welcoming. I figured if they had Octavia Butler, then there would be lots of other Blacks at conventions. But no. It depended on the convention. Out East, it was me and Samuel R. Delany, maybe one or two other people. In the Northwest, for a while, it was me and Steve Barnes. Out West, me and Octavia before she died. Maybe a couple of other people at the bigger conventions. That was it."

"Well," Horatio said. "That's changing now."

"Yes," Zula said. "It is. West Coast cons are mostly better. East Coast cons are too. There're more writers now, and they're actually writing about stuff that I can identify with. Among some folks. But have you looked at this convention? There's maybe four of us. And now, some bigot is using a racist poem to go after fandom. That's weird."

"Spade thinks they're going for memorable," Horatio said.

It felt weird to be discussed in the third person.

"Well, it is that," Zula said.

"I'm a little stuck," Horatio said. "I mean, the fact that the poem is racist is the least of it. Someone's using it to try to kill people. Isn't that worse?"

"Racism kills," Zula said tightly.

I wanted to stop Horatio now, but I had no idea how to do so. I kept forgetting he had pasted a veneer over the blunt socially inept self that had brought him into fandom in the first place, back when he was fourteen, pimpled, short, and scrawny.

"Yeah." Even Horatio's tone was dismissive. "But this is an active crime scene."

"The convention?" Zula asked. "Or the poem?"

My breath caught. Horatio squinted at her. It looked like he was beginning to figure out that her part of the conversation held layers of meaning, while his was deeply naïve.

"Why do you keep coming to conventions if they're so awful?" Horatio asked, and I closed my eyes. That was exactly *not* the question to ask.

"Why do I...?" Zula held some kind of pick tool in her right hand, and she raised it, looking fierce. "Are you saying I'm not welcome here?"

"No!" Horatio's eyebrows went up. "I'm not saying that. It's just—"

"Just what?" Zula asked.

"Well, it's getting better."

Zula closed her eyes. Then she opened them and bent over his leg again. Her lips were thin, her expression cold.

I wouldn't have wanted anyone with that expression working on me. It was a testament to her professionalism that she wasn't going to hurt him, in all his ignorance.

"What did I say?" Horatio looked at me.

"Too much," I said.

I didn't look at his reaction, even though I could feel his confusion as well as Zula's fury.

I took out my phone, and looked up the poem. I found at least three incarnations of it, none of which I liked. The original, with the N-word. The "cleaned-up" 1960s version, substituting the word "Indian" in the poem, which had the "benefit" of insulting Native Americans in the U.S. and people from India in Great Britain. And then the current version which for some odd reason used the word "soldier."

"Okay," I said. "I'm going to read it, and I'm substituting the word 'fen' because I don't like any of this, okay?"

"Do I want to hear this thing?" Zula asked.

"Yeowch!" Horatio said. "What are you doing?"

"I'm going to clean up the wound and stitch you up," she said. "You're lucky it didn't hit any arteries. Damn lucky."

"I'd be dead now," Horatio said quietly, and in all seriousness.

She nodded.

"You don't need to hear the poem," I said to Zula. "I'll just—"

"Yeah, I think I do," Zula said. "I'm used to racism around here. And it's in all the books, up until, I don't know. Lovecraft, you guys revere him and he's awful. And then there's Christie herself. Have you *read* her books? They're... shit, I don't know."

She sighed.

Horatio was looking at her gape-mouthed.

She shook her head, and said, "We need to figure out this poem if we're going to fight whoever it is that's going after us. And it's better if all of us hear it. We might figure something out."

I nodded. I bookmarked the page the poem was on, and then increased the font size so I could read it easily.

"Here goes," I said, and began. "Ten little fen went out to dine; One choked his little self and then there were nine."

"Rogers," Zula said. She knew about the poisoning and the choking.

"Seems like he might be the actual target," Horatio said, "since he was choked and poisoned."

"Let's not jump to conclusions," Zula said. "Maybe *all* of you are targets."

Horatio mimicked a shudder. Or maybe it was real. It was hard to tell. He did look unnerved, though.

"Not sure I want to be a target," he said. "Then again, random victim isn't all that great either."

He started to look at his leg, at what Zula was doing, then clearly stopped.

"I suspect," I said, "if we're dealing with a Christie aficionado, then they'll follow Christie logic. Some of the victims will be random to hide the intent against the other victims."

Zula moved slightly down Horatio's leg, as she worked. "You think they meant to go after Rogers, then."

"No," I said. "But I think they thought all their victims would die."

Horatio shuddered again.

"I suspect the fact that we've thwarted them so far," I said, "has probably angered them."

"Great." Horatio leaned his head back. "That means they'll come after us again."

"I don't know what it means," I said. "All I know is this: We have about twenty-four hours before we even have the possibility of help, and at the pace this...villain...is going after us, they might get the next five victims by then. And one of those victims might actually die."

"Great," Zula said, probably not realizing her tone mimicked Horatio's.

"Ye-owch!" Horatio sat back up. "Do you have a topical anesthetic or something?"

"I already put it on there. I don't have anything stronger." She didn't even look up at him as she said that, but I had the feeling she wasn't feeling bad about hurting him.

He leaned back down, this time putting his elbows all the way down and resting his back on the bed.

"Stop moving," Zula said.

"Yes, Mother," he muttered. Then he waved his hand at me, clearly not following her instruction. "Keep reading."

I didn't need extra encouragement, although I did glance at the time on the upper corner of my phone. It had been ten minutes. I hoped Paladin and Casper would get here soon.

I read, "'Nine little fen sat up very late; One overslept himself and then there were eight.'"

"See?" Horatio said. "Ruth *was* second."

I didn't know why that deserved his tonal *I told you so*. We really hadn't had that discussion.

"Yeowch, Jesus," he said, but this time he didn't flinch. He glared at Zula. "What *are* you doing?"

"The superglued areas were crooked," Zula said.

"So what?" Horatio said. "I'm going to need plastic surgery anyway, right?"

"Only if you want to show off your gams," she said.

He laughed in spite of himself. "Gams. You're good, doc."

"You better believe it," she said.

"Next, Spade," Horatio said. I had no idea how he became in charge of the room, but he had.

"'Eight little fen traveling in Devon; One said he'd stay there and then there were seven.'"

All three of us looked at Jessica-6 after I read that. She was still unconscious, but breathing evenly. Devon was a clue, because someone had to really know her to know the name of her truck.

I put a mental pin in that, and continued. "'Seven little fen chopping up sticks; One chopped himself in half and then there were six.'"

"In *half?*" Horatio squinched up his face, and folded his shoulders inward. "Seriously? That's what the—God, bad guy? Killer?—was going for? In half?"

"There was enough weaponry there to do a lot of damage," I said, "and you're the one who initially said 'chopped.'"

Horatio looked directly at me, a frown between his eyebrows. "I did, didn't I? I guess it was obvious, then, or I already knew it."

"Why would anyone display such sharp blades?" Zula asked. "Shouldn't there have been some kind of cap on them?"

She was right; I'd seen a lot of weapons' displays in the past, and they usually had some plastic guards over the sharp part of the blades.

"I hadn't even thought of that," Horatio said. "I *knew* there was something weird about that display."

"But it's more than the cap," I said. "Those blades are sharp, right? Because the wound was shallow, and you said you got hit with a glancing blow."

I said that last to Horatio.

He nodded.

"Hmm," Zula said. "The wound is shallow. Only a sharp blade would make a wound this devastating on a graze."

"Devastating?" Horatio asked.

"It's long and it's nasty and if Spade hadn't gummed up the works, you would have lost a lot of blood." Zula was working on the lower leg now. She hadn't even looked up as she talked. "I still think you should stay off panels."

"I'm not going to my room and stew about someone trying to chop me up. I'm just not." Horatio sounded even more disturbed than he had a moment ago. "Continue, Spade."

I sighed inwardly at the command, but read the next line. "'Six little fen playing with a hive; A bumblebee stung one and then there were five.' See? I told you there was a bee."

"A bee," Horatio said. "In a fucking blizzard. Wouldn't we know about bees in this hotel?"

"I can't imagine how someone could've brought them here without our knowledge," I said. I supposed it was possible, but it seemed odd to me. If only Ruth was doing well enough that I could check with her. The hotel would probably have asked the convention to approve anything like bees.

I put a mental pin in that too. I'd need to talk with the hotel about it. Maybe they knew who had brought bees here, and that might solve all of this.

Although I seriously doubted it. This killer-villain-evil asshole seemed smarter than that.

As if reading my thoughts, Zula said, "They wouldn't need an actual bee."

She pulled the suture up over the lower part of Horatio's calf. I had promised myself I wouldn't look, and yet I had.

"What do you mean?" I asked.

"All they need is something with the venom," she said.

"Then they'd need to know who had an allergy. Yeowch! For the love of God," Horatio said.

"I'm almost done." Zula was doing all of this without looking at either of us. "And they don't need someone with an allergy, although that would be easier."

"What do you mean?" I asked.

"Some bee venom from different types of bees is more deadly than others. That's why some are called 'killer' bees."

"You're a bee expert now?" Horatio asked. He seemed grumpy, but I didn't blame him.

"I worked in an emergency room in a small town for much too long," she said. "You learn a lot about things that are nearby that cause deadly allergies. Bee venom is a pretty common allergy. Kids, in particular, will go into anaphylactic shock because you don't know if you're allergic to something unless you're exposed. So parents won't know a kid is allergic until he's been stung."

She reached down and grabbed a tiny scissors. Then she snipped the suture.

"That part's done," she said.

"My leg aches," Horatio said. "Are you sure you used a topical anesthetic?"

"Yep," she said, a bit more cheerfully than I would have expected. "And the anesthetic will probably fade away in about an hour. Then you'll really feel this."

"Oh, joy," Horatio said. He was looking pale. His idea of paneling might be just that—an idea.

But I wasn't going to be deterred from our discussion. We had finally moved from the actual attempts to something new.

"How much bee venom would it take to kill someone?" I asked.

"It depends on how much they weigh." Zula moved a little bowl aside. I hadn't realized she had even been using a bowl for her various instruments. "I can't remember the exact number. Something like two to three milligrams per kilogram of bodyweight or something. The average human weighs somewhere between seventy-five and eighty kilograms, but of course, here they probably weigh closer to eighty-five or ninety kilograms. Do the math. That's a minimum of a hundred and eighty milligrams of bee venom. To give you a perspective, the average bee sting contains about five micrograms of venom."

"Oh, for God's sake," Horatio said. "Math. In metric. The horror."

His hand was rubbing his thigh, away from the injury. But he had to be in some pain. I wondered if Zula had some kind of mild painkiller to give him.

"Let me put it to you this way." Zula's tone had a bit of condescension in it. Horatio probably deserved it, since he'd been talking down to her. "You would need thousands of bumblebees to actually kill someone. But if you had the venom, you could deliver the right dosage. Because even though a hundred eighty milligrams is a lot of bee stings, in actual venom, it's less than a teaspoon."

"But it depends entirely on body weight," I said.

"Oh, yeah," Zula said. "That's why some health advocates use bee venom. It's hard to actually kill someone with it."

"Because you'd have to know a person's body weight," I said, more to me than to her, "and administer the right dosage, and even then, it's just a guess."

"That's right," Zula said. "Some people will be really sensitive to the venom. Others won't."

"Does it matter how it's ingested?" I asked.

She shrugged. "I had one kid who swallowed a bee and got stung in the throat as the bee went down. But that kid nearly died because his throat swelled, not because of the venom. So seriously, I have no idea."

I let out a breath. I had no idea how someone would kill another person using bee venom. They'd have to guess and then administer it correctly. But, whoever this was had been using a lot of versions of poison, so I was beginning to think that was the preferred method of killing here.

"This is foul," Horatio said. "It's kinda fun to deal with puzzle mysteries when they're theoretical, but when they stab you in the leg, they're awful. And trying to figure out the next ones are borderline scary."

"Yeah," I said. "I'd always wondered what I would have done in a cozy. But they're generally bloodless."

"This wasn't bloodless." Zula waved a hand at Horatio's leg, then looked at Jessica-6. "If that blade had moved half an inch, Horatio wouldn't be here, and Jessica there would have frozen to death. Even though there is an upside to the cold. It was the only thing that stopped her blood loss. Because head wounds bleed badly."

So, maybe I was wrong about poison being the preferred method. Maybe blood loss counted as well.

"I was just trying to figure out how someone would administer bee venom," I said quietly. "I can't figure it out."

"Maybe because you're not a psychopath," Horatio said. He propped himself on his elbows again. "I can come up with a dozen different ways to use bee venom, now that Zula has explained it."

Zula raised her eyebrows at him. "Does that mean you *are* a psychopath?"

"Well, I don't know," Horatio said. "I'm a writer, which means I'm one of the select few who channels his rage onto the page. I think about a wide variety of ways of killing people, and sometimes, when I devise a method of death, I have a particular living person in mind whom I'd love to see suffer from it."

His eyes weren't twinkling and he was using his serious Horatio voice. He meant that.

"So," he said, "yeah. I can come up with a dozen ways to attack someone with bee venom."

Zula stared at him, as if he had chilled her. I was too tired to be chilled. Or maybe I knew Horatio well enough. Who was it that said every writer had a chip of ice in his heart? One of the literary Brits. Graham Greene, maybe.

It had always seemed like an apt analogy to me.

"Hey! You guys are awfully quiet."

I turned. Casper and Paladin had arrived. Paladin's hair was still wet, but it had been combed back. The points of her ears poked through. She was wearing a heavy black sweatshirt with the words *We Are The Granddaughters of the Witches You Failed To Burn* written in a script font.

If I had to guess, I'd say that the events of the morning had pissed her off more than usual.

"We're just contemplating bee venom," Horatio said.

Paladin shot me an odd look, but came inside. She looked at his leg and whistled. "That's some wound."

"Looks worse than it is," Zula said. "Although it's bad enough."

"All of this is bad," Paladin said.

"How is Ruth?" I asked.

"McCoy thinks she'll recover. We did the best we could with McCoy's medical supplies. I'd be happier if Ruth could go to a hospital though." Paladin looked tired. I understood that. I had left her with the bulk of the work, only to find myself nursing old Horatio there.

"Why were you guys so quiet?" Casper asked.

"Because," I said, "we're going through the poem."

"Poem?" Paladin asked.

"Yeah," I said. "Let me explain."

And so I did.

19

"Okay, that's sick," Casper said when I finished. It had taken me at least ten minutes to explain what was going on, and I didn't even try to recap the bee venom discussion.

"This is sick," Horatio said, running his hand along his leg.

"It's all sick," Paladin said. "But if we can figure out who this person is, based on that little bit of literature, then we'll be lucky. Proceed, Spade."

She plopped herself on the bed beside Horatio, which freaked me out just a little. If I had been a betting man, I would have bet that Paladin would dislike Horatio as much as Zula seemed to. Or as much as Casper did.

Casper stood near the door. She had her arms crossed. She seemed as upset about Paladin's decision to sit beside Horatio as I felt.

Zula went over to Jessica-6 and checked her vitals.

"How is she?" Paladin asked.

"I have no idea, really," Zula said. "If we were in an ER, I'd be ordering all kinds of scans. But I don't have access to anything here."

We were quiet for a moment, probably all worrying about Jessica-6. Or maybe the situation. The air had just an edge of chill, the way that buildings got as cold became so severe that manmade heat couldn't ever keep up.

I hated that kind of weather. It was one of the many reasons I stayed on the West Coast.

"Spade," Horatio said. "The lady would like you to continue."

The lady. That was not how I would ever describe Paladin. But she didn't object. Instead, she smiled ever so slightly at Horatio.

What *was* their relationship? The fact that they were so easy with each other was starting to bug me.

I made myself concentrate on the stupid poem.

"Okay," I said. "Next stanza is—"

Then I stopped myself. Was *stanza* the right word? I was not a poetry guy. Ask me math terms and I had them, but poetry? Hell, I was probably embarrassing myself with my ignorance...

And then I mentally shook my head. I had gone back to high school, where I had become erudite just so that I wouldn't embarrass myself in front of pretty girls.

Pretty girls who always preferred the cool kid, the way that Paladin seemed to prefer Horatio.

"...e...yeeesssss....?" Casper said, obviously trying to get me to continue.

"It's...'Five little fen were going in for law; One got into Chancery and then there were four.'"

"Chancery?" Casper asked and looked at Horatio. "Like in his books."

"No," Horatio said grumpily. "Not like in my books. Same word, different meanings. I was playing off it. I was doing the opposite of Chancery Court."

"But you have a Chancery Court," Casper said.

"I have a royal court that sets its own laws, the way that royalty usually does," Horatio said. "It's almost a pun."

"It *is* a pun," I said.

"So what's a real Chancery Court?" Casper asked.

"It's a court in England and Wales," I said. "It hears business and property cases, finance, things like that."

Casper shook her head. "Well, I don't get it. And it doesn't even rhyme. Aren't poems supposed to rhyme."

"All the other stanzas rhyme," I said. "This one might if I had the right kind of accent."

Horatio tried it, using what the Brits called a plummy upper class accent. "La-ore," he said. "Fo-ur. Yeah. Maybe. We'd need a real Brit to figure it out."

"Is that the original line?" Zula asked.

"I don't know," I said. I was more concerned with figuring out what was going on than I was with pronunciation. "Weren't you having some kind of Chancery thing tonight?"

I directed that last at Horatio.

"Every convention I go to," he said. "We have a meeting of the Chancery Court, usually a brunch the day of the masquerade."

"And here?" I asked.

"We couldn't get a reservation," he said. "Although that might change now."

"Do you want to do that now?" Casper asked.

He let out a small laugh. "Not really, no."

"Seems to me," Paladin said, "your Chancery Court always put on a show at the masquerade. Its own little parade of costumes, right?"

He nodded. "It happens with or without me. It all started years ago, when the books were taking off."

He glanced at his leg, then rubbed it again.

"But the poem doesn't say that the fan boy was killed. Says he went into law, and didn't come back."

"That's the same with Devon," I said, "but we saw what happened there."

"Looks like this is about you," Zula said to Horatio.

He shook his head. "If they're going in order, that doesn't make any sense, because anything to do with the Chancery is tomorrow, and the way this guy is escalating, you'd think he'd want to do it today."

"How do you know it's a guy?" Casper asked.

Horatio rolled his eyes. "You really want to go all feminist right now? I think it's probably a guy because there are more men than women in fandom, and because killers like this guy is trying to be are usually male."

"In *fiction*," Zula said. "There are no killers like this in real life."

"Since when is a con real life?" Horatio asked, and I had to admit, I agreed with him there. If something like this was actually going to happen, an sf convention was the place.

Especially an sf convention in the middle of a blizzard.

The question was: could someone have planned all of this in the week since the news of the blizzard started? Or was that person planning it before the weather cooperated?

SF conventions weren't generally held at remote places. They were in cities or smaller cities, with enough hotel space to accommodate the con-goers and an airport nearby. As much as the fen liked to think of themselves as major travelers, they all started bitching big time when they had to fly into a small airport, and the bitching got even more intense when there was an hour or more drive from that small airport to whatever town had the convention.

"I have no idea how this one would play out," I said. "If he's in a hurry, that is. Otherwise, we're going to have to pay attention to what happens with the Chancery group."

"I'm still trying to figure out what 'going in for law' means in the context of this convention," Horatio said. He seemed determined to take the emphasis away from his books.

"Maybe lawyers," Zula said.

"We have enough of those here," I said, then sighed. "I'm not sure I can think like a crazy person either. Let's just finish the poem, shall we?"

Casper nodded. Zula continued packing up the equipment. Horatio leaned back, closing his eyes, as if this was all becoming too much for him. Paladin was studying her hand, which I found curious. She seemed a little disengaged.

Initially, I had blamed that on the trauma with Ruth, but I wondered if Paladin's reaction meant she thought what we were doing was dumb.

Still, we were nearly to the end of the poem, and I wanted to finish.

"Okay," I said, scanning the poem, and finally finding the next stanza. "'Four little fen going out to sea; a Red Herring swallowed one and then there were three.'"

"Seriously?" Horatio said. "A red herring? Are we supposed to take that literally or metaphorically?"

"Probably metaphorically," I said. "An in-joke for the mystery readers, probably."

"What's a red herring?" Casper asked.

"It's actually a dried herring," Horatio said. "If smoked properly, it'll turn red."

"Well, that's stupid," she said, "because a smoked herring wouldn't be at sea."

"It also means a misdirection, or a distraction," I said. "Mystery novels are filled with red herrings."

"It comes from fox hunting," Horatio said. "The old recommendation was, if you wanted to take the hounds off the fox's trail, run a dead cat along the road. If you don't have access to a dead cat, use a smoked —or red—herring, which is quite stinky. It'll guarantee that the hounds won't find the fox."

"Trust the writer to know that," Zula muttered.

"In mystery novels, it's the same thing," Horatio said. "Only the readers are the hound, and the criminal is the fox. We want the readers to ignore the real clues, so that the ending seems like a surprise. Only when the readers go back, they'll see the trail of red herrings and realize that the author played fair with them."

"Sounds stupidly complicated," Casper said.

"It is," Paladin said. "Especially when there's an entire booth of red herrings in the dealer's room."

"What?" I asked.

"That new plush artist, selling all the soft toys," Paladin said. "Haven't you seen them? They're supposed to be fun. Lots of literary things, like reader cookies—pillows shaped like books, only they're chocolate chip cookies, McGuffins that look like Egg McMuffins, only with a book in the middle, things like that."

"And the booth has red herrings?" Horatio asked.

"A goodly pile of them. Red fish, some that come in a set, with a fox and hounds." Paladin frowned at us. "How did you all miss this?"

"I missed dealer set-up," I said. I was dealing with other things.

"I didn't," Horatio said. "I always sneak in early and look for good deals."

"Only books, though, right?" Paladin asked.

Horatio nodded.

"Well, this booth is across from Escape While There's Still Time, so you probably didn't see it."

Escape While There's Still Time Bookstore always had the front corner of any dealer's room that the owner, Bill Trojan, attended, and he had an amazing collection of books. I always stopped as well, just to see things that I had only read about, not seen.

"Must've missed that," Horatio muttered.

"I was planning to go later," Zula said.

"Well, I would've missed it too if Trojan hadn't been complaining about the way dealer's rooms had devolved from books only to everything else," Paladin said. "Although I have no idea why he's complaining, since he gets more money if there are fewer book dealers."

"Troj always complains," I said, distracted. I was still going back to the original point Paladin had made. "There are actual red herrings in the dealer's room."

I had no idea what that meant, but it had to mean something. Didn't it? Or would the killer-villain-bad-guy actually create a literary red herring for us? Some kind of misdirection, because there was no sea anywhere near this place.

"Does that mean the person selling them is in danger?" Casper asked.

"I have no idea," I said. "Or does it mean that someone will die due to a giant misdirection."

"I can't believe we're actually talking seriously about all of this," Horatio said.

Paladin shifted on the bed so that she faced him. "You always talk seriously about ways to kill people."

"For my next *book*," he said. "Not for actual murder."

We weren't getting anywhere, and I had many other things to do. But I did want this brain trust to continue with the poem because I did feel like we had made some progress.

"All right," I said. "Next we have 'Three little fen walking in the zoo; A big bear hugged one and then there were two.'"

"See!" Horatio said, propping himself up higher. "I *told* you there was a bear."

"And so there is," I said.

"Well, I know there aren't any bears here," Zula said. "We would have heard about it already."

"But there might be a lot of bear costumes," Paladin said.

"Why?" Zula said. "That seems like a very mundane thing to do." Mundanes were non-fans.

And she was right. I hadn't seen a bear costume in all of my years at conventions. However, I had seen them on Halloween and at costume parties. Bear costumes were weirdly easy to come by.

"If we're talking about misdirection," Casper said, "then maybe the killer-guy means death by bear hug."

"Yes," Horatio said. "It says...oh." He looked surprised as the words sank in. "Oh, I see. Well, we can't go through an entire convention without hugging each other."

"It brings us back to poisons," Zula said.

"Or someone being strong enough to crush another person's ribs," Paladin said.

"In front of other people?" I asked.

"Bear hugs don't have to happen in front of people. If you're walking down the hall and see an old friend, you'll probably hug them." Paladin was looking at me.

I was less huggy than I used to be—#MeToo and all that; I didn't want anyone to have the wrong impression—but I allowed myself to be hugged. And the very situation that Paladin had described had happened to me several times at this convention already.

It had happened to her too, when Horatio hugged her.

"I don't like this," Horatio said. "This just takes all the good things from conventions and perverts them. And we don't even know if our guessing is right."

I looked at him. "That's true. If we are right, then whoever is doing this is using the convention against us."

"Which means they're one of us," Paladin said.

"I figured as much," I said, "but this means they might be someone who has been in the community a long time."

"Someone who thinks they're smarter than everyone else," Casper said.

"Well," Horatio said, sitting up and rubbing his lower back. "You just described everyone in attendance here, kid."

Her cheeks flushed. She probably recognized herself in that description as well.

"You said 'and then there were two,'" Zula said to me. "Let's hear the rest of it."

I took a deep breath and forced myself to focus on the words on my phone. "'Two little fen playing with a gun; One shot the other and then there was one.'"

"A gun?" Horatio said.

"This convention isn't weapons-free," Paladin said.

"But we aren't gun people," Horatio said. "No one would have a gun here."

"Why not?" I asked. "What would stop them? We don't have metal detectors and if they have a carry permit, then they could have a gun here."

My words hung over the room like the snowstorm outside the hotel. None of us wanted to contemplate fen with guns, but I'd seen it. There'd been at least three times when I'd had to go to a nearby airport to vouch for someone who flew in with a gun "accidentally" stored in their luggage.

Oh, I forgot to take it out was the usual excuse. And I had always focused on the fact that a gun had made it through all of the airport security regulations rather than the fact that one of "our people" had brought a gun.

"If they have a gun, why not just use it?" Paladin asked, making her

—disturbingly—the third person in this group to ask the question. "If they want to take people out, then this would be the place and time to do it. I doubt many people could defend themselves, and there's no law enforcement backup, so they'd get away with it. Once the snow stopped, they might even be able to escape in Horatio's stupid sleigh or one of the hotel's snowmobiles."

"The hotel has snowmobiles?" Casper asked.

"In case the roads are impassable," I said. "Someone could get out and go to town for supplies or direct a snow plow up here sooner rather than later."

I supposed someone could have escaped on one; after all, that was the ending of the *Shining*—one of the versions anyway. Not the Kubrick one where Scatman Crothers was stupidly and senselessly killed, though. Or was it? I tried to put those movies and that very scary book out of my mind, but the story kept rising to the fore, since we were trapped, in a hotel, in a snowstorm, with a madman.

At least there were no malevolent ghosts...that I knew of anyway.

"And then the poem ends with 'and then there were none,' right?" Horatio said.

I looked back at my phone, making sure I got the exact wording for the last two lines of the poem. "'One little fen left all alone; he went out and hanged himself and then there were none.'"

"No rhyme again. Not only is the poem offensive, it's bad," Casper said.

I smiled at her. "Alone and none *look* like they should rhyme," I said.

"Well, they don't. Not even in Horatio's fake British accent," she said.

None of us laughed. I wasn't sure she wanted us to.

"I have no idea how to protect from any of this," I said. "Do we tell fen to watch out for bees and bears and red herrings? Do we ignore it?"

"We don't ignore it," Paladin said, and looked at her watch. "I think we have very little time to stay ahead of this person. I think we should get busy."

"Doing what?" Horatio asked.

"Well," I said, "you have panels."

"You think I should just act as if everything is *normal*?" he asked.

"You can go to your room and stay there," I said.

"That wasn't safe for Ruth," he said, "and *again*, Spade, this is a *convention*. No one stays in their room."

"There's your answer then," Casper said, sounding annoyed at him again.

"We need to find this person," Paladin said. "You and me."

"What do I do?" Casper asked.

I could see it on Paladin's face; she wanted Casper to stay out of the way. So did I, but I didn't think that was going to happen.

However, people ignored kids. People said all kinds of things around kids that they believed kids couldn't or didn't hear.

Maybe that would be useful.

"I want you to stay with Horatio," I said.

"Hey!" Casper said.

But I kept talking over her. "He's going to be on panels, so you'll be in the audience."

"What if I don't want to hear his panel?" Casper said.

"Yeah," Horatio said. "I told you I wanted to pick my buddy."

"Well, that's not exactly possible," I said. "Paladin and I need to investigate what's going on, and we can't do it with the two of you. Now, you can stay here with Zula or you can go to panels."

I meant that last for Casper, but Horatio opened his mouth, as if he was going to object.

Instead, it was Zula who did. "I don't like being the consolation prize," she said. "And I have things to do at this convention as well."

"I already contacted the two other doctors I know," Paladin said. "They'll be down here shortly. And one of their friends, a nurse, is joining McCoy in his suite, so that he'll have help with his patients there."

"Nurse Chapel to Sickbay," Horatio muttered.

Paladin shot him a nasty glance, which he ignored.

"So," Paladin said to Zula, "you'll be able to wander around if you want, but remember, you'll need a buddy."

Zula nodded. "I'm not even sure it's worth going to panels. This is damn scary."

"It is," I said. "But we'll fix it."

I was promising something I probably shouldn't have. There was no way to guarantee that we could fix this. But I was going to try.

And I had Paladin now. So we'd come up with something.

I had a few ideas.

I only hoped that they would work—and work fast.

20

Paladin and I headed to the service elevator. We left ahead of Horatio and Casper, because Horatio still needed to take his antibiotics and figure out how to use his crutches.

Casper would probably be irritated at him—she wasn't showing a lot of patience today—but they would keep an eye on each other. I knew I could count on them for that.

The corridor outside the medical room was cold, at least compared to the room itself. And the corridor was empty, which I was finding just a bit strange for a convention. Usually you saw people in the hallways everywhere.

Maybe the fen found the daylight basement as creepy as I did with the weird grayish yellow light coming from the snow plastered against all the windows. Yesterday, the windows rattled a bit in the wind. Now the wind was stronger—at least that was what my all-purpose smart watch told me—but we couldn't hear it at all.

Made me wonder just how buried in drifts the hotel was, and whether we were officially impossible to see from above.

Although we would be impossible to see for hours now, as the wind blew and the snow fell and everything swirled in a cascade of whiteness.

"Ruth was awake enough when I gave her over to McCoy to tell me that she hadn't heard anyone in her room," Paladin said. She got to the service elevator before I did, and pressed the button. "The last thing she remembered was guzzling a glass of water before putting popcorn in the microwave. She was going to press the buttons, but they started blurring."

"So those pills were in the water," I said. "Couldn't she taste them?"

"I asked the same thing," Paladin said. "She didn't taste anything. I think that pill bottle was a decoy, and so does McCoy. He said that those sleeping pills wouldn't depress the system the way hers had been depressed. Something about dosage and regulations and pills and I stopped paying attention when he got technical."

"Thanks for taking care of her," I said, and I meant it. It allowed me to help with Horatio, even though that hadn't been my intent when I left Ruth's room.

"I'd say my pleasure," Paladin said, "but crap like that is never fun."

The elevator arrived and the door slid open. The elevator itself still smelled fresh and clean, which meant the fen hadn't discovered it yet. I pressed the button for the first floor.

"What are you doing?" Paladin asked. "Shouldn't we be interviewing people on the mezzanine level?"

The idea of interviewing anyone with Paladin made me smile. She didn't "interview." She demanded. If I was going to interview with her at my side, I would have to remind her of the rules we'd made in the past about such things.

"I want to ask the desk something first," I said as the elevator door opened on the first floor.

The service elevator was located farther from the main guest area than the regular elevator banks, which was probably why the fen hadn't found it yet.

The first floor had what I was beginning to think of as its distinctive odor of woodsmoke. It was darker back here, with no windows and only interior lighting on dark discouraging carpet.

We hurried toward the desk. There seemed to be a lot more people downstairs than I had expected, almost as if more congoers had arrived.

I knew that wasn't the case. What it probably meant was that we were past noon now, and everyone who was at the convention was awake and doing whatever they normally did at a con.

Normal for a lot of them was hall costumes, something I normally loved. But now, seeing Klingons with bat'leths hanging off their backs or Borg walking in lock-step or a small group of dwarves and elves and hobbits probably heading to defend Mordor, I felt as nervous as a mundane who had never seen anything like that before.

I kept wondering how the weapons would be used or if someone had a gun or if there was an angry psychopath in the group. And that really, really, really wasn't like me.

We got to the desk, but there was no Betty. I asked for her only to be told she was on a mandatory lunch break. Instead, I had to work with a slightly less sympathetic Russell Cairns, who shared desk duty with Betty. Russell had been there as long, but he preferred not to be part of the convention. While other hotel staff dressed up or wore a Bajoran earring or a Chancery scarf in solidarity, Russell never did. Usually on day two of a convention, he wore his best suit, a way of showing his superiority over us (at least according to Ruth).

I leaned forward. "You've heard about the problems we're having," I said.

"Yeah." He spoke softly. "Sounds like the playacting isn't play for someone."

That was a lot more prescient a comment than I expected from Russell. He didn't even say it judgmentally, which I appreciated. Just as if it were an absolute fact—which it probably was.

"Tell the staff to use the buddy system," I said. "This seems to be directed at the con itself, but just in case it's not, make sure none of your people go anywhere alone."

"Betty already instituted that," Russell said. "But I'll make sure everyone follows it." Then he tilted his head—somehow making that movement seem supercilious and superior at the same time. "Is that it?"

"Not even close," I said. "I have a couple of weird questions."

"Only a couple?" he asked, and smiled. I wasn't sure I liked it when he smiled. The smile seemed a little too sincere, which was weird, since I knew he didn't always appreciate what we were doing.

I ignored the smile and the attitude.

"I know our people come in with a lot of strange things," I said, "and it wasn't my job to pay attention to those requests."

Russell folded his hands on the top of the desk. His gaze shifted to Paladin ever so briefly, then back to me.

"Has anyone arrived with, say, a container of bees?" I asked. My cheeks heated. The question sounded stupid as soon as it was out of my mouth.

"Bees?" Russell said. "As in bumble?"

"As in bumble," I said.

"Container," he said, "as in *real* bees?"

"Yes," I said. "As in a hive."

And as I said that, something bothered me. I raised my head and glanced around, trying to figure out what had triggered me.

"I'll check, but I doubt it," Russell said. "We certainly wouldn't be responsible for them, and I'm pretty sure the hotel would have frowned about them. So many people are allergic, after all."

"Yeah, I know," I said. "But humor me."

"You said you had a few things," he said.

"Yeah," I said, knowing now that I couldn't ask about a bear or a bear cub. Or any other wild life. Because his reaction to the bees was enough. We all would have known about a bear, anyway. "But let's go with the bees at the moment."

He nodded and left the desk. He went to the middle of the reception area and began a computer search of some kind. That made sense to me. A hotel would have asked a guest to fill out some kind of waiver or asked the convention to do so, if something like bees were brought in.

"What were you looking for?" Paladin asked me.

"Borg," I said to her, almost before I realized what was coming out of my mouth.

"Borg?" she asked.

"They're a hive," I said. "And they are Bs."

"Not bumblebees," she said.

"No, but their name. It begins with a B. It could be a pun. He was stung by a bee and then there were five."

She sucked in air. "In a hive."

"Yeah," I said. "Are the Borg gathering at this convention? And could that fairly be called a hive?"

At that moment Russell came back. "No one brought a container of bees or some kind of beekeeping equipment or a portable hive. I looked at our regulations, and we wouldn't have allowed it anyway. If they did bring bees, they would have had to keep them outside, and I don't know much about bees, but I do know they do not favor winter conditions. So if anyone brought bees and said bees were in, say, a van, then said bees would probably be dead bees by now."

I had to agree with that.

"Is that all then?" Russell asked.

"For the moment," I said. "Thank you."

He nodded a tad too formally, and then turned to something else at the desk.

Paladin had turned away from me. She was scanning the pocket program, which she had apparently folded up and put in her pocket.

"That thing's worthless now," I said. "We've really changed it up."

"For special events?" she asked.

By specials, she meant the fan-group meetings, gaming rooms, and meeting room for the various professional groups, like the SFWA Business Meeting, which was—I think—scheduled for Sunday morning.

"I didn't change any of those," I said. "But that doesn't mean that Ruth let them stand."

Paladin pointed at one. "Star Trek fan groups," she said. "Section 31 meeting (maybe)."

Then she chuckled. Section 31 was supposedly a secret organization within the Federation. So whoever had taken that *(maybe)* on had been evidencing a fannish sense of humor.

She continued reading. "Klingon High Council meeting. Star Fleet Academy Red Shirt training." She giggled again. "Someone had fun with this."

I was having issues with Paladin giggling. It showed me that we were all getting punchy, and it was only Friday afternoon.

"Here it is," she said. "Hive Maintenance, ordered by the Queen."

"We have a Borg Queen here?" I asked. I always found the one in *Star Trek: First Contact* terrifying on some very deep level.

"Apparently so," Paladin said.

"When do they meet?" I asked.

"Starting at half past the hour," she said.

"I guess we go there, then," I said.

"What are we looking for?" she asked.

"I wish I knew," I said. "I really wish I knew."

21

The Star Trek Fan meeting room was on this floor, in a group of badly designed rooms that could be united to form a rather dismal ballroom. I suspected, when I first saw them, that they were the original function rooms for the hotel.

The rooms on the mezzanine and also in the daylight basement were probably the result of some remodel in the last thirty years or so.

But these rooms, dark and a little dank, without windows, were uncomfortable, but part of our hotel package.

So I had done what I always did with dismal rooms; I gave them to the fan groups and costumers, the gamers and the business meetings, the gatherings that cared less about the function space and more about their own agenda.

As we got closer, I saw half a dozen Borg striding through the corridors. They all had the grayish bodysuits, and—unusual for a convention—they could wear them. Many of the Borg had fake prosthetics glued to their faces and wore some kind of face makeup.

That, and the movement, was eerily like the Trek Borg—creatures whose individuality had been removed and replaced by a hive mind led by a somewhat vicious queen. In Trek lore, the Borg could communicate with each other like any hive could do.

I had no idea what the fannish Borg used to substitute for that. Probably some kind of earbud.

This part of the hallway smelled of pancake makeup and a slight whiff of gamer. It was early in the convention, so the gamers were still benefitting from last night's or this morning's shower.

That wouldn't last, of course. They would get involved in whatever they were doing, and they would forget the basics...like hygiene.

The Star Trek fan room was just off the corridor. The room was one of the smallest rooms. At the moment, its door was squared off, and covered with gray blocks that had fake wires going through them. Or maybe not fake wires, since some had lights that illuminated as we walked through.

About ten Borg stood in the room. Whoever had decorated it for this particular meeting had done a fairly creative job. A three-foot tower that looked like something that would have been a control center on a Borg vessel stood in the middle of the room. There was at least one Borg "sleeping" chamber—basically a sarcophagus with a Borg design instead of an Egyptian one—and something that hung from the ceiling with thick wires and electrodes.

The only real disappointment in the decorations was the walls. They were covered with cloth that had been silkscreened with images of the walls inside a Borg cube.

The lights were low, just like they were on a cube.

I shivered, and not because of the cold. This was one of the warmer places in the hotel—which, I suppose—if you had asked me before what the temperature was on a Borg cube, I would have said that it was warm and stuffy. Guess I wasn't the only one who thought that.

Paladin glanced at me, and made a tiny judgmental noise, kind of a barely audible "whelf." I nodded. I understood a lot of fannish traditions. I loved a good Time Warp dance at any con that hosted a Friday night dance. I even understood a Regency ball, and fannish nicknames (since I had one), and medieval dinners, complete with jesters and a dismaying lack of silverware.

I knew why so many of my friends dressed up in costume for an entire weekend; it was a great escape from their daily lives, which weren't always good. Or hadn't been good, back in the day when they first started coming to conventions.

I understood people who dressed up as Klingons, because Klingons were strong and proud. I understood those who preferred to be the intellectual and emotionless Vulcans. I actually loved those who wore hobbit feet instead of shoes, because I thought that kind of costuming fun and a bit sly.

But I never understood people who dressed like the villains. The Voldemorts of the world or the Emperor Palpatines (why not Darth Vader? he at least was intriguing. Palpatine was just...slimy) did not seem inspirational or even that frightening outside of their literary and cinematic contexts.

The Borg I did find frightening, though, because of the hive mind. It was, maybe, my biggest nightmare. That someone could co-opt my brain and make it do their bidding.

So people who dressed like Borg were damn close to the exact opposite of me.

Then, this group of Borg reinforced that sense of creepiness as they all turned to face me and Paladin as if they were one unit.

"EarPods," Paladin said ever so quietly to me.

I squinted a little, and then I saw them. Apple EarPods, painted gray, hanging out of every ear. Someone was giving this group instructions, just like I thought, telling them how to move and how to be.

I couldn't help myself. I said, "Take me to your leader."

Paladin punched me in my left arm, but as she did, I thought I heard a guffaw.

"Your queen," she corrected.

A slender woman swanned out from behind one of the curtains. I had thought they were against the wall, but that one, at least, was set so that there was space between the curtain and the wall.

She had gone full Alice Krige, with her head mostly bald except for pointy things sticking out of her skull. In this Borg Queen's instance, though, the pointy things might have been made of twisted hair.

Her form-fitting suit ended at her ribcage. From there down, she wore a gray robe that matched the walls. A black spine-like thing hung out of her chest. If I remembered the ickier part of my Trek lore properly, that was the part of her that was supposed to "plug into" the whatever it was that attached the queen to the hive.

There was no whatever it was here, in this cramped little hotel space, but the illusion was just creepy enough to make me uncomfortable.

"If it isn't the great Spade," the Borg Queen said.

"I need to see your badge," I said, not because I really needed to, but because I wanted to memorize the badge number. I wanted to know who to avoid at normal conventions.

She reached under that gray robe and dangled a badge at me. I got closer than I wanted to—close enough to smell the glue in her costume —and got the number, which I memorized. I had to, because the name on the badge was exactly what I had expected: The Borg Queen.

"To what do we owe this honor?" she asked as the badge receded into the folds of her clothing.

I had no exact idea how to approach this, so I decided to go for half honesty, and hoped I would be covered by stfnal weirdness.

"Are you going to be doing anything that would require someone to get pricked or stung at this convention?"

She lifted her head as if contemplating the question. "Are we?" she asked the others. Her Alice Krige imitation was pretty good. I could almost hear the lines delivered by the actress, instead of by a fan.

"New initiate later," said one of the Borg in sepulchral tones.

"Oh, for God's sake," Paladin said, and I cringed a little. Here came the bulldozer. "Stop roleplaying for a minute. This is serious. Do you prick their skin when you 'initiate' them?"

Everyone's posture changed. The uniform look left immediately. One guy still stood ramrod straight, but the rest either slumped their shoulders or bent slightly as if their backs hurt.

"It would be kinda stupid to do that," said the person closest to me. She had been facing me directly and unlike many of the Borg costumes on TV, hers did not emphasize her breasts. In fact, they kinda blended into the rest of her. I probably wouldn't have realized she was female until she spoke.

She waved a hand in front of her face. "If the prosthetics pricked, we'd all be scarred up when we went to work on Monday."

"Or we'd keep them on like Seven of Nine," said one of the Borg in the back. Then he giggled nervously. I couldn't tell if he was intimidated by me or by Paladin or by expressing his own opinion in the middle of their Borg meeting.

"We glue everything on," said a third Borg, another male. "Unless someone already has a piercing. If that's the case, then they usually bring their own face art."

Paladin sighed in frustration.

I said, "Did anyone give you anything, like to drink?"

"What's going on, Oh great Spade?" the Borg Queen asked.

"You've heard that we're having incidents," I said, as honestly as I could. "You were all told to use the buddy system, right?"

They laughed as one, creeping me out again. And then the Borg Queen said, "A hive mind does not need a buddy system."

"You are not a hive mind," Paladin snapped. "You are playacting a hive mind using very expensive earbuds and some kind of group phone call. Which will not be enough to protect you if you're walking alone in a hallway."

The third speaker, a little thinner and smaller than the others, took a step back as if to get out of harm's way.

"You were told, right?" I asked, hoping the concom had made it down here.

"We thought it was some kind of blizzard rule," said the female Borg.

"It's a little more serious than that," I said. "Someone is assaulting fen. We need to find the person, but until we do, we're warning everyone."

"Consider us warned," the Borg Queen said.

"But you're not." Paladin's tone was a little too charged. "Someone has made a direct threat against you."

"Us?" the Borg Queen asked, no longer channeling Alice Krige.

"A hive, to be more precise. You're our only hive," Paladin said.

I wasn't sure if she was correct, but if they knew of any other, I'm sure the Borg would inform us of it.

"What kind of threat?" One of the male Borg asked.

"Some kind of harm that might include a sting and venom," I said. "Anyone bring you drinks, maybe?"

I wanted to ask them if they injected anything, some kind of drug or something. Drug use wasn't that common at modern cons. In the 1980s, there was a lot of cocaine among the professional writers (thanks to a Big Name agent, who eventually fried his own mind and whose behavior ensnared one of the most famous writers in the world so badly that he went off to rehab). The 1990s had a helium party fad. And of course, there was always some marijuana as folks tried to relax in their own rooms.

But mostly, the fen didn't do drugs. Their fan moments were too precious to waste on an altered state. The fan moment itself *was* the altered state.

And if they chose a real altered state, most of them just drank too much, probably because they didn't have the opportunity in their real lives—at least, not to drink in a social situation, among like-minded people.

"In case you didn't notice," the female Borg said, "people don't *give* us things. They stay away from us."

I straightened just a little. Maybe that was the hook for them. A way of being with like-minded people, and keeping everyone else away. The ultimate in stand-offishness, even at a convention.

"So I take that as a no," I said.

"Yes," the female Borg said. "It's a no."

"Do you use any liquid in your..." Paladin waved her hand. She apparently didn't have the word for what she wanted. "...your...rituals?"

The Borg Queen squeaked. She pulled back the curtain—literally —and held up a tube of greenish liquid.

"I use this," she said. "When we initiate a new Borg—"

"Create a new Borg," one of the others mumbled, clearly correcting her.

"We sometimes have me come out, re-enacting one of the scenes from *First Contact*."

"Does that liquid touch your skin?" I asked.

She nodded. Finally the calm Borg face was gone. She looked terrified. "What do you think it would do to me?"

I had an idea, and I didn't like it. But the greenish liquid was in a protected vial, not your basic plastic tube.

"You have a bowl or something?" I asked.

Someone brought out a cup with a Star Trek logo on it.

"Where's a garbage can?" I asked.

Paladin understood what I was going to do. "You probably can't use a plastic one," she said.

She stepped outside and dragged one of the big ceramic cans in, the kind that had an area for cigarettes. The hotel didn't allow smoking as of last year, but it hadn't gotten rid of its gigantic ashtrays yet.

She peeled off the lid, made sure there was a lot of sand, made sure that there was metal beneath the sand, and then shoved the entire mess closer to that tube.

She placed the mug on top of the sand.

"Anyone got thick rubber gloves?" she asked.

Lo and behold, someone did. Which kinda surprised me. But one of the Borg held out the gloves. I didn't want to touch them, but Paladin did. She slipped them on—even though they were too big for her small hands—and then she took the vial.

"Stand back," she said.

She spun the top, so that there was a slight opening, and a few green drops escaped into the cup. For a moment nothing happened, except that the smell of rotten eggs and something worse filled the air.

Then green smoke started rising out of the mug.

"Is that supposed to happen?" she asked the Borg Queen.

"No," she said, sounding panicked.

"I didn't think so." Paladin moved the tube away. "I think it's time to clear the room."

She didn't have to say that twice. The Borg did not act like one brain. They acted like a group of panicked fen, fleeing from something evil.

The smoke was continuing as the green fluid ate through the sand. I had no idea if the metal would hold it.

"Acid?" I asked.

"Some particularly nasty kind," she said. "We have to block off this room. I suspect you'll need a hazmat team to clean this up properly. We don't have that."

Fortunately, I'd been in enough hotels to know how to shut down a room and to shut down the air vents. Normally, I did that on day two of the convention in the gaming areas, so we didn't export the stink to the other parts of the hotel.

We needed to do it here and now. And for good measure, we had to move the gamers.

I told all of that to Paladin. Normally, I would have had her talk to the hotel while I shut down, but we didn't dare separate.

"That would've been an ugly death," she said, making a face. Her eyes were watering.

"It might not have been a death," I said. But it certainly would have led to a terrible wound and horrible disfigurement.

We shut down the air flow, made sure that the tube was back in its holster, where it was facing upward and wouldn't do any real damage, and then we locked down the room.

I took the sign that said *Star Trek Fan Room* and crossed that off, and scrawled *Moved! Check at Registration for new location.*

Then I locked the room, and headed to the gaming rooms.

"We're moving you upstairs," I said. I gave them the only open room number I knew.

I'd moved gamers before. They got angry and groaned and bitched, but they always cooperated, and this was no different.

In fact, there was less bitching than I expected, maybe because the stench from the other room had already reached them.

They trooped out. I locked their room too for good measure, and then Paladin and I headed to the desk.

As we walked, I contacted Judita, and told her to set up that extra room as the Star Trek fan room. I also warned her that gamers needed their overflow room.

"Oh, joy," she said, and then signed off.

I couldn't have agreed more. But I was also relieved I wasn't the one dealing with them.

As we got closer to the desk, I was stunned that there weren't more people on this level. Usually folks roamed around. Not everyone attended panels, which had just started about fifteen minutes ago.

In fact, a lot of people never attended panels (and were proud of it). Generally speaking, pros only went to the panels that they were actually on, unless the panel had some expert whom they needed to listen to for a project they were working on.

As if to confirm my assumptions, the first group I saw on this floor were the Usual Suspects. They were sitting near the fireplace, drinking from mugs (although I couldn't assume they were drinking coffee) and conversing casually. I had no idea if they had already gone upstairs to registration. I hoped someone had told them about the buddy system

The Borg huddled nearby, talking animatedly—too animatedly for Borg. Their costumes looked ridiculous now.

And, except for a handful of people still finishing the World's Greatest Breakfast Buffet in the café, that was all of the people connected to the convention on the ground floor—at least that I could see.

Betty was back at the desk. She glanced over at the Borg.

"You scared the gamers and the Borg," she said. "What did you do?"

"*I* didn't do anything," I said, and then I explained what we found.

The blood left her face and for a moment, she looked utterly terrified.

"What should we do?" she asked, her voice trembling.

"First, I need a way to lock that room so that no one can get in, not even someone with the master keys that you gave to the convention," I said. "You probably want to block off the entire area. I don't think the acid is going to go through any of the stuff it was stored in, but I'm no expert."

"How much of the area?" Betty asked.

"I'd do half the floor," Paladin said. "I have no idea if the toxic fumes could be a problem."

"And move anything that's above that area," I said. I knew there was nothing below it. The daylight basement did not extend back that far.

"Maybe we should throw that stuff in the snow...?" Betty said.

"If you have police level hazmat gear," Paladin said. "Then that's a good idea."

"You know," Betty said, "we just might. We have a lot of search and rescue stuff up here, and other things for emergencies. We might have something like that."

"A robot would be better," I said, thinking of those robots they used to take bombs out of an area.

"We have a lot of robots here," Paladin said. "I could get someone—"

"No," I said. We had no idea who was behind all of this, so we didn't dare trust someone outside of our little group. "Let's just block off that part of the hotel. Let's be as conservative as we can."

Then I leaned a bit closer to Betty. "You need to call the authorities yourself, and tell them things have gotten worse here. Cite the toxicity. Say you've got that part of the hotel cordoned off, but say you have no idea how long all of this will protect us."

She nodded, her mouth turned downward, her eyes big dark holes in her face. When she volunteered to work a convention in a massive snowstorm, she probably hadn't expected to have a deranged killer added to the mix.

"Okay," she said. "I'm on this. But can you figure out who this person is? Please? Or maybe we should just lockdown all of your people, and keep an eye on them."

"That might be what that person wants," Paladin said. "It'd be easier to attack people."

I shook my head. "I really think they're following the poem."

"Poem?" Betty asked.

I waved my hand dismissively. "That's just too complicated to explain. I'm hopeful we'll find this person today. If things get worse, then we will have to move everyone to a large space for their protection. But we're not there yet."

And, I almost added, I hoped we would never be.

Betty let out a large sigh, then glanced at Paladin, almost as if expecting her to disagree with me.

But Paladin was done with this conversation. She was eyeing the Borg, as if she wanted to say something to them.

I tapped my hand on the desk, getting Paladin's attention, and also letting Betty know the conversation was done.

"Thanks, Betty," I said, and then I headed down the hall toward the Borg.

They were not close enough to the Usual Suspects to loom over them, but it was pretty clear that the Borg were making them nervous. Perry Stevens and Wyatt Edwards were standing on the far side of the fireplace, watching me and Paladin and the Borg and the Usual Suspects. I couldn't read the expressions on the faces of those two men. They always made me nervous because they were so real-world competent.

I didn't think either of them could be involved. They seemed twice as sane as everyone else at the convention, but more than that: they were young writers at the beginning of their careers, and as such, they had a lot to lose.

I had a growing sense that the person I was looking for had been in fandom for a long time, and felt like they had nothing left to lose.

"Why were you watching the Borg?" I asked Paladin.

"Because, they said they had an initiate, but so far, I'm not seeing anyone new." She was walking much faster than I was. Even though my legs were longer, I was having a heck of a time keeping up.

"Let me ask them," I said.

She looked at me sideways, then grinned. "Afraid the bulldozer will scare them off?"

"Actually, yes," I said.

She nodded and didn't protest, which surprised me. We stopped next to the Borg. I was standing beside the queen which, I had to admit, made me a lot more nervous than I expected.

"What are we supposed to do now?" the Borg Queen asked me. Her tone was very un-Borglike, and un-Alice-Krigelike as well. She was whining—justifiably so.

"I see nothing wrong with continuing with your hall costuming," Paladin said, already forgetting my admonition to let me talk.

"All of our ceremonial stuff is in that room," the queen said. "We can't do anything. And what if it's ruined? It's not cheap, you know."

I felt a tug of empathy. For so many in fandom, getting to live their fantasy took all of their resources. Many in fandom weren't rich or even truly middle class. Every last dime went into their costumes or their games or their con membership.

"I know," I said. "If something happens, we'll see what we can do."

That was the best I could promise at the moment. We had liability insurance, but I wasn't sure it had any kind of crazed killer clause—either allowing payments because of one or denying payments for the same reason.

She gave me a worried look, but nodded.

"You mentioned that you had—I believe the word you used was 'initiate'?" I said. "Someone who was going to join your group? Are they here?"

"No," she said. "We've been waiting for her, too, but she's nowhere around. I was just about to send someone to that room upstairs where you moved the Star Trek fan room."

"We're going to have to call off the ceremony," said the female Borg who had spoken earlier. "We can't do it now with our stuff locked away."

"Not that I want to," said one of the male Borg. "I think I'm going to just call it a con and head back to my room."

"With a buddy," I said. "We need you all on the buddy system right now."

"Oh, yeah," said the male Borg, who sounded a lot more shaken than I liked. "I forgot."

"Who is your initiate?" Paladin asked, with an edge in her voice.

The Borg Queen looked at her in surprise, apparently hearing that tone.

"So if we see them, we can send them to you," I said placatingly. I wished I was close enough to Paladin to nudge her with my foot and remind her that I was going to talk.

"Camille Smudge," the Borg Queen said. "Do you know her?"

Oddly enough, I did. I had known her for years. And if there was anyone in the world whom I did not believe would want to be a Borg, it was Camille Smudge.

"Really?" I said. "I thought she disliked Trek."

Twenty years ago, she ran panels on the scourge that was Star Trek. As the Trek-verse grew, so did her protests about Trek's effect on sf. She would often scream things at pros who had award-winning careers and for monetary or fannish reasons (or both) wrote Star Trek novels.

"She said she disliked it until the Borg were introduced." The Borg Queen sounded a bit more like Alice Krige, now. "She didn't believe that the Borg were the bad guys. She thought they were a metaphor."

"For what?" Paladin said as she started to cross her arms. Then she stopped herself, and let her arms drop.

"For conventions and life, and oh, so many things," the queen said.

She made it sound like that metaphor was a good thing, but I didn't think it was meant as a compliment.

I frowned, trying to sort all of this. Paladin was shifting slightly, as if she wanted to leave. Having a name seemed to be enough for her.

"I didn't realize Camille was coming," I said. "I don't remember seeing that she had signed up."

And I would have noticed. We'd had a lot of trouble with Camille over the years. When she was young and thin and as pretty as she would ever get, Camille slept her way around the field. She had that *je ne sais quoi* that all crazy people seemed to have in a relationship—apparently, the sex was good. At first.

And then she got possessive and what we would call stalkery now, but back then, she was just "a problem."

We had an entire list of male pros that she was supposed to stay away from. Then a couple got smart and took out protective orders against her. She couldn't attend conventions in the Bay Area because it violated the protective orders. The cons weren't big enough to have the pro in attendance and Camille. Since the pros drew fans, and Camille caused trouble, choosing between them was not an issue.

The Borg Queen shrugged. "I don't know who is a member of the con and who isn't," she said. "I assumed when she asked to join us at SierraCon, she would be in attendance. Maybe she's not here at all. Maybe that's why she wasn't in the room."

That was a logical assumption, one I would have to check. Maybe someone blocked her and forgot to inform the Borg. Or Camille forgot to inform the Borg.

"All right," I said, "I'll see if she's here, and if she is, I'll tell her to contact you for initiation at the next convention."

Paladin looked at me sideways, her expression impassive. Apparently she knew about Camille as well.

"Yeah, okay." The Borg Queen didn't really sound that interested. She still didn't sound much like the Borg Queen. The Borg were shaken, just like the rest of us. "I don't feel like a ceremony anyway, especially not a half-assed one."

Then she turned to her little group.

"We have a choice," she said. "We can do our hall costume thing, or, you know...regular clothes."

"Wait," Paladin said. "Before you get all technical, I want to know one thing."

I glared at her, but she ignored me.

The Borg turned to her as one unit. It really bothered me when they did that. When they were operating as individuals, I was fine, but those group movements were just damn creepy.

"Who had access to your equipment?" Paladin asked.

The Borg Queen blinked at her.

"Who put it together and assembled it, and got it ready for use?" Paladin asked.

"Those are all different questions," the Borg Queen said.

They were also damn good questions, ones I had been too preoccupied to think of. Normally, I was good at multitasking, but this situation was stretching me to my limits, and, apparently, what I was shedding was my ability to concentrate on the smallest of details.

"So answer all of them," Paladin said. "Where'd you get that stuff?"

"Charity auction at Comic-con," The Borg Queen said. "Or maybe it was Dragoncon. Evan, do you remember?"

The male Borg who had been speaking up shook his head. "It was years ago."

"So you've had the equipment a long time," I said.

The Borg Queen nodded.

"Who donated it to the auction?" I asked.

"The Trek people," Evan the male Borg said.

"I actually think it might have been one of the Las Vegas things," the Borg Queen said. "You know, like the ride or a Creation convention or something. I don't know. I can check receipts."

"That's not necessary," Paladin said, although I begged to differ. Whoever donated it might know how to manipulate it. "Did you notice anything different about it when you set it up?"

"No," the Borg Queen said, "and if you think I put the acid in, you have another think coming. Because I wouldn't—"

"We don't," I said. "We're trying to figure out how that acid got in there."

"We set it up yesterday morning," Evan the male Borg said. "We knew we had the fan room first. We always ask to go first because we do the most setup. Then we have an hour for teardown and we move on with the convention."

"Always?" Paladin asked before I managed to parrot the same word.

"Any convention we're at," Evan the male Borg said. "We set up, we start when programming starts, then we tear down."

"For how many conventions?" I asked.

"Better to ask how many years," said one of the female Borgs.

"How many years?" Paladin asked, sounding vaguely annoyed. I knew what had annoyed her. She figured they could have answered the question before it was asked.

Which was why I usually handled the questioning. There was a lot less exasperation that way, a lot fewer ruffled feathers.

"I don't know," the Borg Queen said, sounding as annoyed as Paladin. "Five?"

"Are you asking me or telling me?" Paladin said.

I put my hand on her arm. We were actually trying to get information from these people, not trying to shut them up.

"It doesn't matter exactly how long you've been doing it," I said. "The key is that you've done it for a long time. You know what you're doing."

"Damn straight," the Borg Queen said, with an amazing glare at Paladin.

"And nothing seemed off to you yesterday?" I asked. "The equipment didn't feel weird, didn't look different?"

"No," she said. "And I would have noticed. I've called off the ceremony before when something wasn't right."

"What was that?" I asked.

"Oh, nothing major," the Borg Queen said. "Not like this, anyway. Once or twice I forgot a piece, so we couldn't do the ceremony right."

I nodded as if I understood. "Did that ever happen at any California or Nevada convention?"

"No," she said. "Otherwise I could've sent someone home to get it or gone myself. Twice it happened on the East Coast, because I forgot to pack stuff. But that was early on. I have a checklist now."

Of course she did. That actually made sense, even for Borg. Especially for Borg.

"After you set up, then what happened?" I asked.

"I locked the room," she said.

"*We* locked the room," Evan the male Borg said. "We double-checked everything and then locked up and left it for today."

"Was that how you normally did things?" I asked.

"Absolutely," the Borg Queen said.

"And who knew that?" I asked.

"Oh, hell, I don't know," the Borg Queen said. "Everyone here, that's for sure, and past Borg, and the concoms of every convention we've been to, not to mention the other users of the Star Trek fan room. Sometimes they protest, you know."

I didn't, but I was going to keep that in mind. First, I had to ask something else, though. "Past Borg? You've lost members?"

"They de-assimilated," said the female Borg, sounded disgusted. "One of them even became a Klingon, which I think is antithetical to Borgness."

I supposed it would be.

"They didn't start as a Klingon, then?" Paladin asked with a straight face.

"No, of course not," the female Borg said, sounding peeved. "Klingons aren't real, you know."

Paladin's eyes twinkled. "I wouldn't want to tell the local Klingons that." she said.

I put my hand on her arm, and this time, I kept my hand there. I wanted her to be quiet for a moment.

"Are any of the past members here?" I asked.

"I haven't seen any of them," the Borg Queen said, "but then, I haven't been in any major parts of the convention. Most of the past Borg last for a convention or two and move on. Many of them aren't even in fandom anymore."

I wasn't sure if that was important or not. What was important was that a lot of people knew that they set things up the day before, and then locked the room.

Contrary to what the Borg Queen said, a lot of people had access to the room, from members of the concom to the hotel staff. We had a plethora of suspects.

"I hate to ask you this," I said—and I sounded sincere because I was, "but does someone hate you enough to want to hurt you badly?"

"Or permanently disfigure you?" Paladin added, with a little too much intensity.

If someone in Borg makeup could get paler, then the Borg Queen managed it.

"I'm the Borg Queen," she said without the bravado she probably should have used for that sentence. "Of course, people don't like me."

"I mean in your mundane life," I said.

The Borg Queen frowned. "Oh, jeez," she said, "I don't know. I never thought about it." Then she took a deep breath. "I am an attorney."

"Well, then," Paladin said, as if that settled it. Apparently in

Paladin's mind, all attorneys had enemies.

I knew better, thanks to all the time I'd spent in various courts. "What kind of attorney?" I asked.

"A tax attorney," the Borg Queen said in a small voice.

"Working for the IRS?" I asked, because if she did, then she would have prosecuted tax scofflaws, and that would have made people angry.

"No," she said. "I advise people on tax law, settle tax disputes, and sometimes help with tax relief. It's not glamorous, but it usually doesn't make people mad at me, not like—you know—divorce attorneys."

As she said that, she looked at the other female Borg.

"Past life," the female Borg said. "I teach law now."

"Yeah," said Evan the male Borg. "Teaching in a law school *never* pisses anyone off."

"Not enough to travel from Mississippi," the female Borg said, and now that she wasn't even trying to sound Borg, I could hear the faint music of the Deep South in her voice. "If they wanted to kill me, they'd've had plenty of opportunity on campus."

"This really isn't a joke," Paladin said.

The female Borg glared at her. Paladin glared back.

I decided to ignore both of them, and return my attention to the Borg Queen.

"No messy divorces?" I ask. "No crazed relatives?"

She shook her head. "Never married. Only child. Quiet job filled with numbers."

That all sounded distressingly familiar.

"I can't think why anyone would want to kill me," she said.

"What about the rest of you?" I asked, then realized I wasn't being specific. I didn't mean to ask whether or not *they* wanted to kill her—but they all took it that way, judging by their expressions.

"We're *Borg*," the other male Borg said. "We want to assimilate, not destroy each other. Why is that so hard to understand?"

He asked that question of the other Borg, as if they were all dealing with that very disturbing problem.

"I meant," I said, "do any of you use that device that the Borg Queen was going to use?"

I actually had planned to ask a slightly different question, but I felt like I had to soothe some ruffled feathers. (And the mixed metaphor amused me ever so slightly, which meant I was getting punchy.)

"Only if she didn't show up," said the female Borg former divorce lawyer. "And as you can see, she's here."

"But it was possible," I said, not sure where I was going with this.

"Not today," the second male Borg said.

So that ruled out my next question, at least for the moment. I had wanted to know if any of them had enemies.

"I did have car trouble," the Borg Queen said. "I almost didn't make it here."

I turned back toward her.

"Yeah," Evan the male Borg said. "She had me pick her up."

"And all of her equipment?" I asked.

"No," he said. "We ship that. It was already here."

So many people shipped their supplies to a convention. Sometimes, particularly at a remote convention, it was easier than dragging a van or a truck up a mountain or on isolated roads.

That was the mark of an experienced congoer.

Paladin zeroed in on what I would have asked as well. "Had someone opened the boxes before you got to them?"

"No," the Borg Queen said. "And to be more precise, there were boxes, but inside those boxes, the equipment was in its own boxes, and those had a combination lock."

"Combination?" Paladin asked. "Those dinky things that are built into any kind of luggage? Or an actual padlock."

The Borg Queen looked down. I was beginning to think that Paladin intimidated her. "I think you would call it a dinky thing."

Paladin looked at me. "I can break into one of those things in a New York minute."

Actually, I could too, and I wasn't as good with those things as Paladin was. It was yet another piece of information to have.

I was beginning to feel restless, which was how I often felt when it became clear that an interview would no longer yield good information.

"Let me know if you think of anything," I said to them. "Otherwise, we'll be back if we have more questions."

The Borg Queen nodded sadly. The others crowded around her, almost too close, in my opinion. But then, I never wanted to be assimilated.

I thanked them and headed back to the desk to bother Betty again. As I walked, I grabbed my walkie-talkie. I was about to press the send button, when I realized I didn't want Smudge's name broadcast.

It bothered me that she hadn't shown up. It also bothered me that she wanted to be involved with the Borg at all.

That was important, although I still wasn't sure how or why.

"I wish we could check that equipment," Paladin said to me.

"I'm not sure we would know what we were looking at," I said.

"Yeah, and it's dangerous right now," Paladin said. "But that's our answer, somewhere in this Borg conundrum."

"Maybe," I said, but I wasn't going to say much more. My brain was making connections without consulting me yet, and I didn't want to interrupt its thought processes. And one of those processes was checking in with Betty again, to see if Camille Smudge had even shown up at the hotel.

Then I would go to the Tower of Terror and look up Camille Smudge, as well as her fannish aliases.

"Something's bothering you," Paladin said. "I mean, even more than it was earlier."

"Yeah," I said. "I think we may have figured this all out."

"What?" she asked. "I haven't figured anything out. So there's no 'we' here, Spade."

Oh, but there was. And if we hadn't decided on the buddy system, I would have sent her to check a dozen different things.

Instead, we were glued at the hip as we went about our investigation. And as much as I liked being glued to Paladin, right now, the gluing wasn't that efficient.

I wished I felt secure enough to send us both on our way.

But I didn't.

I didn't feel secure at all.

22

Betty could not find Camille Smudge's name in the hotel registration for the convention. Or even for the handful of people who had arrived after the snow started, searching for a place to stay in the middle of a crisis. There wasn't a "Camille" of any spelling in the hotel—at least, according to legal documents, like driver's licenses and credit cards.

Which meant exactly nothing. Fen often crowded into hotel rooms, as many people as possible, some on the much-too-hard couches, some on trundle beds, and some sleeping five to a King-sized bed. It was a way for people to attend a convention without spending a lot of money.

Folks usually didn't mind, because most of them—particularly the gamers—rarely spent time in the room. For the non-gamers, the line-up for the shower could be inconvenient, but the gamers just decided to become...well... gamey.

Because that was a dead end, Paladin and I headed to Con Ops and my Tower of Terror. As we ascended the wide staircase, and said hello to a lot of people neither of us had seen since the last con, Paladin said, "After I deliver you to Con Ops, I'm going to check in on the panels."

"Only if there are people in Con Ops," I said. "And really, you need to maintain the buddy system for yourself."

"The panels are not even twenty yards away," she said. "If I can be assaulted and kidnapped by someone connected to fandom in fewer than ten yards, I deserve what I get."

"No one deserves what's been happening, Paladin," I said.

She sighed. "You know what I mean."

And, strikingly, I did.

As we walked past the main programming area, I peered into the rooms. They were more packed than usual. I wasn't sure if that was because of the snowstorm, unnerving everyone, or if that was because we had hit the programming out of the park at this convention.

I liked to think it was the latter, but I'd noticed at other conventions where the weather or the outside conditions were weird, the fen tended to crowd together.

It also helped that Horatio was on a panel in one of the ballrooms. Horatio wasn't just famous, he was an interesting panelist. It was amazing how often those two things did *not* go together.

Paladin and I rounded the corner, and peered into Con Ops. Judita was in there, along with Bryan Bessemer and Cindy Ismay. I wasn't happy that there were three of them, instead of four.

"Who's missing a buddy?" I asked.

"Chill, Spade," Judita said. "We all three walked here together."

"So Con Ops was empty?" I asked.

"No-o-o-o-o," Cindy said with that tone people sometimes used when they were feeling snotty. "Two security people were here. They left when we got here."

"Good," I said, and stepped inside.

It was beginning to smell like Con Ops, all sweaty feet and day-old pizza, even if the pizza was the microwave variety. Apparently no one here knew that the café's pizza wasn't half bad.

That made me hungry, even though I'd had a good breakfast, and I cast around for munchables. There was healthy stuff—apples, bananas, gluten-free muffins from the hotel, and the ubiquitous peanut butter, with a butter knife stuck in the open jar like a stake to its heart.

"Let's order some room service," I said, and grabbed the phone. No one disagreed, except Paladin, who said, "Anyone interested in seeing some panels? I need to walk that way."

"I have to check on something," Bryan said, maybe not because he had to, but because he always kept a chivalrous eye on Paladin. She never noticed—not that she needed the chivalry at all, anyway. "I'll walk with you."

"As long as you buddy up with someone to go elsewhere," I said. Then I frowned at Paladin. "What are you going to do?"

"Check on Chancery and the law," she said. "Isn't that next?"

It was, but the Chancery gathering wasn't for hours. I figured we could buy some time.

"I would prefer if you stayed here," I said.

"I don't twiddle my thumbs well, Spade," she said. "And nothing can bore me faster than watching you do computer work. Text me if you find anything."

Then she waved a hand at Bryan. It was an odd almost ambivalent movement, a kind of...*if you're coming with me, come now.* I had no idea how she managed to pull that off, but that was Paladin. She always managed to be different.

I called room service and ordered two pizzas, nachos and the char-cuterie plate to be delivered to Con Ops. I gave the kitchen my convention code, so they automatically charged everything, along with the gratuity to the convention.

Then I climbed onto my exquisitely comfortable custom-built captain's chair, and turned on my Tower of Terror. It bonged and binged as it returned to life, something akin to much-beloved music in my life.

I inputted various passcodes after making sure no one was looking over my shoulder—even though it would be damn near impossible for them to copy down what I was doing. I had the ability to memorize long threads of numbers and letters, something I learned as a kid to impress girls (before I learned that being a smart-ass impressed no one).

Then I dug into various files.

I started with registration for the convention. I wanted to see if Camille Smudge was on the list. She was not, which surprised me. I had thought, if she was going to be initiated by the Borg, she would be registered.

That made me even more uncomfortable than I had been. It was a weird red flag, one I didn't entirely understand. But part of me knew something, from very, very, very long ago.

I had a lot of old files. Back in the days when conventions were young(er) and computers had less memory, the Secret Masters of Fandom had developed a system for archiving old information. Those of us with access to computers with larger memories kept the archives.

As computers became smaller and developed so much more memory, the practice continued. Nothing got tossed. Somewhere along the way, it had become a habit for SMoFs in different parts of the country to have all of the archives.

Some of the archives were in a cloud database, but not all of them. The most sensitive stuff was still scattered among SMoFish computers. We have a lot of white hat hackers in fandom (and a few black hat hackers, who haven't yet [as far as I know] turned their evil intent on the rest of us), and those hackers could easily break into our cloud system.

It's tougher to break into individual computers. My Tower of Terror, for example, has one entire hard drive that I opened on a secondary computer, one that never got networked with anything, from another SMoF's computer to the cloud to hotel Wi-Fi. Over the years, I had become so paranoid, I didn't even let that hard drive network with my other computers.

That was the hard drive I opened now. I used the dedicated keyboard that I had connected to a dedicated screen that was hard to read if you weren't looking at it directly.

I tend to concentrate pretty hard when I'm working, and someone could easily look over my shoulder without me knowing it. Which was why I had that dedicated screen.

I set everything up, looked over my shoulder to make sure the others were busy, and then dug into the old files, searching for Camille Smudge.

I found a few things.

She had been flagged by the SMoFs in the early part of this century because of all the complaints against her. Turned out that Camille

Smudge had a history of sleeping with men, usually once, and then obsessing about them. She would stalk them at conventions, and make their lives a living hell.

Finally, enough of the men complained about her that the East Coast wing of SMoFdom decided she wasn't welcome at conventions anymore.

That rarely happened, and almost never happened to someone who hadn't made a physical threat against anyone. Stalking, especially before the anti-stalking laws got passed in several states, usually needed some kind of physical endangerment charge to stick.

SF conventions had a problem with dealing with bad actors who didn't violate an actual law. Because hotels were separately owned businesses. A convention could ban someone from the convention proper, but couldn't prevent them from coming in the hotel.

And the hotel, aware of liability problems from all angles, usually required proof of criminality or threatened endangerment to proactively ban someone from the premises.

The smell of fresh garlic and melted cheese caught my senses. I smelled the arrival of room service before I actually heard someone cry, "Room service!"

The waiter showed up with another waiter in tow, just like I had suggested to the hotel. Apparently they were doing the buddy system too.

I stood, walked over to the room service delivery table, and lifted the lids off the food.

"No one touched this after it left the kitchen, right?" I asked.

"That's right, sir," said the scrawny waiter who had waited on me at breakfast. "And I was told that everyone was extremely careful in the cooking, making sure no one got in the kitchen either."

The hotel was feeling sensitive about the poison, as it probably should have been.

"Here," Cindy Ismay said, holding out a plate. "Sample this for us."

The waiter looked startled, and so did the other waiter. But I understood where she was coming from.

"I'll give you an extra fifty if you both do it," she said.

"Each?" the second waiter asked.

Cindy rolled her eyes. "Fifty each," she said.

She grabbed her purse, as the waiters took plates, and served themselves a bit of nachos, a little of the charcuterie, and split one slice of pizza.

I appreciated Cindy's efforts enough that I didn't want to tell her that it was possible for only part of the food to be poisoned. Just like you'd order a pizza with half mushrooms half pepperoni, you could probably prepare one with half poison and half none poison. She shouldn't have let them choose what part of the food to serve themselves.

But I didn't say anything, because it was okay. The kitchen didn't dare poison anyone else, even if the poison had come from someone in the kitchen. The hallmark of this wannabe killer was unusual methods, and I didn't think he (or maybe she) would use the exact same method twice.

Both men chewed and looked nervous and chewed some more. I got it. They weren't supposed to eat guest food. I also knew none of us would tattle on them.

They finished, and we all waited for Cindy to remove $100 from her wallet, which she actually had. She handed them the money, thanked them for their time, and was about to dismiss them, when Judita stopped beside her.

She swept back the tablecloth over the little delivery table. She'd seen too many movies, in which the bad guy (or the good guy) had hidden underneath one of those tables.

This one had no one, and I found myself relieved too. I had seen those movies as well.

"All right," Cindy said. "I appreciate your indulging our paranoia."

"We get it," said the second waiter. And that's when I realized he had been as afraid to eat food served to us as we had.

"Hey," I said. "Tell me one thing. Is the kitchen concerned about what happened last night?"

"Everyone's terrified," said the second waiter. The first one shushed him, but the second waiter took a step toward me, so that he could ignore the first waiter. "They don't know what happened to that meal or how any poison got in the food."

"It might not have," I said. "We can't test everything, and Rogers was on some medication. So it might have come from elsewhere."

"Well," the second waiter said, "I've never worked at a place that's this tense, and frankly, I'm done when the snow clears. This has been the worst twenty-four hours of my life."

I was pretty sure it wouldn't get better, not for the next twenty-four hours anyway, but I didn't want to tell him that.

"Thanks," I said, and grabbed one of the small plates. Either I was going to be scared all the time or I was going to be scared all the time and take risks, with my food and with my person.

I opted to be a scared risk-taker.

The waiters left, pocketing their money. I served myself some pizza, ham, and a stack of nachos, all from the area near where the waiters had taken their food. Apparently, I was a little more nervous than I let on, even to myself.

Then I grabbed a Coke from the cooler, rooting in the ice for one of the cans near the bottom. I carried it all back to the Tower of Terror. Before I started eating, I looked up the order the East Coast SMoFs had written up, banning Camille Smudge from conventions.

The order was straightforward, as these things went. They cited disruptive behavior "unbecoming a science-fiction fan," and stated that she was no longer welcome. That was a copy that was given to her. Those copies, given to individuals, were often sparse on the details. We always figured that the individuals already had an in-depth listing of whatever had precipitated this.

Also, we didn't want them to see who had complained about them or what incidents had actually incited the ban. We had never really had anyone go after their accusers for actual revenge—at least not on the sf side—but we didn't want that to start.

Although, a few of the banned did see their accusers...in court. In the 1990s, there had been a group of truly insidious pedophiles who had infiltrated Southern Fandom, and those assholes ended up in jail. And considering that the laws against their crimes were not as harsh in the 1990s as they are now, that was actually saying something.

So, I dug deeper into the archives. I wanted to see the copy of the order that went to the various concoms all over the world.

That order would have a lot more information. There would have been more detail about her behavior, a listing of which cons the problems had occurred at, a listing of the actual legal cases (if any) that arose from her behavior, and a listing of any other properties (if any) that had banned her. That order would also have a list of all of her fannish names, and maybe a grainy photograph or two, as well as the convention activities that she liked to participate in.

If she had committed actual crimes, the order would have a cc: notation at the bottom because the order would also go to whatever law enforcement jurisdiction that covered the convention area, as a kind of CYA for the convention. That way, if they had to toss her off the premises—with or without the hotel's permission—they could more easily get law enforcement backup.

I'd only seen that happen once or twice, although I'd heard about it a lot more often. (See that stupid pedophile ring.)

Behind me, dishes clanged, and low conversation continued. The other two were talking about something that didn't interest me. I ate my nachos, wiped off my fingers, and continued working.

I was digging for that copy, and maybe, just maybe the original file —something that showed in depth what the incidents were that caused Camille to get tossed from conventions.

It took more digging in the old files to find it. That order was also straightforward and not that much different than the one that she got. But I was relieved to find this order because it had the identifying information that I wanted.

It had her fannish names—and her real name.

I had always thought that her real name was Camille Smudge. I just figured she had British ancestors or something, not that she had actually chosen a name that sounded like it had come out of a British drawing room mystery.

And to be fair to me, Camille Smudge was her legal name now. She had changed names about twenty-five years ago. Initially, her name was Ludmila Cesgue. Camille Smudge was an anagram of Ludmila Cesgue.

She didn't have a lot of other names. But back in those early years, she also went by the fannish moniker Luddite. According to the notes, the name Luddite had been an inside joke.

Ludmila Cesgue had been an engineer. She had started coming to conventions when she was an MIT post-doc, working on some highly classified research, a fact that she used to brandish about like a verbal whip, cowing anyone who dared suggest she wasn't smart or wasn't capable.

There were some early photos in the file, many of them of some Fen Bowl competitions—based on the whole collegiate quiz bowl models. Fen Bowls were more intense than the average trivia contests. Some Fen Bowls split into categories—science, science fiction "science," balonium, fannish history, fandom history, convention history—you get the idea.

Ludmila seemed to play in the science categories of the Fen Bowl series. With the rise of actual trivia contests in bars and other places about twenty years ago, Fen Bowl competitions faded out due—according to Big Name Texas fan Groot—to the influx of idiots who thought Fen Bowls were about trivia instead of about knowledge.

Ludmila's file indicated she participated in quite a few Fen Bowls. She'd been pretty active for a few years, before disappearing from fandom altogether.

I enlarged one of the grainy photos, just to double check my memory—that the Camille I remembered looked something (anything) like the Ludmila that I wasn't sure I had met.

The photo I clicked on showed two tables lengthwise on a dais. In the middle, a man in a Viking cap stood at a podium, holding some index cards in his hand.

The index cards alone showed that this photo came from at least the 1990s. There was no laptop, no tablet, no smart phone—nothing that would make things easier electronically.

The people at the tables—Team Red Dwarf and Team Farscape— were either in some kind of costume (which was hard to discern from the photo) or in fannish casual, a T-shirt and jeans, with the name badge around their necks.

Ludmila was on Team Farscape, in the seat closest to the podium. She was as thin as I remembered, almost skeletal, and she was looking up at the moderator with an expression that I couldn't quite read.

I looked at the other faces, though some seemed familiar, and was about to go back to the archives, when I stopped.

That moderator did look familiar too.

I enlarged his face. Half of it was cut off by the Viking helmet—which was apparently a size too large—but the rest of it seemed truly familiar. Even if the enlargement hadn't caught his badge, I would have figured out that I was looking at a young Rogers Carren.

I let out a breath. Rogers, connected to Ludmila/Camille. The Borg connected to Ludmila/Camille. I needed to find some others connected to her as well, and I had a hunch I would.

I opened a few more files, and then backed up. The orders usually had to come from someone—either on letterhead (back in the day) or through an official fannish email account.

The order banning Camille Smudge was just early enough in the century to have an email address attached to it, but that email address was an AOL address. And AOL addresses, like gmail addresses, were often someone's name.

I peered at this one: RuthHarshSMoF. Ruth Harshaw. Our Ruth, who nearly died last night.

I swore, not creatively, not even profoundly. Just one short four letter f-bomb that I said a bit louder than I expected to.

I turned around to apologize, and then realized that I was alone in Con Ops. I had no idea how that had happened. Someone might have talked to me, and I might've answered, but I had been deep in my work, and that often meant I didn't really hear anything anyone said.

I needed to get a buddy in here, and fast. But I was probably safe enough with the door closed. Still, I needed to follow my own rules.

I texted Paladin.

Hey. Just realized that I'm alone in Con Ops. Need you to send me a buddy.

If she didn't respond, I'd find a buddy on my own.

I was a little nervous. I grabbed the cold piece of pizza still on my plate, and chomped down. Yes, I'm a stress-eater. It was amazing that I hadn't eaten more at this convention than I already had.

I went back to the list of members of the convention, seeing if a Luddite had registered or a Ludmila Cesgue was here. Neither name was on the list nor was there another obvious anagram of Camille Smudge.

But that didn't mean she wasn't in attendance. I knew she couldn't check into the hotel as Luddite, but she could use an old identity.

I scrolled through my contacts until I found the number for whoever was running the front desk. I always programmed that number into my phone at any convention, because it saved time. There was the official number for the hotel and then there was the hey-we're-paying-you-a-small-fortune-and-we-need-you-to-do-something-quickly number.

The phone rang for a minute, and I was beginning to think I was going to have to try again, when Betty answered. She identified the hotel, but sounded both stressed and distracted.

"Bad time?" I asked. "This is Spade."

"I'm beginning to think this entire convention is a bad time," Betty said, sounding annoyed.

I was going to ignore that. "I have a quick question," I said. "I need you to look up a name on the guest registration for me."

"Another one?" Betty said.

"You want me to find this creep or not?" I asked.

"Find 'em, of course," Betty said, sounding almost defeated. "What's the name?"

"Ludmila Cesgue," I said.

"Oh," Betty said. "That's easy. She's not registered at the hotel. She works here."

I went cold and the hair on the back of my neck stood up. Literally. That had never happened to me before, not ever, not in all my years of doing detective work.

If Ludmila worked for the hotel, she had access to all the function space, and she could make keys that would let her into guest rooms.

"Doing what?" I asked, trying to keep my voice level.

"Normally, she's front desk," Betty said, "but she offered to be on rotating assignment here. Mostly she's been helping Assistant GM Shaye."

"Doing what?" I asked again, trying to keep my voice just like it had been before. I thought I sounded a little off, but it seemed like Betty wasn't paying attention.

"Whatever he needs her to do," Betty said, "which probably means everything."

I didn't swear. I didn't really alert Betty, either. I mean, what could I say? I only had suspicions at the moment.

I really needed Paladin. I needed some muscle at my side.

"Should I let her know that you're looking for her?" Betty said.

"Um," I said. "Not yet. I have a few other things to do first."

"Okay." Now Betty sounded a little strange. Which meant that she heard how odd my tone was.

"Um," I said again, cursing my own verbal ineptness. "One question. Was she one of the people who came back to the hotel when the weather service started predicting the snowstorm?"

"No," Betty said. "She's been here for two years, almost to the day. What's going on, Spade? She's one of our best employees."

My brain froze. My brain never froze, but it did this time. I couldn't come up with a passable lie.

"I...um...found her name on a file," I said, "and I just wanted to check something with her. I misunderstood what I have. I thought she was an attendee. My mistake."

"Okay." Betty said. "You sure you don't want me to send her to you."

"No," I said a little too quickly. "I'll find her."

And then I hung up before I made things even worse.

A hotel employee. I hadn't even thought of that. But it made access easy, and it also made setup easy. She had the ability to create the booby trap that hurt Horatio. She had time to change out the fluid in the Borg equipment. She had access to the kitchen, so she could drop poison (and that number) in Rogers' food, without creating any suspicion.

And she either could have been waiting in Ruth's room or slipped in when Ruth wasn't paying any attention.

That meant that she might have booby traps waiting for the Chancery celebration, and God knows what she had planned for the bear hug thing.

I thumbed my phone until I found Paladin's number. My heart was pounding.

"Pick up, pick up, pick up," I said softly.

In less than a minute, Paladin did. "Hang on, Spade," she said. "I'm in a panel."

I heard the murmur of voices, and then a door creak, followed by a bang.

"You're not alone in the hall, are you?" I asked.

"You're alone in Con Ops for some reason, so stop being the damn pot."

It took me a moment to get the reference, which just told me how crowded my brain was.

"I asked you to send someone," I said.

"On it," she said. "Anything else?"

"Yeah," I said. "I think I found our culprit."

I gave Paladin the short version—the banning from conventions, the different names—and then I said, "We have to figure out what's going to happen next, and stop it."

"Well, we have a better chance of that now," Paladin said. "I have a couple of ideas."

And then she hung up.

If Paladin hadn't done that to me a million times in the past, I would have been freaked out by it, thinking maybe she had been attacked by Ludmila Cesgue or something.

But that was just the way Paladin did business.

I clutched my phone for a moment, trying to figure out my next move. Call Betty back? Tell her that a "good" employee was trying to kill the guests?

Who else would I tell?

Con security, but not on the walkies.

I flicked on the walkie at my side, and asked for security to come to Con Ops. We could all figure this out together.

Somehow while I was doing all of that, I also finished my piece of pizza. I was feeling a bit calmer. I would have help figuring out how to handle this mess.

I sipped my Diet Coke, and thought about what Betty had said. What *I* had said. I had known we were dealing with a longtime fan, with someone who held grudges, with someone who planned.

Ludmila-Camille had joined the staff here almost two years ago to the day. Which meant that she had been targeting SierraCon.

I sat in my chair and spun back toward my Tower of Terror. Usually cons announced future guests on the last day of the convention. Local cons announced one year out, but some cons, particularly cons like SierraCon that were destination cons, announced two years out.

I went back to the last day file for SierraCon [43] two years ago. Sure enough, they had announced the guest of honor roster for SierraCon 45 at closing ceremonies.

They didn't have an editor guest of honor yet or a fan guest of honor, but they did have a writer guest of honor.

They had Horatio. The current biggest draw in all of fandom.

And he had been that big a draw then, too.

"Son of a bitch," I said quietly. "Son of an ever-loving bitch."

23

I went back to the actual order that went to the various cons. I didn't see any mention of Horatio. So I dug into my files, hoping I could find the inciting incidences that kept Ludmila out of fandom.

The last straw was an actual knife fight in the hallway at Dinocon. Ludmila had actually stabbed someone. But the concom hadn't called the police, even though there was hallway video footage from hotel security. Apparently, it was impossible to tell who had started the fight.

There was a notation as well. Dinocon was not yet weapons-free and was worried after that event (and the Martha Stewart thing I had dealt with the year before) that the hotel would kick them out, and no other hotel would take them.

The convention had died a year or so later anyway, because of fan attrition—dinosaurs stopped being cool a few years after *Jurassic World* —so the entire convention rebranded and moved to a different hotel.

But by then, Ludmila-Camille had had enough complaints against her that the concom and the local SMoFs decided enough was enough.

I sighed. That lack of information really didn't do me a lot of good.

I needed to know what Horatio knew.

I glanced at my watch. We were in the ten-minute break between panels. I thought of hurrying to his panel, but that meant leaving the safety of Con Ops, and venturing alone into the hallway. I wasn't going to do that.

So I decided to try the phone. The worst thing he could do was not pick up.

I found Horatio's number in the con files, and updated my phone. Apparently my contact information for Horatio was a few years old. Then I dialed the updated number.

He picked up right away. "Jesus Christ, Spade," he said. "I'm going to another panel. Your girl is just fine. Don't be a mother hen. She's with me."

It took a moment for me to realize he meant Casper.

"If I want to know how Casper is, I'll call her directly," I said. I wasn't sure if he had become more annoying over the years or if I was just noticing. "I have a question for you. Can you step somewhere private?"

"Hey, adoring masses," Horatio said loudly in his con voice. I had to pull the phone away from my ear. I could still hear him. "I've gotta take this. It's my agent."

And then the noise slowly diminished.

I cautiously moved the phone back, just in time to hear him say in his normal voice, "Your girl is still with me. She sticks like glue."

"I'm supposed to!" Casper said, sounding indignant.

"She's supposed to," I said at the same time.

Horatio grunted. He wasn't telling me about Casper to brief me on how she was doing. He was telling me as a passive-aggressive protest to having Casper as his buddy.

"Clock's ticking, Spade," he said.

"Oh, knock it off," I said. "You have plenty of time. You only have to get back up on the dais. You're in the same room all afternoon."

"Still," Horatio said.

"Still," I said mimicking his tone, "I only have one question for you, and I don't want you to let anyone know I asked it."

"Not even the sticky kid?" he asked.

"Not even," I said.

"Hey, kid," Horatio said, "I need a second of privacy. Go sit over there."

"I will not," Casper said.

"As if the panel has already started," Horatio said.

I could hear Casper's voice, but her words weren't audible.

"Okay," Horatio said into the phone again. "You got maybe thirty seconds before some fan gets too close."

He wasn't exaggerating. His fans were probably leaving him alone because he asked for privacy, but soon someone new would enter the room, and make a beeline for him.

"Back in the day," I said, "did you know a fan named Camille Smudge?"

"I don't think so," Horatio said. "But you have to know, Spade, I've met thousands and thousands of congoers over decades."

I did know that, and he knew I knew that, and I didn't have time for these verbal power games. So I just...powered on.

"What about Ludmila Cesgue?" I asked.

"Says goo?" He said, sounding odd. "Spell that."

I did.

"Oh." His voice went flat. "You mean Ches-coo."

And with the correction, he confirmed that he had known her. "What's the history, Horatio?" I asked.

"Wasn't she banned from cons?" he asked.

Wow. He really did know her. "What's the history, Horatio?"

"How long have we known each other, Spade?" he asked, his voice even lower. "Did you know me in the dark years?"

I'd heard his go-to speech, particularly for young writers. The dark years, as he called them, were the years between his rapid beginning, back when he was a hot young writer who won every award in the industry, and his spectacular crash, after the failure of a "big" book.

He would still come to conventions in those years, but he drank a lot and slept around. Fortunately for him, that behavior wasn't unusual for pros at the time.

"I was there," I said. "And we were both thinner."

He barked a laugh. "True."

"I take it Ludmila was one of your conquests?" I said.

"Better to say I was one of hers. She pressured me for three cons before I got too drunk to say no," he said. "And then it got worse."

"What do you mean, 'it'?" I asked.

"The pressure," he said. "In today's parlance, she stalked me. She was everywhere. Thank God there wasn't social media. She would have proclaimed herself my fiancée online if she could. She did that, and more, at conventions I didn't attend. Lucky for me, or them, or someone, I was broke and not all that popular, so what perks she thought she could get didn't really exist. If I had done something like that now..."

He whistled, which made me pull the phone away yet again.

"So you were one of the complainants who got her banned," I said.

"Yeah," he said. "But I wasn't the only one. Every hot young Turk from those years had his Ludmila story. It was worse for Rick Silver."

That was a name I hadn't heard for a while. He had had a hot career, writing hard sf, and then his much-vaunted trilogy got caught in a distribution war, and he couldn't sell another book. Last I heard, he was a professor of creative writing in Arizona.

"What happened to him?" I asked.

"He was on a break from his then-girlfriend, and—you know." Horatio's voice got lower. I supposed that meant some fans were getting closer. "I don't know the timing of all of this, but somewhere along the way—the next convention maybe—he told Ludmila that he was back with his fiancée and Ludmila lost it. She spent half the convention excoriating him and the other half claiming she was going to commit suicide."

I felt a chill. I had said suicidal. I wasn't sure I liked how all the pieces were lining up.

"Some of the newer writers, who didn't know Rick or Ludmila, took her side, and the whole fight at that con got ugly. Finally, someone— and I don't know who—got Ludmila out of there. Last I heard, she was in some court-ordered treatment center, getting help. That was years ago."

I let out a sigh. Years ago, and apparently the treatment didn't take.

"I hesitate to ask why you want to know," he said.

"She's here, Horatio," I said.

He swore, viciously. "Who lifted the ban?"

"No one," I said. "She's on staff at the hotel."

"Spade," he said with great urgency. "You have to tell them to fire her. She's toxic. She's—"

"I know," I said. "I haven't said anything yet. I don't want them to tip her off. And I don't want you to say anything either. I'll have it handled by opening ceremonies, okay? You just do a panel as if nothing is wrong. And if you see her, text me."

"I don't like this, Spade," he said.

"I don't either," I said. "But, honestly, how is this worse than having an unknown assailant? At least we have a good idea who is doing this."

"I *know* her," Horatio said. "She's smart. She's devious. She's way ahead of us, which is exactly not where she should be."

"I understand," I said.

"You don't." Horatio's volume was starting to go up. "It took me years to shake her off. *Years.* You have to do something."

"I will," I said. "Now trust me. I'll talk to you at Opening Cere-monies. You go entertain people."

"Yeah, like I can do that now," he grumbled.

"You better," I said, and hung up. This was going to be tricky. For the first time, I regretted the fact that Con Ops had no windows. I wanted to see how the storm was doing.

Because once we caught Ludmila, we were going to have to hold her somewhere until the authorities could get here. We needed a way to do that, without causing even more problems.

I sat back down at the Tower of Terror, but instead of digging through the archives, I looked at the weather.

The storm—now an official blizzard that covered half of the Sierra —actually had a name, an irritating practice the National Weather Service had started to make winter storms more like hurricanes. With so many names floating around, the storms became impossible to remember.

So I ignored the name of this one, and looked at its trajectory. On satellite radar, it looked like a gigantic blue and pink comma, the fat end over us right at the moment. Blue was the weather service's radar color for snow, and it looked like there was more to come.

We were in the early afternoon, and there was going to be snow for another twelve hours, minimum. The high winds were supposed to increase, not decrease, until the band of snow vanished. Then we had about twenty-four hours of sunshine with no wind before another band of snow and "wintery mix" found its way here.

I didn't like "wintery mix." That meant snow and ice and a bit of rain, all scheduled to hit on Sunday, when everyone wanted to go home.

But that was a future problem. I had hit the website, trying to get answers about the big storm. Once the winds died down and the snow vanished, the authorities would get here, especially considering all the calls they'd had from us. If nothing else, they'd show up with medevacs and then we could reiterate that we needed some kind of law enforcement ASAP.

Which meant, of course, that we needed a place to store Ludmila once we found her.

And subdued her.

And then we'd have to guard her.

I wasn't sure what the legalities of any of that were, but none of us were law enforcement, so I hoped that whatever we did wouldn't prevent her from being properly prosecuted.

In the meantime, though, I'd try to figure out the remaining stanzas of the poem. I'd have to let the concom know that we needed to cancel any events that had to do with the Chancery and Horatio's books.

I had been right about that: this entire thing was focused, in an odd way, on Horatio himself, with the others as collateral damage.

But that bear hug. I still didn't know what that was.

I needed to dig deeper in the archive. Since Ludmila-Camille was actively getting revenge against Horatio and Ruth, with Rogers also suffering for a reason I didn't yet know, but could probably guess, I needed to figure out who the others might be who would suffer Ludmila-Camille's wrath before she turned her gun on herself.

As I dug, I found references to Jessica-6. Turned out she was one of the girlfriends of an obsession of Ludmila-Camille's. Nearly a decade ago.

That woman could really hold a grudge.

I was getting deep into my digging, when a sound caught my attention. That was weird, because I usually didn't hear anything when I was working. But something felt odd.

I swiveled my chair around, and there she was: Ludmila Cesgue, Camille Smudge, or whatever she wanted to call herself.

She was standing in the middle of the room. She had a gun in her right hand—and the gun was pointed at me.

24

"Hello, Spade," she said in the cheeriest tone imaginable. She was almost chirping.

The cheer and the chirps were completely at odds with her face. She looked like a ravaged version of the girl I'd seen in the Fen Bowl pictures. Her cheeks, which had been round back then, were sunken inwards now, making her eyes larger.

She had lines around her mouth, and streaks of white in her hair that looked natural. If she hadn't had a gun pointed on me, I would have thought that she was an older woman—a mundane—whose life hadn't gone how she planned.

Exactly the type of woman you'd expect to see in a hotel off the beaten path. The kind of person who worked her way to the middle of some local operation, and stayed there, because, for her, there was nowhere else to go.

"Imagine finding you alone. I guess the buddy system doesn't apply to the Great Spade, does it?" She smiled, and the smile actually did reach her eyes. They twinkled.

She was enjoying herself.

And we were alone. The doors to Con Ops were closed, albeit not tightly, and there was no one else in the entire large room. I wasn't sure if what I had heard was a door easing open or closed, or maybe I had just noted her perfume.

Because the smell of it—cloying lilacs—had grown stronger in the last few minutes. I was used to tuning out sounds as I worked, but smells always caught my attention. I was hypersensitive to them, and usually asked people to move away from me if their scent interfered with my concentration.

Although, to be fair, at a convention, the smells were usually overpowering body odor and, lately, that skunky stench of some kind of pot that had become legal in so many states.

Perfumes and colognes were usually not in a fan's hygiene regimen.

Yet another way for Ludmila-Camille to hide in plain sight.

"Or were you waiting for me?" Ludmila asked. "Did you want me to be your buddy?"

I wasn't sure how, exactly, to respond to her taunts. Because I didn't want to make her angry. I'd never stared down the barrel of a gun before, and son of a bitch, it was as distracting as all the studies said it was.

I had to keep telling myself to look at her face, not at the gun, but then my gaze would slip back down to it.

Her hold on that gun was steady, her expression delighted. Somehow, she was focused on me, and I wasn't sure exactly why.

"You have a problem," I said.

"Really?" Her tone lost its cheer and became withering. "Because I'm not the one with a gun pointed at me."

"That's the thing," I said. "I think you've skipped over a few stanzas of your poem."

"*My* poem," she said. "That's *your* poem."

I shook my head just a little. I wasn't sure what she meant.

"I didn't write that poem," I said.

"No," she said. "But great minds work in patterns. I used the poem, and the number one, to get you started on your journey. You figured it out a little too early. Kudos on the Borg. I did not expect that to tip you off."

"Thanks, I think," I said, trying to figure out how she knew that.

And then I realized what she had said. My brain was working sluggishly. I was not trained for this kind of thing.

I did my thinking alone, with my Tower of Terror, not in the middle of some kind of emergency.

"Why is this about me?" I asked. "You and I have met, sure, but a long time ago, and I wasn't involved in anything that had to do with you."

I had almost said I wasn't involved with banning her, but I was really terrified of setting her off—worse than she already was.

She smiled at me. The smile was warm and friendly. I didn't like how changeable her moods were. That was the third—I thought, anyway—in the last few minutes.

"The Great Spade," she said. "I'd been hearing how very smart you are, how no one can put anything past you. I figured I could. I figured I could outthink you. I wanted to prove it, and there's no longer anything like a Fen Bowl. So I devised a little test all my own."

"It would have been nice to know I was playing," I said. I was so pleased my voice was staying steady. I hadn't expected that, especially considering how hard my heart was beating.

I really did not know how to get out of this. I couldn't outrun her. I couldn't hide under my desk. I couldn't even *fit* under my desk. There was nothing I could throw at her to distract her.

I had to keep her talking, as if she were some kind of supervillain. And I had to trust everything I'd read about average people and guns. Most people, no matter how skilled they were with a weapon, had trouble actually shooting someone.

It wasn't an instinctive reaction.

Although it could be trained. And it could really be trained with practice hunting cute cuddly things, like rabbits.

I had no idea if she trained. Hell, I had no idea if she actually had fellow feeling for other people, buried underneath her rage.

I hated that my mind was wandering everywhere but where I wanted it to be. I needed some kind of solution here, some kind of plan, and I wasn't coming up with anything.

"I assume the fact that you're here means the next two traps are set," I said.

"That would be a fair assumption," she said. "I debated about coming here at all. I wanted to see your reaction when you realized you had not interpreted the poem correctly. But you figured out the Borg. That was surprising."

"Is that why you're here?" I asked.

"I'm here because you made a mistake," she said. "You told Betty you were looking for me."

Damn. I thought I had told her to keep that to herself. But Betty was nothing less than helpful, and she probably thought she was helping.

"When I realized you were using my real name," Ludmila said, "I realized you were farther along in our little duel than I had planned for this stage."

"You had always planned it to be you and me at the end?" I asked.

"Cat and mouse," she said. "It's the staple of cozy mysteries everywhere."

"Only we're at a science fiction convention," I said.

"Science *fiction* is *fiction*, Spade," she said. "Mysteries are real life. I just took a fictional construct—a killer loose at some kind of house party—and made it my own."

"So," I said, "are you planning to end this the way the poem ends?"

My mouth was dry and I wasn't being as coherent as I wanted to be.

"I don't believe in hanging," she said. "There's too many ways that could go wrong."

Of course she wasn't going to do it. She wasn't going to kill herself after all.

"I don't know," I said. "It seems to me it would be fairly easy here. The mezzanine has sturdy oak beams in that railing. You'd be able to hang yourself quite easily there."

"Yes," she said. "I thought of that. But there's a convention going on. Someone would stop me. I'm much more focused on the last few words than I am on the hanging."

And then there were none. That chill was back.

"You're going to kill everyone in the hotel?" I asked. "That seems impossible. It was built at different times. No part of the hotel shares a ventilation system with other parts."

Her mouth thinned. "You're not as creative a thinker as I thought," she said. "There's a blizzard, Spade. If you had been doing your job, you would have shut down programming, and herded everyone to a single room."

I had thought of it. Good Lord, I had considered putting everyone together because I was afraid they were at risk. But I knew fen, and they would have gotten bored. They would have protested. They would have fought me.

It was better, as I had told the concom, to keep programming going as long as possible, while I tried to find the potential killer.

Well, I had found her. Or, rather, she had found me.

"You know," I said, "once you shoot me, the entire convention will know something is going wrong."

Her smile widened. "That's what I'm hoping for," she said. "Then we really can get them, and the entire staff in one room."

My mouth was dry. I probably looked nervous, because I *was* nervous. My mind was racing a mile a minute and not finding any answers.

I'm large, but I'm not strong. And I had no idea how to correctly subdue someone with a gun.

"It would be easier if I told them," I said. "They'll listen to me. I'm the acting chair."

I didn't believe me. I knew she wouldn't either.

Then she tilted her head, and smiled at me. The smile was creepy. It was warm, it was wide, and it was...off somehow.

"You'd do that for me?" she asked.

She sounded sincere. Why would she be sincere?

Because, my brain told me, apparently relieved it had a question that it was able to answer. *She's a stalker, a woman who gets obsessed with people, and while she's after Horatio, she's obsessed with you. That's why she wants the challenge.*

"Yes, I'd do that for you," I said. "I'm really impressed with you."

That tilt went the other way, and the smile faded. "You're humoring me," she said.

Yes, I am, I nearly blurted. "No, I'm not," I lied. "I'm being honest with you. You've been planning this for years. Not even the blizzard is knocking you off your game."

"But you have," she said. "I'm here sooner than I wanted to be."

I shrugged. "I'm sure you have contingencies," I said.

Her mouth opened, and then closed. Contingencies. Apparently, she didn't have any.

She was now officially winging it.

She tilted her head the other way, again. "Hmm," she said. "If I let you talk to anyone, then you'll warn them."

I started to say that I wouldn't, but she held her hand up.

"Spade," she said. "You know you will. That's why you offered."

"I *am* impressed," I said, and oddly, I wasn't lying about that. "It's taken a lot of work to get to this point. You don't want to screw it up now."

"That's right, I don't," she said. She took a step toward me. "I think I need to get closer just to make sure I do this right. I'm a good shot, but I am a bit distracted."

I swallowed against my dry throat. I backed up involuntarily, and my legs hit the captain's chair. If I wanted to escape her, I had three directions—left, right, and forward. My chair and the Tower of Terror were in the way behind me.

"I'm sorry, Spade," she said. "I wish we had met sooner."

"We did," I said, sounding as desperate as I felt. "We met years ago. Don't you remember?"

"It doesn't count," she said. "You weren't the Great Spade then."

She took another step toward me. I couldn't run. She'd shoot no matter what.

But I couldn't stand here like a willing victim either.

"And you were interested in Horatio," I said, grasping.

"*Interested?*" She waved the gun, indignant. "I was his *lover*. I was the most important person in his *life*. And then he threw me over for that *bitch*."

Guess I had unleashed the crazy. I wasn't sure if that was good or not.

"The fact remains," I said calmly, "you were promised to Horatio back then."

"*And he threw me over!*" She took a deep breath. "You understand, Spade, that I should be at his side, right? He wouldn't understand anything about the law if it weren't for me. He would never have been in court without me. He would never have written the Chancery Universe without me."

She took another step toward me. I wanted to keep backing up. Maybe if I dove down, and rolled under the desk. Only the desk had some weird metal supports. I might hit my head.

As if that mattered. I needed to—

The lights went out.

The entire room was dark. Finally, the storm had blown out the power, just like we suspected it would.

Only there was weird light that was circling like spotlights at a movie premiere. It took me a second to realize that the circling lights came from the Tower of Terror's screen saver, which meant the power wasn't out, which meant someone was here.

I dove to the floor. Okay, not really. I bent to the floor and my arms slipped out from under me. I landed with a thud and an involuntary grunt—that was echoed with another, larger bang. There was more groaning—not me—and some grunting.

I crawled away, around my desk, and headed toward the doors in the back of the room. There was a gigantic slap, and another thud, and a thud, and yet another thud.

"Spade! Get her Goddamn gun!"

That was Paladin! Paladin was here. Paladin was the source of the thuds and the slaps.

I looked around in the weird light of the screen saver, and saw the gun only a yard or two from me. In the middle of the floor were two women, that looked like a single woman with a lot of limbs.

I gingerly grabbed the gun by its muzzle, terrified that I was going to set it off. I didn't know how to turn off the safety. I didn't know if it *had* a safety. I just remembered all that stuff I'd read about people accidentally shooting themselves, and moved the gun as carefully as I could, as far away from me and the fighting women as possible.

I didn't want Paladin to be fighting her. I would happily have died here if Paladin would be all right. But I didn't say anything. My breath was loud and obnoxious.

A woman rose up and then there was another thud, a meaty thunking sound, and for a moment, no one on that two-woman pile moved.

Then: "Spade, it's okay to turn on the light."

I exhaled loudly. God, Paladin.

I got up, faster than usual, my knees popping and complaining, my back hurting, and managed to make it to the door, and the bank of lights.

I slapped them on.

Over the Tower of Terror, I saw Paladin kneeling on Ludmila's back, holding her head down with one hand.

There was a light spatter of blood on Paladin's elvish features. It seemed to have come from her own nose, which had a trail of blood along the side.

She grinned at me.

"Hey, Spade," she said. "You're an I.T. guy. Got any zip ties?"

25

I did have zip ties, but it took me forever to find them. (Or maybe a minute or two, which just seemed like forever.) They were in a box underneath my desk and I banged my head on the desk twice, before Paladin said, "Hurry, Spade. I have no idea how long she'll be out."

Out. Paladin had turned out the light, rushed Ludmila, and after some kind of struggle, during which the gun slid over to me, managed to knock Ludmila out.

I found the zip ties, and I handed them one by one to Paladin. "They're not the kind cops use," I said.

"Doesn't matter," she said. "They'll do for now."

Ludmila was pressed against the floor, on her stomach, eyes closed, and I worried—I really worried—that she was faking it.

Until Paladin yanked her arms back like a pro, held the hands together with one hand, and looped a zip tie around them with the other.

"Hold her down," Paladin said.

I crouched, and gingerly put my hand on Ludmila's neck.

"*Hold* her down," Paladin snapped. "Use some force, for God's sake."

So I did, even though it felt weird. Her hair was thin and her skull felt fragile and there was blood on her face.

Paladin didn't seem to care about any of it. She moved to Ludmila's feet and zip tied them together.

"Thanks," she said to me, and moved me aside, sitting astride Ludmila's upper back, effectively holding her down. "Call Zula, would you? We need some kind of tranquilizer. Because this isn't going to last."

As if she heard that, Ludmila moaned. Paladin grabbed the back of her neck in one hand, and smashed her head against the floor. Now I knew the source of that meaty thud earlier. I wasn't sure I could ever hear that sound again without thinking of skulls and floors.

Ludmila didn't move.

"Spade," Paladin said. "Call Zula."

So I did. I called her. I asked for tranquilizers, and as I was trying to explain why I wanted them, Andelusia Tran and another con security person whose name I couldn't remember arrived.

They didn't need briefing. They just consulted with Paladin about what to do with "the prisoner" while I discussed with Zula the ways of keeping "the prisoner" unconscious until the storm ended.

Zula had all kinds of objections that I wasn't really paying attention to. I wasn't paying attention to much, because—I figured out later—I was in some kind of shock. Words rolled over me and around me and I responded, but I felt very distant from myself.

I had nearly died, and Paladin had saved me, and she was now trying to deal with a prisoner and a storm and the entire crisis, and I couldn't quite explain why I needed something to keep someone unconscious, until Paladin—leaving Ludmila in the custody of Andelusia and the other security officer, a big guy with muscles on his muscles, who probably could dive to the floor when the opportunity arose—grabbed my cell phone from my hand, and said into the phone, "For Gods' sake, Zula, people nearly died. I don't give a rats about your qualms. This damn storm means we won't have police here for hours, and I'm not going to keep punching Ludmila in the head to keep her unconscious."

Then Paladin handed the phone back to me. Zula was talking, promising to come up now that we no longer needed the buddy system, right? And I wondered about that until I realized Ludmila was not the kind of person who worked with anyone. No one liked her, and someone would have reported her, and I said, "Yeah, right. Hurry," and probably hung up a bit too abruptly.

I pulled myself into my chair and sat there while Paladin and Andelusia discussed where to squirrel Ludmila away while they waited for the authorities.

I couldn't shake the feeling that I was missing something. I grabbed my now warm Coke, and sipped it, and the sugar helped. I guzzled it, and felt even better.

And that's when I realized: we had to call off the Chancery events. And figure out what room she had set aside for the entire convention to go into.

There was only one room like that. It was the largest ballroom, where we would hold the masquerade tomorrow night. Usually, we would hold opening ceremonies in that room too, but SierraCon wasn't known for its opening ceremonies attendance. Rather than embarrass ourselves, we had moved opening ceremonies to one of the smaller convention rooms.

"Spade?" Paladin said. She looked so tough and mighty, still sitting on Ludmila. Now, I realized there was blood on Paladin's T-shirt and along her arms.

"Someone needs to move that gun out of here," I said.

"Gun?" Andelusia asked.

"Oh, yeah, I forgot," Paladin said. "It's probably loaded, so be careful."

"Probably," I said.

She shrugged. "Nothing else has really gone Camille's way, so I figured this might not either."

Andelusia moved around my desk, found the gun, and expertly handled it, ejecting a clip just like people did in the movies, and then opening the chamber and removing a bullet.

Yep, loaded.

My heart hurt, and I had trouble catching my breath. She really was going to shoot me.

"It's okay, Spade," Paladin said softly.

But it wasn't. We both knew that. I would probably lose sleep for weeks after this.

"We're not done," I said. "We have whatever she was planning for the Chancery events. Then there's the red herrings. And she was going to do something with one of the ballrooms."

I explained what she had said about gathering everyone together.

"She seems to like poison," Paladin said. "As soon as she's secure, we'll look for gas."

"Okay," I said. "But what about the zoo? The bear hug?"

"I think this *is* the zoo," Paladin said. "The convention. That would make sense."

"And the bear hug?" I asked.

"Bear spray, maybe," Andelusia said.

"It won't kill someone," Paladin said. "Mace and pepper spray are much more effective."

"Maybe she didn't know that." They all looked—we all looked—at Ludmila.

We'd have to ask her, I guessed. Or we'd have to search the hotel.

"I'll cancel the Chancery stuff," I said. I thumb-dialed Judita, and told her that the Chancery stuff needed to be canceled, and she reminded me that we had already discussed some of that. I warned her to let Horatio know.

Horatio. He needed to tone down all Chancery events, or make sure they weren't going to happen, not at this convention.

I also told Judita to make sure that the red herrings in the dealer's room hadn't been tampered with.

Before I called Horatio, I called Betty and warned her that someone had booby-trapped the large ballrooms, and security had to find the problem. If it was a bomb or something beyond them, they weren't to touch it. They just needed to isolate it and make sure no one went in the rooms.

Betty sounded scared but purposeful. She knew what was going on, more or less. I hadn't told her about Ludmila yet, but the entire hotel staff would find out soon enough.

At that point, Zula showed up. She hurried in with a medical kit, saw the blood on Paladin's face, and insisted on examining her.

"After you take care of her," Paladin said.

Zula looked at Ludmila, who just looked like a battered middle-aged woman now. Then she looked at me.

"Are we sure this is the person we were looking for?" Zula asked.

"She had a gun on me, so yes," I said. "She's the one. Oh, and she confessed."

"People don't confess in real life," said Zula, still looking at Ludmila as if trying to figure out what was going on.

"You think a convention is real life?" Andelusia asked.

Zula barked out half a laugh. "How long do we want her out?"

"As long as it takes," Paladin said.

"The storm is supposed to ease twelve hours from now," I said.

"So I'll have to administer this at least twice." Zula grabbed Ludmila's arms, slid one sleeve up, and stuck a needle in a vein with as much expertise as Paladin had used on the zip ties.

I really had to rethink my skill set, which was pretty damn useless when it came to facing a villain with a gun.

"What are we going to do with her?" I asked.

"We need to keep her down," Paladin said. "I'm not sure where we will store her."

"We're putting her in the medical room," Zula said. "We have one free hospital bed, and the nice thing about those is they come with restraints."

She looked at the security officer, the guy whose name I still couldn't access, and said, "Get me a wheelchair."

"We're going to need a guard on her at all times," I said. "And what about Jessica-6?"

"Didn't I tell you?" Zula asked. "She's awake. She's concussed, and she'll need someone with her at all times, but I called Zombie Killer. He came to get her, and he's going to keep an eye on her. She's not in the office anymore."

"Oh, good," I said, relieved that she wasn't hurt worse.

"Still," Zula said. "I'm sure as hell not babysitting anyone. You all are going to have guards on her at all times."

"I was planning that," Paladin said.

Ludmila seemed to melt even more. Paladin rolled off her, and Zula grabbed Paladin's face with her fingers. Paladin looked tiny next to her. I'd never seen anyone handle Paladin quite like that.

Zula tilted Paladin's face from side to side. "You're going to have a hell of a bruise on the left side of your face. You'll need ice. After you wash the blood off your face."

"Blood?" Paladin asked.

"Yeah." Zula grabbed a wipe from her medical kit and handed it to Paladin. "Did you get an elbow in the face?"

"How did you know?" Paladin asked.

"I worked in an ER. There are telltale signs," Zula said.

She touched Paladin's nose. Paladin winced. Then Zula ran her fingers over the side of Paladin's face.

"The good news is that nothing's broken," Zula said. "You're lucky."

"No," Paladin said. "Spade's lucky."

My gaze met hers. She was very serious now.

"He kept her talking, which gave me time to get here, get the door open, and plan my assault. If he hadn't been talking to her, this would not have worked." Paladin swallowed. Apparently she was feeling a little shaky now. "She would have shot him."

Her words calmed me just a little. I didn't feel as useless as I had a few minutes earlier.

"Thanks," I said quietly.

"No need to thank me," Paladin said. "You're the one who figured this out."

"But you're the one who stopped it," I said.

And, at that moment, the lights went out.

Only to come up a minute later.

The lights were dim and brown, though. Half power, or maybe even a quarter power, from the hotel's generator. Apparently the worst of the storm had hit.

And I had had the Tower of Terror running. I worried that my entire computer system was ruined, and then I grinned at myself.

A lot worse could have happened. We could have lost Paladin. Hell, we could have lost everyone at the entire convention.

And then there were none. That had been what Ludmila had been aiming for. Taking out all of us. And probably herself.

Only she had failed, because we all worked together.

And because we were not predictable. Because we were fen. And the most important thing to anyone in fandom wasn't what was going on in the real world.

It was making sure that the fannish moment—the panel, the camaraderie, the costuming, the masquerade, the books, the movies, the convention itself—went on as planned. No matter what was happening around us.

Blizzard, power outages, psycho killers.

We managed to somehow survive them all.

26

Or rather, we survived them by the end of the convention. The hotel was on generator power for five hours. The medevac teams arrived about the time the power came back on, and they brought a detective, a grizzled sheriff's investigator who told me privately that he had thought he had seen everything until he came here.

Only I wasn't sure if he was talking about Ludmila or the group of middle-aged women in Clan of the Cave Bear fur bikinis that he was staring at as he uttered that sentence.

Ludmila was arrested and hospitalized, since Paladin had given her a few broken ribs, two dislocated shoulders, and a collapsed cheekbone. The detective was pretty certain, after he looked up Ludmila's record, that we wouldn't even have to testify. He doubted there would be any kind of trial. She had a history of going in and out of mental institutions. If he could get her to plead, he might be able to put her away for life.

We would see. I wasn't worried about that part. I was more worried about the publicity. We didn't want to be the Agatha Christie convention. And I wasn't sure how to prevent it, particularly since Horatio was involved.

Although I really didn't need to worry: he didn't want to discuss that period of his life where he slept with anything that moved.

Some things don't belong in the gossip columns, Spade, he said to me, which took me aback. Because I had forgotten that Horatio occasionally got written up *in* gossip columns.

Apparently, he had enough of a reputation out there in Hollywoodland that he didn't want to screw it up.

I spent most of my time at the convention quelling rumors. I spent most of my time afterward making arrangements with the hotel. Michael Shaye, the idiot assistant GM, threatened to sue us for bringing a psycho to their hotel and endangering their reputation and staff.

I just went over his head, told his boss that he had threatened that, and reminded them that they had hired Ludmila without, apparently, doing a proper background check.

The con ended up with a credit for next year's convention, and we all decided never to speak of this again.

We never did figure out the "bear hug," and Ludmila never confessed to that part. She had a partially assembled canister of poison gas in her hotel room, but she hadn't set it up yet (thank heavens). And nothing else was boobytrapped throughout the weekend.

The rest of the con went as well as a con could go in a blizzard, without its chair, and with a somewhat subdued Guest of Honor.

The roads were clear by closing ceremonies and everyone seemed happy with their experiences.

It wasn't until the Dead Dog Party that I actually slowed down enough to start shaking. And then I couldn't stop.

Casper was the one who calmed me. She took my hands in hers.

"You know what I like about you?" she said, sitting in a chair next to me in the remains of the con suite.

I shook my head.

"You solve things with brains," she said. "You're the one who saved us."

"Paladin is the one who saved us," I said.

"Oh, no," Casper said. "You're the one who did it. You figured out who was doing this. You thwarted her. You outthought her."

She squeezed my hands, then grinned at me.

"You're my hero," she said, as she stood up, and walked away.

I watched her cross the room to grab something to drink. Then she ended up talking to one of the gamers. I had no idea how she could get so close, because I could smell the kid from here. Although he looked like he was her age.

Conventions were never real life. They were never normal times. They were always something above and beyond what we usually lived with.

Whether it was the loss of parents and some really mean kids in school, like Casper was dealing with, or the scum of the Earth that Paladin defended us against, or just a rather boring day job, which was how I started, a convention distracted us and made us stronger.

Usually through the fiction of a questionable character like Horatio. I wasn't going to tell him that no one really cared that he slept with half of fandom back in the day. I wasn't going to tell him that his rude mouth was probably going to be more of a problem going forward.

Because I wanted him to finish the Chancery series just like his fanbase did. Whatever he was—pain in the ass, opinionated ass, or just an ass—he was also a hell of a writer, and writers like him were the backbone of fandom.

We wouldn't gather if it weren't for the stories.

The stories were more important than the storytellers.

Horatio knew that.

We all knew that.

All except Ludmila, who had forgotten it. Because if she had thought it through, she would have realized that the worst thing I could have done was take away the fantasy. Putting everyone together in the same room would have meant that every single sf fan would have had to confront their fears without their fictional crutches.

And that would have been untenable for all of us.

Fiction got us through.

And if she had thought of that, she would have planned differently.

But she was past that. She had been lost in a delusional story of her own.

She wanted to be the best, to best a "great detective" just like villains did in fiction. And then, apparently, she could have died happy.

But even that plan wouldn't have worked.

Because if she had killed us all, no one would have told of her exploits. No one would have known what, exactly, she had done.

I thought about that in the days after. I wondered if that long speech wasn't about gloating, but about stalling—on her part. So that she could get credit. So that she could be done with her so-called crimes.

I wasn't going to ask her. No one would.

She was done. And so was the talk of Agatha Christie at conventions.

I went to conventions to see my friends, enjoy science fiction, and follow fannish traditions. I went to *science fiction* conventions. I wasn't a big mystery convention fan.

I had just lived through a cozy, in a blizzard.

It was not an experience I ever wanted to have again.

AFTERWORD

As I wrote this book, I thought about all the friends who've moved on, and who we will never see again. Not everyone below died of Covid-19 or its complications (although too many did). Something else took them, and often before the pandemic itself. But the losses have accelerated in recent years. In fact, the losses have been so great, that I probably have missed someone, either because I hadn't heard yet (in the deluge that was 2020) or because I forgot. I started this list early, and I still think I'm missing someone.

So, here they are, the friends, acquaintances, mentors, and idols. Some I loved, some I had complicated relationships with, some I hadn't spoken to enough, but all of them—every single one of them—I miss.

Mike Resnick, Jack Cady, Susan Casper, Gardner Dozois, Harlan Ellison, Susan Ellison, Len Wein, Mary Rosenblum, Kate Wilhelm, Damon Knight, Octavia Butler, Dave Bischoff, Ben Bova, Fred Pohl, Elizabeth Anne Hull, Jack Williamson, Gene Wolfe, Kent Patterson, Ed Bryant, Richard Lupoff, Bill Trojan, Keith Farrell, Martin H. Greenberg, Vonda McIntyre, Betty Ballantine, Carrie Richerson, Stan Lee, Rowena, David Willoughby, Ursula Le Guin, Kit Reed, Jerry Pournelle, Brian Aldiss, Larry Smith, Ed Gorman, Bob Weinberg, David Kyle, William F. Nolan, Tanith Lee, Melanie Tem, Suzette Haden Elgin, Alice Turner,

Genie DiModica, Stu Schiffman, Frank Robinson, Lucius Shepard, Kelly Cairo, Debra Doyle, Anne Jordan, Steve Utley, Janet Berliner, Josepha Sherman, Ray Bradbury (even though I could never bring myself to speak to you, I enjoyed listening to the conversations you had with our friends), Julius Schwartz, Jay Kay Klein, Judi B. Castro, K.D. Wentworth, Mark Bourne, Jack Whyte, Rusty Havelin, George Scithers, Algis Budrys, Kage Baker, Ken Rand, Roger Zelazny, Brian Thomsen, Alan Lickiss, Storm Constantine, Kathleen Ann Goonan, Stephen Hickman, Geri Jeter, and so many others.

Keep a chair warm for me at the amoeba table. I hope to be late, but I'll be there eventually—and I'll be very happy to see you all.

New York Times Bestselling Author

KRISTINE KATHRYN

RUSCH

Spade
Paladin

THE EARLY
CONUNDRUMS

A Spade/Paladin Collection

If you enjoyed Ten Little Fen, *you might also like the
Spade/Paladin short story collection,* The Early Conundrums.
Available from your favorite bookseller.

I value honest feedback, and would love to hear your opinion in a review, if you're so inclined, on your favorite book retailer's site.

Be the first to know!

Just sign up for the Kristine Kathryn Rusch newsletter, and keep up with the latest news, releases and so much more—even the occasional giveaway.

So, what are you waiting for? To sign up go to kristinekathrynrusch.com.

But wait! There's more. Sign up for the WMG Publishing newsletter, too, and get the latest news and releases from all of the WMG authors and lines, including Kristine Grayson, Kris Nelscott, Dean Wesley Smith, *Fiction River: An Original Anthology Magazine, Smith's Monthly,* and so much more.

To sign up go to wmgpublishing.com.

THE SPADE/PALADIN CONUNDRUMS

NOVELS

Ten Little Fen

COLLECTIONS

The Early Conundrums

SHORT STORIES

"Stomping Mad"

"The Case of The Vanishing Boy"

"The Karnikov Card"

"Pandora's Box"

"Trick or Treat"

"The Really Big Ka-Boom"

"At Witt's End"

"Unity Con"

ABOUT THE AUTHOR

New York Times bestselling author Kristine Kathryn Rusch writes in almost every genre. Generally, she uses her real name (Rusch) for most of her writing. Under that name, she publishes bestselling science fiction and fantasy, award-winning mysteries, acclaimed mainstream fiction, controversial nonfiction, and the occasional romance. Her novels have made bestseller lists around the world and her short fiction has appeared in eighteen best of the year collections. She has won more than twenty-five awards for her fiction, including the Hugo, *Le Prix Imaginales*, the *Asimov's* Readers Choice award, and the *Ellery Queen Mystery Magazine* Readers Choice Award.

Publications from *The Chicago Tribune* to *Booklist* have included her Kris Nelscott mystery novels in their top-ten-best mystery novels of the year. The Nelscott books have received nominations for almost every award in the mystery field, including the best novel Edgar Award, and the Shamus Award.

She writes goofy romance novels as award-winner Kristine Grayson.

She also edits. Beginning with work at the innovative publishing company, Pulphouse, followed by her award-winning tenure at *The Magazine of Fantasy & Science Fiction*, she took fifteen years off before returning to editing with the original anthology series *Fiction River*, published by WMG Publishing. She acts as series editor with her husband, writer Dean Wesley Smith, and edits at least two anthologies in the series per year on her own.

To keep up with everything she does, go to kriswrites.com and sign up for her newsletter. To track her many pen names and series, see their individual websites (krisnelscott.com, kristinegrayson.com, retrievalartist.com, divingintothewreck.com, pulphouse.com).

kriswrites.com